The NEBADOR series:

Book One: The Test

Book Two: Journey

Book Three: Selection

Book Four: Flight Training

Book Five: Back to the Stars

Book Six: Star Station
2012

Book Seven: The Local Universe
2013

Book Eight: Witness
2014

NEBADOR

Book Five
Back to the Stars

an epic young-adult science fiction adventure

by
J. Z. Colby

and the short stories

Buna's New World
by Karen Buchanan

and

First Taste of Freedom
by Katelynn Persons

Nebador Archives

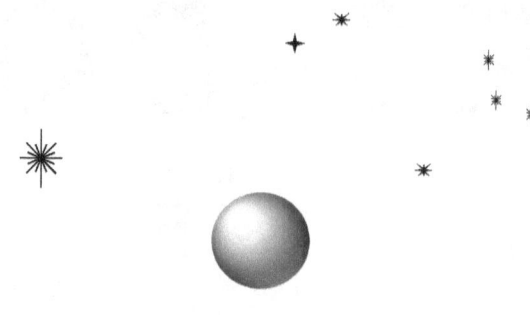

Cover art by Rachael Hedges
Illustrations by J. Z. Colby and Mireille Xioulan Powers

For other print editions, ebooks, dramatic audiobooks, previews, samples, biographies, comments, questions, artwork, writing contests, Ask Kibi advice, deep learning notes, Nebador citizens, and more, please see:

www.nebador.com

Nebador Archives
Kelso, Washington, USA

Library of Congress Control Number: 2011918932
Manufactured in the USA

ISBN: 978-1-936253-38-8
NEBADOR5PBG: paperback, 6" x 9", 174 pages, global edition
    (10-point Georgia type)

Greetings, young people of planet Earth,

This grand, life-changing, soul-building adventure continues as the new crew of the deep-space response ship Manessa Kwi heads for interplanetary space. Will Satamia Star Station await them, just around the corner? Of course not. Those readers looking for *quick and easy* left the Nebador stories behind, probably several books ago. Those of you about to sink your minds into this book are made of sterner stuff.

Space separates the children from the grown-ups. Your age doesn't matter. If you are nine, and you are aiming your life toward standing on your own two feet and dealing with hard, cold reality, you are leaving childhood behind. One of the critiquers who helped make these stories possible started at age eight.

Interplanetary space is like the twenty feet of air that separates the bird nest, where the little birdies must first spread their wings, from the ground, where cats await their next meal. In interplanetary space, we will grow up or die.

But beware the temptation to gaze at the stars and planets too much. The first step into space starts on the ground, on the good fertile soil of planet Earth. We visited our moon in 1969 and the early 1970s, but have not been back, and have not done much else in space, because our "house" is not yet in order. We knew, in the 1970s, that energy and other resources would soon run short, and we decided, as a whole people and a whole planet, to ignore the warnings and do nothing.

The crew of the Manessa Kwi will see and understand many things as they journey outward from their original home to the stars. If you, young readers, have your eyes open, you will learn much from their journey, perhaps more than many people learn in a lifetime.

J. Z. Colby
2011

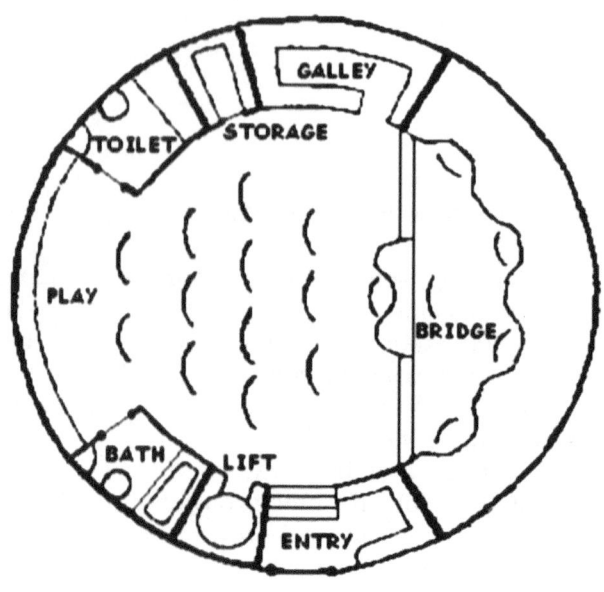

Acknowledgements

Wonderful people throughout the author's life provided unique and irreplaceable lessons and inspirations:

Juniper Russell
Vicky Ball
Linda Dezzutti
Jennifer Carolyn Gates
Rachael Bleich
Paula Wells
Sarah Satterthwaite
Ashley Riddle

Esther Smith
Dottie Frisbie
Martha Higgins
Susanne Koller
Charleen Cox
Meredith Herzog
Patricia Sharp
Antonya Pickard

Valuable readers gave the author feedback after digging through early drafts of the book:

Deborah Meier
Cecelia Harper
Shelley Johnson

Ardith Libby
Karen Oster
Jimmy Johnson

Excellent critiquers commented on thousands of passages, then provided reactions during in-depth interviews:

Sidney Oster, 11

Sarah Bray, 12

Dylan Oster, 12

Hannah Li Powers, 17

Rachael Hedges

Catherine "Cat" Harper, 12

Jessica Johnson, 12

Alex Chalcraft, 16

Elwin Aragorn

Careful publishing assistants, proofreaders, and technical helpers brought the final manuscript as close to perfection as possible:

Deborah Meier

Tim Kutscha

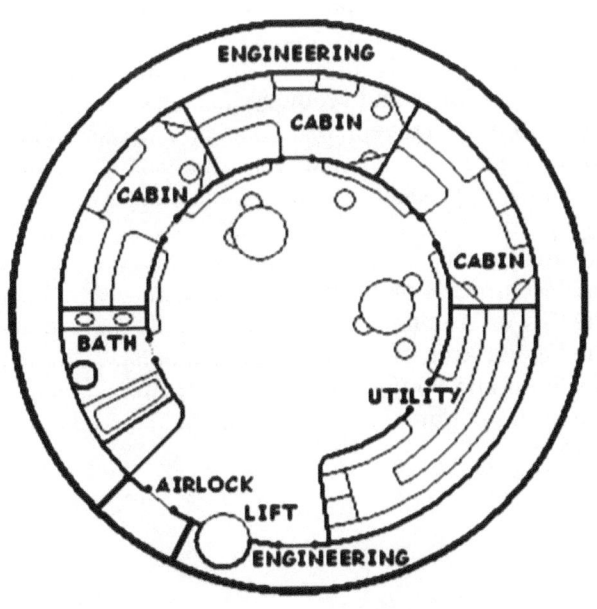

Contents

"The most beautiful and most profound emotion we can experience is the sensation of the mystical. It is the sower of all true science. He to whom this emotion is a stranger, who can no longer stand rapt in awe, is as good as dead."

— Albert Einstein

Chapter 1: Beauty Isn't Everything

Once again, Rini was embarrassed.

Earlier, during his low-orbit excursion, he was having so much fun playing with his suit thrusters, he accidentally induced a spin he couldn't correct. Mati smiled as she guided the Manessa Kwi into a matching spin so Rini could get into the airlock. Ilika gave him a mild lecture, but let it pass.

Rini's geo-stationary orbit excursion was worse. Since he wasn't paying attention to which way he was going, his suit thrusters quickly put him into a lower orbit, which rapidly began to decay. The Manessa Kwi came to his rescue, and Ilika made him do the excursion again.

But during his high-orbit excursion, Rini committed a crime he knew no one on the ship was going to easily forgive.

"Um . . . Sata? It's really beautiful out here with the world turning below and the stars above, but I just remembered something. A few minutes ago, my half-fuel alarm chimed and I forgot to start back."

"Oh, I see!" Sata said through the intercom with a taunting voice. "Actually, your half-fuel alarm was eleven minutes ago. Is that a problem, Rini?"

"Um . . . yeah. This is so embarrassing. I can't get back to the ship now. Manessa looks really small, and is getting smaller all the time."

Rini heard some giggling over the intercom, but didn't get an immediate response. He watched the ship continue to shrink with distance as he used his thrusters to slow his movement as much as possible.

Sata's voice came again. "Rini, we've discussed the situation, and since you've got enough air for about an hour, we're going to do a review of language lesson twenty-two. You don't mind, do you?"

Several voices in the background chuckled.

"Um . . . okay," Rini said with a sigh. "I guess I'll . . . be here."

The minutes passed slowly as Rini used the remainder of his thruster fuel.

He knew it wouldn't help, but doing something about his mistake brought some comfort. Finally his thrusters sputtered and died.

The silence was profound. He looked at the blue and green world below, but it no longer gave him pleasure. He looked at the stars above, but they now seemed dim and lifeless.

Tapping a code into his mission bracelet, he was informed he would be out of air in about half an hour. Helpless to do anything else about his situation, he began to recall scenes from his life. Moments of both joy and sorrow came to him, memories that had somehow touched him deeply.

Somewhat later, he tapped the code again. Twelve minutes of life left. He could see Mati's face clearly in his mind, her hair tangled like it usually was during their journey around the kingdom. He felt an intense desire to wrap his arms around her once more before he died.

Three minutes of air, and perhaps another minute after that as he suffocated inside his space suit. Tears formed and began to roll down his cheeks. Blinking them away, he made one last effort to see the ship, but found only blurry stars.

Forty seconds. His mind raced, struggling to find something to do with his remaining moments of consciousness. Fear crept all throughout his body, making his skin cold and tingly. His stomach churned and tightened.

Eight seconds. Suddenly he knew. "Mati! Nothing else in my life has ever mattered! I love you!"

"I love you too, Rini. So get yourself into the airlock so Boro can do his high-orbit excursion."

The tears in Rini's eyes blurred the golden sphere in front of him, with a dark opening close at hand. After one final alarm sounded in his ears, the air in his suit rapidly became stale. A suited arm reached out and pulled him into the airlock. He blinked away the tears and glimpsed his teacher and captain behind a face plate.

*

After gasping and crying in Ilika's arms for several minutes, Rini slowly extracted himself from the space suit, trembling all the while. No one else came to talk to him on the lower deck. He didn't blame them. After stumbling into the toilet room to wash his face, he kept one hand on the wall as he rose in the lift.

All his shipmates were seated at the big oval table in the passenger area, sipping cups of fragrant tea. Looking at the floor, Rini shuffled forward and slipped into the empty seat beside Mati. Ilika took another seat.

"I really do love you, Rini," Mati said, "but you screwed up again."

"I ... I know."

"When he's surrounded by beautiful things," Kibi began, "Rini loses track of time. It's not that big a deal, seems to me."

"He also loses track of directions," Boro said.

"And warning alarms," Sata added.

"And people who love him and are waiting for him to come back," Mati said with a tender frown.

Rini took a deep breath and looked up. "I'm sorry. I'll do my excursions all over again. I'll do better, I promise."

Ilika had been sitting quietly, listening and wearing a subtle smile. "I think you finally heard us, Rini. There are several planets coming up. If you practice every chance you get, I think we can let Boro do his excursion, then move on."

Rini took several slow, thoughtful breaths. "I will."

"Fantastic!" Boro said, hopping up. "I'll be in a suit in eight minutes!"

* * *

Chapter 2: Leaving Home

With a tasty casserole of beans, rice, and vegetables on their trays, along with sticks of hard cheese and cups of sweet tea, the entire crew of the deep-space response ship Manessa Kwi gazed at the large display screen above the steward's station. For five of them, the world of their birth filled the screen and turned slowly as they watched.

After journeying the entire width and length of the small kingdom where he found his crew, Ilika was almost as attached to the place as they were. He recalled the many faces in the room full of slaves he had tested.   He remembered Kodi and his sticky fingers, Miko's leap from boulder to boulder, and sweet Neti who was left to grieve and find a new partner. Toli had tried very hard toward the end of the journey, but was just not Transport Service material. Buna had chosen another path, and Ilika would always miss her.

"Our business here is done," he began. "This beautiful planet is the only place in the Sonmatia solar system with good air to breathe. The people who live here will not appreciate that fact for a thousand years or more, and will probably come close to destroying their atmosphere before they learn to take care of it."

"That's stupid," Kibi grumbled. "If anyone even *looks* funny at Manessa's air system, they'll have to get through me! I kind of like breathing."

Everyone around the table smiled or chuckled. They also knew their beloved steward wasn't joking.

Ilika grinned at his lover. "So . . . if everyone is ready to say good-bye to this little planet for a while . . ." He stopped and looked around the table.

Rini smiled, but still carried a measure of guilt about his recent orbit excursions.   Boro nodded slowly, trying to hide his nervousness about warming up the ship's interplanetary engines for the first time.   Mati sparkled with longing, knowing that only a few planets separated her from healers who could fix her knee. Sata, leaving parents and a brother behind at not quite twelve years of age, took a deep breath, planted her feet squarely on the floor, and grinned.

Ilika saw that Sata's grin was a bit forced, but after a moment, he continued. "Interplanetary space is scattered with countless wandering molecules, bits of rock and ice, and occasionally bigger things that Rini can detect and we will avoid. The ship uses a very slender shape, a repulsion field, and high levels of ion drive. You have all studied the necessary engines, controls, and instruments. Now it's time to use them.

"As you know, we measure interplanetary space in light-minutes. It's about eight light-minutes from here to the sun — an hour at one-eighth the speed of light, Manessa's cruising speed in space. I've started a new flight list. We're at navigation point one, and I've entered a proposed flight plan. See what you think of it."

Ilika collected empty trays and stepped into the galley.

※

As the captain of the Manessa Kwi did the dishes and started a pot of soup, he didn't have to look to see what his crew-in-training was doing. He had been through the process himself, and from words he overheard now and then, could clearly imagine their thoughts.

For a while, they huddled around Sata's navigation console. Then they moved to the engineer's station, where Boro slowly and carefully expressed his concern. Back at the large table, no less than three knowledge pads were in use, with Kibi routing their displays to the big screen when one of them had something to share. Ilika kept his eyes on his galley work.

More than an hour after starting, they spent a few minutes at Rini's watch station, then returned to the table.

Ilika could tell by the dead silence behind him that it was time to cover his soup pot. Rather unfriendly looks greeted him when he turned around, but he had expected as much. "So . . . what do you think?"

The others looked at Kibi.

"We don't like it one bit," the steward said in a firm voice.

Ilika held in his smile. "What's wrong with it?"

"There's nothing wrong with the trip from here to the sun," Mati explained.

"It's the part about hovering over the surface of the huge thing," Boro went on, his voice getting louder.

"At that distance, the gravity will be so great," Sata declared with despair, "that we'll need the anti-mass drive at level seven!"

"That will take all three anti-mass inducers," Boro explained, almost gasping for breath, "and leave us nothing extra for an emergency."

"What about orbit?" Ilika asked, trying to keep a straight face.

"Orbiting the sun at that distance would require one-quarter the speed of light!" Rini squeaked. "Manessa can't go that fast."

Ilika smiled. "You guys are good! We might take a risk like that in a dire emergency. We certainly won't any time we can avoid it. A good flight plan includes at least two paths to a safe destination. After a break, you can rewrite it so everyone's happy."

All five crew members sighed with relief. Kibi shooed Ilika out of the galley so she could find snacks.

✳

After a few calculations, Boro was happy with the new hover altitude, giving him anti-mass power to spare. Rini, however, reminded them that if the anti-mass drive failed, they'd have to use space thrusters.

Mati frowned and grabbed a knowledge pad. "Thrusters only give me a thousand meters per second," she complained. "That's not escape velocity anywhere near the sun."

Ilika scrunched his face for a moment. "You're confusing velocity and acceleration, Mati. Manessa's thrusters can give you that much *change* in velocity, per second."

"Oh . . . yeah . . ." Mati mumbled with embarrassment as she tapped at the knowledge pad again. "Okay, I'm happy."

"But . . ." Sata began with a cringe, "wouldn't that much acceleration kill us?"

Mati frowned again and looked at Ilika.

"Yes," Ilika replied, "but Manessa wouldn't use maximum thrust with anyone on board. Look at emergency acceleration curve two."

Mati worked with the hand-held device, peering at its screen in silence for a moment. Kibi stepped to her station and sent Mati's display to the big screen so everyone could see.

"Okay, I get it," Mati said with a much happier voice. "It starts slow so we can get into inertia straps, or grab something, and backs off after eight seconds, but builds plenty of speed."

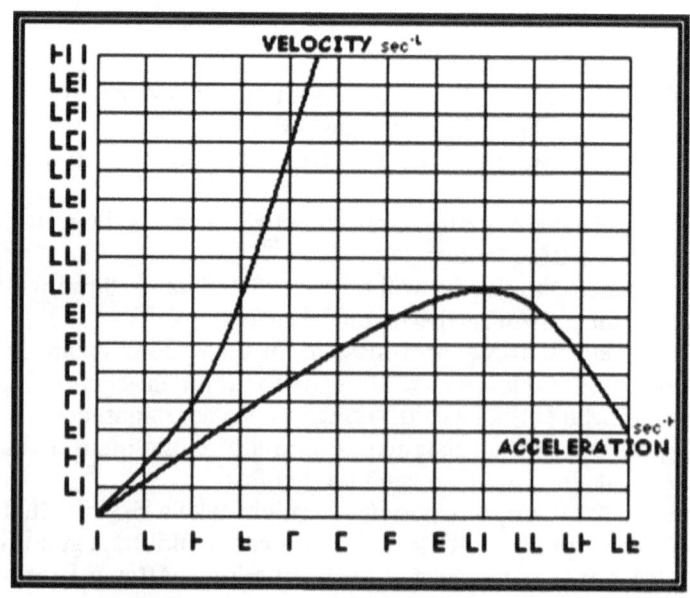

"Right. Your planet has a gravity of about twelve meters per second squared," Ilika explained. "This curve gently takes us to about six times that. We'd be moaning, but we'd live."

After Rini presented his chart of all objects along the way larger than a grain of sand, Ilika looked over the entire new flight plan, smiled, and said, "Stations."

Slipping into their console chairs, the crew began pre-flight checks while Ilika secured the soup pot. As soon as he took the command chair, he spoke. "We will no longer be working Mati to death on every flight. She will be on-duty at the beginning and end of each flight leg, and Manessa will remind her eight minutes before each navigation point so she has time to climb out of the bathtub, or wherever, and get to her station."

Mati grinned and gestured toward her crutch. "For me, make it twelve minutes. But I think I'll stay close this time. Leaving my station with the ship moving feels scary."

Ilika nodded. "Sata and Boro are also off-duty once we get moving, but Rini's job is critical."

The freckled lad smiled, turned back to his console, and started a solar wind chart.

"All stations, report flight-plan readiness," Ilika commanded.

"Pilot has the plan," Mati reported, "an elliptical course ending in a solar hover. Um . . . I want everyone in inertia straps."

"Good use of flight command, Mati," Ilika said. "Continue with reports."

"Manessa likes the plan," Sata announced. "Universe transponder on."

"Ion seven is green," Boro declared. "Full inertia canceling and repulsion field."

Rini touched another symbol on his console. "Flight path is clear, and I'll be watching it like a hawk."

Kibi finished looking over the inside of the ship from her console. "Ship is secured for flight."

✳

Evening light was fading as Noni leaned on her staff and looked up at the crystal clear winter sky. It would be a bitter cold night, and she envied her sheep their thick coats. Suddenly she saw a shooting star streak away toward the lingering sunset light in the west. She smiled and made a wish.

Just then Bo barked, signaling he needed help with a stray, so she pulled her old cloak tightly around her and went back to work.

✳   ✳   ✳

Chapter 3: Solar System Primary

"Oh ... my ... god," Sata said under her breath as she stared with wide eyes. On her display, a huge loop of orange fire slowly arched up from the boiling yellow surface, almost reaching their current altitude.

"All crew members are on-duty in a situation like this," Ilika stated calmly.

Boro's mouth hung open as he gazed at the inferno below. "Y ... yeah. Thrusters are all warmed-up, just in case."

Mati continued to stare at her fiery display. "The sun ... is burning!"

"The ... um ... temperature and ... um ... radiation ..." Rini whimpered in a thin voice.

"You feeling okay, Rini?" Kibi asked from her console.

"N ... not really. Um ... I promised I'd practice orbit excursions every chance I got ..."

Kibi got a bowl from the galley and took it to the watch station with a motherly look of concern.

Ilika held in a smile. "Do you think a space suit could handle these radiation levels?"

Rini looked up the answer with sweating, shaking fingers, bowl in his lap. Soon he started breathing easier. "Whew! Not by a long shot!"

Ilika smiled, then tapped at the controls on the arm of his chair and a diagram appeared on the main bridge screen.

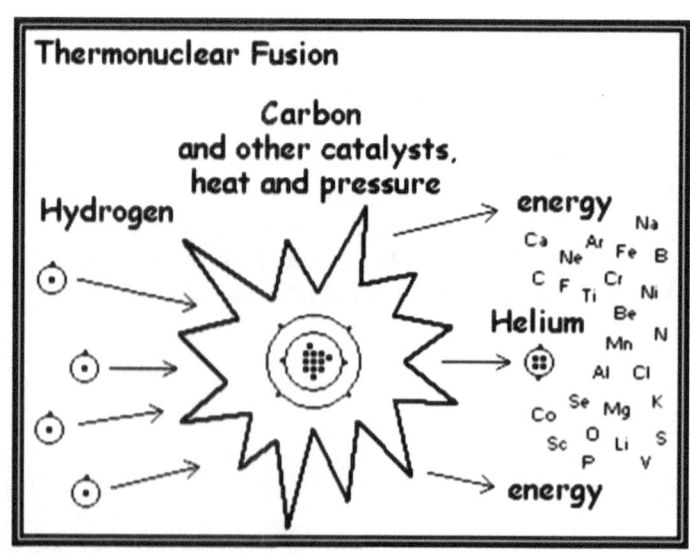

"Let's peek at what's happening down there. The chemical reactions you've studied involve the electrons around each atom. This is different. Here, great heat and pressure are forcing changes to the nucleus of the atom. There are several types of stars, but all of them burn hydrogen. Carbon is most often present as a catalyst, a helper that isn't changed by the process. Helium is created, a sprinkling of heavier elements, and a huge amount of energy."

As Ilika spoke, five pairs of eyes went back and forth from their visual displays to the diagram.

"The energy comes out as heat and light?" Boro asked.

"Every kind of energy you can imagine, Boro, and some particles too strange to classify. Rini, give us a full-spectrum graph."

Rini touched a small part of his display. "Channel four."

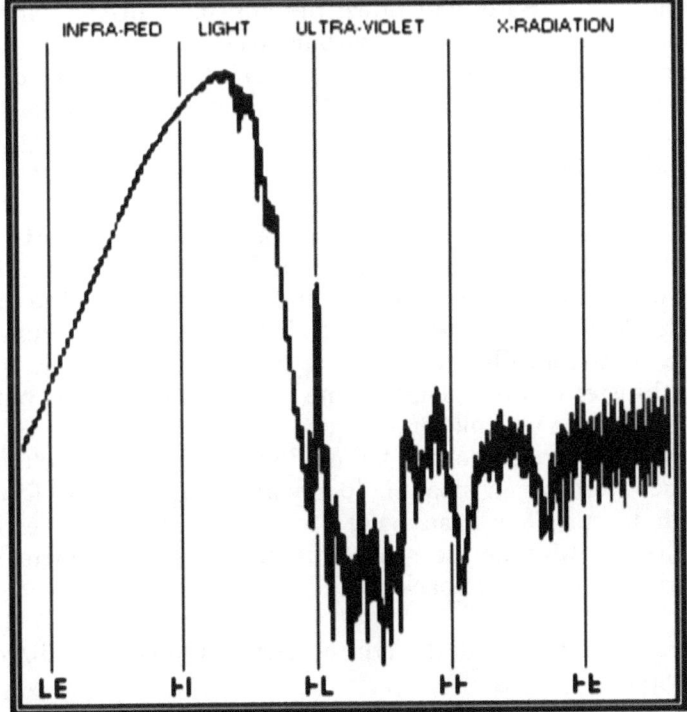

Ilika spoke in a calm voice as he went from station to station checking on his crew. "Even though visible light from the sun has the most energy, it's easy to deal with."

Rini chuckled nervously. "I just imagined Manessa wearing a sun hat!"

Ilika grinned. "See that sharp spike in ultra-violet? There's a layer in our space suits just to deal with it. But the x-rays are far worse, even though they have less energy, because they can penetrate so deeply. It's not the heat that keeps Rini from doing an excursion here, it's the x-rays."

The freckled lad smiled at his captain.

"Manessa's hull is the only part of this ship that can withstand all that radiation. As Boro knows, Manessa can't use atmospheric engines here, even though a fair amount of matter is present, because that would draw the hot solar material into the ship. Space thrusters use fuel very quickly, so we rarely use them. This is the best place to see what they'll do. Prepare for anti-mass failure drill."

Mati swallowed, then selected the emergency escape course and put it on her display.

Ilika stowed Rini's bowl in the galley, returned to the command chair, and pulled down his inertia straps. "Normally Manessa would begin the escape plan automatically if Boro shut down the anti-mass drive. I'm canceling Manessa's safeguards. We have to save ourselves."

"I'm ready," Mati declared. "All I have to do is touch one symbol."

"We're going to lurch straight up as the ship drops toward the sun," Ilika pointed out.

Mati nodded. "We've practiced that."

"Anti-mass off," the captain ordered.

None of the new crew members were prepared for the gut-wrenching sensation of the ship dropping out from under them. Sata and Rini both screamed with fright, and Kibi couldn't think of anything but the contents of her stomach. Mati cried out with pain as her bad knee hit the underside of her console, and tears filled her eyes as she tried desperately to see her emergency thruster control. Time seemed to stand still as she blinked and forced her hand down with all her strength.

Suddenly they were no longer falling, but the forward acceleration was almost worse. Boro began moaning loudly and couldn't stop. Kibi used all her strength to turn her head before losing her snack. Everyone else, including Ilika, howled as the space thrusters pushed them to six times normal gravity, then began to back off.

✻

"Status reports," Ilika said when the acceleration finally stabilized at twice normal gravity.

"I . . . th-think . . . I pr-pressed it," Mati stuttered.

"You did," Ilika reassured. "Sata?"

"Um . . . don't know where we are."

"You work on that, and I'll come back to you. Boro?"

"Alive . . . I think. I can *see* the fuel level dropping."

"We'll switch engines soon. Rini?"

"Wow. Um . . . nothing on the flight path, until we get to that little planet without an atmosphere."

"Kibi?"

"This is embarrassing . . ."

"Report now, feel later," Ilika reminded her.

"I . . . um . . . have a mess to clean up. I'm just not sure where it is."

✳   ✳   ✳

Chapter 4: Orbital Velocity

When the ship finally quit accelerating, Boro looked at his thruster fuel gauge with a worried frown. "I hope that's all you need."

"We'll know in a minute," the pilot said as she and Sata studied the orbital entry diagram on their screens.

Sata entered another number and the diagram changed slightly. "According to Manessa, this should work. You just need to adjust speed and nail that entry point."

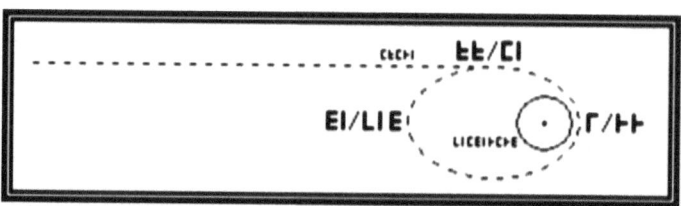

Mati glanced at her console. "Yeah, Boro, I need a little more. We're going too slow."

"Oh, okay. But you're doing the dishes next time I cook!"

Pilot and engineer exchanged grins.

For the next two hours, Ilika worked in the galley to finish the soup and make biscuits. Kibi got cleaning supplies from the lower deck and began the long process of washing all the passenger seats, the floor, and the walls. When Ilika pointed out a bit of the ceiling that also needed work, she burst into tears. He surrounded her with his arms, and they worked together to finish the job. The four other crew members stayed at their stations, or slipped quietly into the lift.

Finally Mati called everyone back and raised her flight control. "Inertia straps."

Ilika remained silent as he pulled down his straps, but as he turned to glance around the ship, Kibi noticed he was holding something in.

Mati remained focused on her work. "The speed matches our calculations perfectly. Just a slight course correction, and we'll slide right into an elliptical orbit around the first planet. Does it have a name, Ilika?"

"No, just Sonmatia One. No one on your world even knows it exists."

Mati continued working with her flight control. "Maybe we could name it. Course looks right. Check me, Sata."

"Um . . . looks good. Orbital entry in twenty-five seconds."

Everyone watched their displays as the Manessa Kwi approached the planet, a bright ball of rock floating in space with no water or atmosphere, and no visible surface features.

"Orbit in three . . . two . . . one . . ." Sata narrated.

Everyone watched the course diagram on their screens as the ship flew right past the planet with only a slight change in direction.

※

Mati and Sata fussed and fumed over the orbit calculations for the next half hour, trying to figure out what went wrong.

Ilika let the others go off-duty, but otherwise remained silent. He stepped into the galley and added a few more spices to his soup.

Kibi joined him to help with trays. "You knew, didn't you?"

Ilika nodded so only she could see. "Two biscuits for each person."

Soon the pilot and navigator came to the table. "We give up," Sata moaned.

Ilika poured bowls of soup. Kibi added biscuits and dried fruit, then carried out the trays.

"Are you *sure* Manessa knows how to calculate orbits?" Mati asked with a slight pout.

"Yes . . ." Ilika said slowly.

"Mati . . ." Kibi began hesitantly, "I . . . don't know quite how to say this . . . and I don't know the math like you guys do . . . but as we passed the planet, it just *felt* like we were going way too fast."

Rini nodded agreement but kept his expression soft.

"But Manessa says the speed was just right!" Mati defended herself with a tone of despair.

"What speed did Manessa calculate for your orbit entry?" Ilika asked calmly as he sat down.

Sata craned her neck to see her display. "Fifty-three thousand five hundred and twenty."

"And what was our speed?"

"Fifty-three thousand five hundred and twenty!" Mati blurted out with frustration. "We've checked it over and over, even reviewed the flight log!"

Ilika took another spoonful of soup. "Relative to what reference point?"

Suddenly both pilot and navigator became deathly quiet. They looked around the table, then at each other. "Um . . ." Mati began in a tiny, sheepish voice, "based on our last navigation point . . . when we were . . . hovering over the sun."

"And what does a speed relative to that point have to do with orbiting Sonmatia One?" Ilika asked.

Sata swallowed. "Um . . . nothing?"

Ilika nodded. "Let's eat a good dinner, then Mati and Sata can put us into that elliptical orbit . . . and I bet it will be perfect this time!"

✳   ✳   ✳

Chapter 5: Baked and Frozen

The two girls who worked at the front of the ship quickly finished their dinners and dashed to the bridge to recalculate the ship's relative speed. When they discovered it was four times too fast for any orbit around the first planet, they looked at each other with sad faces for a moment, then both started snickering.

Boro moaned when they began using his precious thruster fuel again, this time to loop back to the planet and slow down.

The orbit Mati achieved needed a few minor adjustments, but both the captain and the ship were soon happy.

"This little world has lost its rotation," Ilika explained as they all peered at their displays. "One side always faces the sun, so its surface is nearly molten. The other side is close to absolute zero, the temperature at which all electron activity stops. Neither situation allows an atmosphere to develop.

"Tomorrow we will learn how to do landings and excursions in these extreme environments. It's been a long day and we've experienced many things. Have a relaxing evening."

When Rini came up in the lift after a deep sleep, he found Ilika leaning back at the engineer's station and Kibi asleep in a passenger seat. "Didn't you . . . get any sleep?" he whispered to his captain.

"Yes. Kibi and I took turns."

"I'll make breakfast," Rini offered as Kibi began stretching.

Soon others arrived and Rini set out mugs of tea. As soon as everyone was at the table with hot cereal and honey, Ilika looked at the knowledge pad beside him.

"We have four kinds of excursions we can do here, two in the shadow of the planet, and two in the much smaller shadow of the ship. Rini and Mati, you are doing an orbital excursion together. Rini and Boro, you two will take some readings on the daytime surface. Rini and Kibi will look for the little creatures that live in the thin cusp between day and night. Finally, Rini and Sata will explore the dark, frozen night side."

Rini grinned.

"Rini is in command of each of these excursions. As we all know, he is practicing awareness of the situation. He is responsible for getting his companion, and himself, back to the ship, alive and well."

Everyone smiled at Rini.

"Here's the score," Ilika continued. "Eight seconds of exposure to the x-radiation from the sun at this distance, and you can forget having children."

Kibi looked glum.

"Twenty seconds, your hair will fall out and you won't be able to keep your food down . . . for months."

Mati frowned.

"Thirty seconds, you'll make it back to the ship, but quickly die."

Sata cringed.

"Forty seconds, your suit will be breached and you won't even get back inside."

Boro moaned.

"Rini, will you go down and get two space suits ready while we do the dishes? Mati will be down in a minute."

"Sure," Rini said, put his tray on the galley counter, and stepped into the lift.

As soon as he was gone, Ilika whispered further instructions to the other crew members.

*

Mati leaned on Rini until the outer airlock hatch opened. "I love excursions in orbit," she said through the intercom. "It's the only time my knee doesn't matter."

They both took a moment to hook their three-meter safety lines to the outside of the hull, then looked down at the little porch Manessa had created for them just outside the airlock.

"Nice," Rini said. "We can just stand here and look around at the stars and the beautiful little planet, without any danger of going outside Manessa's shadow."

Mati launched herself through the hatch. "Who needs a porch? We're weightless, remember?" She floated and slowly tumbled out to the end of her short safety line.

"Mati, I don't think that's such a good idea. They're just safety lines . . ."

"It's the only time I can forget I'm a cripple. And it's fun!"

Rini stood on the little porch, shuffling his feet and looking around. "Ilika just said these lines were about the right length. He didn't promise they'd keep us out of the x-rays . . ."

"I'll be careful, and if I feel any x-rays, I'll come in."

"But you can't feel . . ." Suddenly Rini stopped in mid-thought, seeing one of Mati's booted feet become brilliantly lit by the direct rays of the sun for a split second. He waited a heartbeat, then saw the same thing happen with one of her gloved hands. "Mati! On the porch! Now!"

Somewhat to his surprise, she said nothing, but immediately pulled on her safety line and a moment later was beside him on the porch, arms around him and a smile on her face. "Thank you, Rini."

✳

After Mati carefully brought the ship to a one-meter hover over the blazing daytime surface of the planet, Rini and Boro attached short safety lines and stepped out onto the little porch in the shadow of the ship. The slender lad had a complex instrument attached to the right arm of his suit, and the larger boy carried a sample container with several tools attached to the outside.

"Wow. I can feel the heat," Boro announced, shielding his face with a gloved hand.

Rini did the same. "Lucky for us, rocks don't re-radiate x-rays."

Boro raised his eyebrows. "They sure do a good job with infra-red! What shall we do first?"

"Um . . . instrument readings."

Both boys knelt down at the edge of the porch.

"We're still too high," Rini said. "Mati, can you take us down another half meter?"

"Sure," Mati replied from her station.

Boro shook his head with discomfort. "I'm starting to sweat, and my suit cooling system's doing all it can."

Rini thought for a moment. "Um . . . you move back from the edge while I get the readings, then you can get a sample."

Boro did what Rini commanded without hesitation. Rini didn't see his friend's slight smile.

Rini lowered the instrument's probe to the ground. "Ilika was right — it's so hot, it's almost liquid. I'm getting a bunch of weird numbers Ilika will have to explain. Okay, I'm done."

Rini moved back from the edge and Boro moved forward with the sample container.

Rini was leaning against the hatch, blinking to keep the sweat out of his eyes, when he saw Boro reach for a small loose rock with his gloved hand. "No! Stop!"

Boro jerked his hand back. "Oh, yeah, I forgot. I'm supposed to use the spoon." After detaching a sampling tool from the side of the container, he carefully scooped up the rock, placed it inside, closed the top, and replaced the tool.

Rini breathed again.

"All done!" Boro said in a happy voice.

*

Rini was the first member of the new crew to set foot on another world. Kibi came close behind.

The Manessa Kwi perched in the shadow of the planet, on the perpetual night side, but just barely. The intense solar wind streamed by less than a hundred meters over their heads. On the horizon, a short walk away, barren rocks blazed with light and heat. Even though no sound could be heard in the airless vacuum, both crew members felt a subtle vibration coming through the ground as the deadly solar wind slowly ate away the rocks, and anything else it touched.

"This is creepy," Kibi said with a shaking voice. "Let's go find those critters, make a painting, and get back to the ship."

"Photo . . . graph," Rini corrected, still struggling with the word himself. "We're safe as long as we stay out of the light."

"I suppose you're right. I never thought I'd say this, but I'd rather be in our ship than on *this* solid ground."

Rini chuckled as they began walking toward the glowing horizon, the home of the only living things on the planet.

A few minutes later, less than a kilometer from the blazing rocks, tiny flashes of blue light greeted them from the ground. "Don't step on them!" Rini shouted. "Ilika said they're sentient."

"I won't," she said, stooping down to look closely at one. "Wow, they're like little gems. No water, no carbon, just rocks and stardust." She opened the cover of her mission bracelet, made some adjustments, and took a picture.

Kibi stood up and gazed toward the bright horizon. "Looks like they get bigger closer to the light." She began walking slowly, avoiding the crystalline creatures on the ground. "I want to get a photograph of a big one."

Rini followed silently, watching where he placed his feet.

A little way ahead, Kibi stopped in front of a sparkling clump of blue crystals. "This is about as big as they get." She knelt down in a clear place and opened her mission bracelet again.

Rini looked all around at the crystal life forms, the glowing rocks on the horizon, and the solar wind streaming by not far over their heads. He smiled. When he looked back at Kibi, he saw blue crystals beginning to cling to the legs of her space suit. "Kibi! Run!"

She instantly jumped up and ran back toward the ship. The blue creatures on her legs quickly fell to the ground. Rini met her just outside the narrow habitat of the only living things on the planet.

"Thanks, Rini!"

✳

Flying solely by instruments, Mati landed the little ship on a level place deep in the perpetual darkness of the planet. Only dim starlight suggested where the horizon might be, until the pilot activated external ship lights. Strange rock formations of all sizes, some taller than the ship, surrounded them in every direction.

"The rocks are built up over millions of years by frozen stardust," Ilika explained. "They are very fragile, and may crumble if touched, but weigh very little."

Rini and Sata were soon in space suits, ready to explore. As soon as they left the airlock, both activated their bracelet lights. Sata carried a sample container.

Rini was soon immersed in the mystery of the place, gazing open-mouthed at the eerie rock shapes all around, sometimes turning circles to look up at the star-studded sky above, occasionally even laughing out loud at the sheer wonder of being on another planet.

Sata felt the same joy and wonder, but remembered her task. About fifteen minutes into their exploration, she spotted what she wanted, a tiny stardust formation that would fit whole into her container. "I'm stopping for a sample, Rini."

With some difficulty, he stayed within sight while she worked.

Sample container closed, Sata was back at his side, ready to follow wherever he led.

About half an hour later, Rini began to slow his pace. "Um . . . Sata, have you been paying attention to which way we were going?"

Sata took a few seconds to remember what she was supposed to say. "No. I got the sample. You're the leader."

Rini swallowed. "I just realized . . . we've been walking a long time."

"Yeah. Almost an hour."

"Ilika, can you hear me?" Rini asked over the intercom. "I . . . um . . . think we're lost."

He heard nothing but their own soft breathing.

"Mati? Boro? Kibi? Manessa?"

Again, only silence.

Sata cleared her throat. "I remember Ilika saying the stardust rocks might block our communications."

Rini was silent for a long moment, then spoke in a broken voice. "I'm . . . sorry. I'm not a very good leader. You can lead now . . ."

"No way!" Sata replied instantly. "I just came along for the sample."

Several more minutes passed as the two explorers stood among the eerie rock formations that all looked alike. Neither spoke. Rini stood slowly turning, looking this way and that. Sata stood calmly and patiently, not offering suggestions or encouragement.

Suddenly Rini began stomping around like a furious animal, sometimes growling with anger, at other times sobbing with guilt. Soon he bumped into a large formation and it came slowly crashing down, doing him no harm but knocking him to the ground.

Seeing he was okay, Sata said nothing.

His anger at himself spent, Rini began to pick himself up, and happened to shine his bracelet light onto the impression of his own boot in the stardust on the ground. A moment later he began laughing and couldn't stop, even while getting to his feet.

"I'm so stupid! We can just follow our tracks back to the ship! It's crumbly stardust the whole way! It may not be a perfectly straight line, but we'll get home."

Sata smiled. "I knew you could do it!"

✳

When Rini and Sata returned, it was no simple meal of stew and bread that greeted them, but a feast from Manessa's original supplies. Rini started to tell what happened, but soon realized from everyone's expressions that they already knew.

"I think Rini has made great progress at situational awareness here on Sonmatia One," Ilika announced happily. "He has to keep practicing, of course, as we all must do. His biggest challenge will be when he is alone, with no one counting on him."

"The way I see it," Boro began, "when we're alone, we're *always* in command."

Mati sipped her tangy beverage. "And he has to learn that bringing himself home safely is just as important as leading others home."

Rini grinned and blushed. "Thank you, all of you, for helping me . . . um

. . . grow up."

"You've always been there for us!" Mati said with sparkling eyes and a smile.

Rini leaned toward her. "And I always will be." Then he leaned farther and kissed her.

She wrapped her arms around his neck and didn't let him get away for a long time.

✳   ✳   ✳

Chapter 6: The Sad Tale of Sonmatia Two

When Sata opened her sample container, the little stardust formation was nothing but a spoonful of sparkling gray powder on the bottom. Kibi and Boro insisted on an excursion to see the strange things up close and try to get a good one for a souvenir.

Ilika smiled, but said nothing. He had never walked on this planet, so he joined them.

Mati stuck out her lower lip for a moment, then grinned.

Ilika returned her grin, and put her in command.

✳

Mati watched on the large bridge display from the commander's chair as Kibi, Boro, and Ilika wandered among the strange formations. She laughed when Boro touched one, then found himself standing in a pile of stardust.

Both the steward and the engineer brought back small formations. Furrowed brows and sad faces gazed into their sample containers, until Rini called them over to the watch station and explained the pressure difference between the near-vacuum of the planet and the atmosphere inside the ship.

Kibi looked thoughtful. "So . . . if we brought a little blue crystal creature into the ship . . ."

Ilika shook his head. "Same thing would happen as soon as you opened the container. This is their home, a strip of this planet just a few hundred meters wide, a little indirect warmth from the solar wind, and a pinch of stardust. Anything else and they'd die, as surely as we would die here without a ship or a space suit."

✳

An hour later, Sata, Boro, and Ilika very carefully walked among the blue crystals, letting them cling to their legs for a moment before gently shaking them off.

Mati again watched from the ship, and silently counted the planets that lay between her and the healers of Satamia Star Station.

✳

"We've learned many things from this little planet," the captain said after a hearty breakfast the next morning. "I'm glad Boro is feeling protective of his space thruster fuel. We won't use it often."

Boro smiled.

"I can see that Mati and Sata are anxious to calculate another orbit . . ."

Both girls nodded. "And get it right this time!" Sata said with a big grin.

"Good. The next planet we will visit, Sonmatia Two, is going to test us in very different ways because it contains the ruins — and even a few survivors — of a civilization that collapsed several hundred years ago. It's closer to the sun than your planet, and tends to overheat with any instability in the climate, just as your planet tends to cool off. Sonmatia Two is currently overheated because of the conscious choices of the people who lived there. They could have avoided the destruction of their civilization and the death of most of their population. They chose not to."

"That's stupid!" Mati spat out with a growl.

"They were much more intelligent than the people on your planet," Ilika pointed out.

Mati clamped her mouth shut.

"But they weren't smart enough. Every sapient race goes through this test, arranged by the overseers of the universe. Every planet full of people eventually discovers enough knowledge and power to change their climate. If they have also gained enough wisdom, they survive. If not, they die, or regress to a level that can survive on . . . whatever is left of their planet. It's like the little birdie that mother bird has to shove out of the nest, to fly or fall to the ground and be eaten."

A long silence followed.

"Um . . ." Kibi began, "those . . . overseers of the universe. Are they in . . . the Nebador Services?"

"No. We, in the Services, are just their helpers. None of us have the wisdom to manage a universe. Sonmatia Two is a perfect example, on a very small scale. The people who lived there were, as people go, quite wise. Now their world is a wasteland of corroded metal and poisonous fumes, with a few sickly mutated people surviving in deep tunnels, eating old food and a few mushrooms they grow, barely able to have children before they die."

Several crew members closed their eyes tightly and shuddered.

✻

Mati and Sata planned the flight quietly and thoughtfully. They paid close attention to the orbital entry, wanting to get it perfect. Boro watched and asked a few questions. Rini worked alone at his station, then sent them a chart with a couple of asteroids to avoid. Kibi started a stew for lunch and dinner.

Boro smiled as he checked and warmed up the anti-mass and ion drives, both of which used very little fuel. After securing the ship, they floated up a thousand meters, then streaked off across the black sky on an elliptical course toward Sonmatia Two.

During the half-hour transit, they peered at maps of the planet, got a feel for the locations of gentle mountain ranges and shallow valleys, and were quite amazed at the number and size of the cities — all now ruins. As they approached the haze-enshrouded world, Mati instantly changed the ship's relative speed to match their calculations. "I *like* the anti-mass drive!" the pilot declared.

Sata double-checked everything and judged the ship ready to slide into a circular orbit.

"Finished with ion drive," Mati said to Boro as she concentrated on her three-dimensional flight plan.

"Ion drive off," Boro replied. "Maneuvering thrusters green."

Mati made a slight course correction. "That should do. Anti-mass to standby."

"Manessa is happy with the orbit," Sata announced.

Ilika turned to the watch station. "Anything up here with us, Rini?"

"Not this high. Several pieces of junk lower, all made of metal and in slowly decaying orbits."

"Update Manessa's satellite list, as we'll be going down later."

Rini went to work.

"Wow . . . um . . . Ilika . . . er . . . um . . ." Sata began, searching for words as she stared wide-eyed at her display.

"Report," Ilika said, "preferably with words."

"Um . . . the universe transponder . . . um . . . says there's another Nebador ship down there!"

Ilika stood up and stepped to the navigator's station. "Well, well. I'm not too surprised to see a life-monitor ship here. Also . . . you could use some practice at ship-to-ship communications."

"Me? Um . . . what do I say?"

The captain reached down and made a selection on Sata's main console. "Here's your outline. First, who you are calling, ship type and name. Second, who and where you are. Finally, what you want. For example, life-monitor Tirilana Kril, this is deep-space response Manessa Kwi in high orbit, request planetary information and practice at ship-to-ship communications. They'll know from the transponder that we're a crew-in-training."

"Um . . . okay . . . I'll try."

"Everyone, activate your station cameras so they can see us," Ilika instructed, then walked around to make sure each was ready. "Go ahead, Sata. Communications is primarily your job."

Sata touched the transmit control with trembling fingers. "Um . . . life-monitor Manessa Kwi . . . no, I mean Tiri . . . lana Kril . . . um . . . this is life-monitor . . . I mean deep-space response Manessa Kwi . . . um, what's next . . . oh, yeah, in high orbit . . . um . . . request ship-to-ship information . . . no, communications . . . sheesh!"

"You're doing fine," Ilika said from behind her with encouragement. "Keep going."

"And . . . um . . . planetary information. Whew!"

Suddenly Sata's display changed to a visual of her counterpart on the other ship. The ship's interior was much larger than the Manessa Kwi, and several other crew members could be seen working at consoles or tables.

"Greetings, Manessa Kwi! I am Drrrim-na, navigator of the Tirilana Kril, at your service, bok."

"Hello . . . um . . . I'm Sata. Um . . . everyone else say hello."

Each of the other crew members managed to say their names and add a smile or a little wave. Only Kibi kept her words untangled.

"Ilika Imni Zalara Sim, captain," he said, last of all.

Sata tried to collect her thoughts when Ilika looked back at her. "Um . . . what does a life-monitor ship do?"

"Bok. On this planet, the remnant of the sapient race is in a very dangerous transition. Their population is only about five hundred and falling, bok. They are running out of food, and are very hesitant to try new things, even though we often give them, bok, seeds and spores. They have an offer of relocation, but have not yet accepted."

"How many . . . um, people . . . work on a life-monitor ship?" Kibi asked from her station.

"Twenty, bok, with cabins for eight more visiting specialists or students. We are a mixed crew. I see that you are all, bok, what do you call yourselves? Monkey mammals?"

Hurt expressions came to Sata, Mati, and Boro. Kibi managed to hide her feelings. Rini just grinned.

"I am sorry, bok. I can see that I offended."

"It's okay," Ilika said. "They're still getting used to the variety of people in the Nebador Services."

"I have read about deep-space response ships," the other navigator said. "You have every kind of engine, and get to have mates on board, bok."

"Yes," the captain said as the other five blushed. "Are there any areas of the planet we should avoid?"

"Yes," Drrrim-na said, touching a control. "The inhabited areas are sensitive, bok. I will send you a chart."

Sata noticed the chart flash onto a small part of her display. "I have the chart."

"I must go now," Drrrim-na said. "I am cooking the next meal."

"Bye!"

"Thank you!"

"Bye!"

"I hope to talk with you again, perhaps meet you someday, Sata. Tirilana Kril closing, bok."

"That would be wonderful. Manessa Kwi . . . um . . . closing."

Everyone was silent for a moment as they absorbed the experience.

"Good work, Sata," Ilika said.

"Wow. I can't believe I just talked to another navigator, on another ship, and she's a bird!"

* * *

Chapter 7: Watch Your Back

Mati made use of Rini's orbital junk chart as she carefully lowered the ship toward the planet. She took them near one of the metallic objects, almost as large as the Manessa Kwi, just to satisfy everyone's curiosity.

"It's a communications satellite," Ilika explained, "designed to receive audio or video signals from one place on the planet and send them back down to another place." He worked with Rini for a minute, and they detected a working energy source within the huge device, but no signals coming or going.

Mati continued the descent and soon entered the noxious yellow atmosphere. "Real-time surface topographics, Rini."

"Channel four."

"Synchronized map is on channel five," Sata added.

Mati arranged the new information on her display. "Atmospheric thrusters, level two."

"Warming . . . green," Boro reported.

"Kibi has command," Ilika said, standing up.

Kibi swallowed once, glanced at a few things on her console, then stepped down to the command chair. "You have that chart of the places we're not supposed to go, Mati?"

The pilot poked at her display selector. "No. I need that, Sata."

"I'm adding it to the map on channel five. There."

"Got it. Where to?"

Kibi thought for a moment. "I'm sure we all want to see a city. Other requests?"

"Any oceans or lakes?" Boro asked with a twisted grin.

"Not any more!" Rini replied. "It's so hot down there, all surface water is now just vapor mixed with the foul air."

"So this . . . sickly soup I'm flying through . . ." Mati began.

"Is a mixture of smoke and fog," Rini finished.

"Smoke from a million factories," Ilika explained. "By the time they realized the planet was overheating and they could never get the stuff back out of the atmosphere, it was too late."

The interior of the ship was quiet for a few minutes as Mati guided them toward a large ruined city. Ilika went from station to station, giving little reminders or pointing out new controls.

Their visual displays were useless until the Manessa Kwi was almost on the ground. Huge metal skeletons of crumbling buildings appeared in the putrid yellow mists, most of them towering over the ship.

Ilika went to the steward's station. "I suggest inertia straps."

Kibi nodded and everyone strapped themselves in.

Boro moaned as twisted metal seemed to reach out toward them when the yellow vapors parted for a moment. "Ugliest place I've ever seen. Makes Rumble Town look nice."

Mati guided the ship between crumbling towers, some partly collapsed, others leaning. Brownish fumes lurked at the base of one ruined building.

"Why did they make them so tall?" Rini wondered aloud. "Were they trying to touch the sky?"

Ilika was silent for a moment as he gazed at the statue of a sea creature in a bone-dry fountain. "I don't know, Rini. Most sapient races seem driven to crowd themselves close together, then compete violently for the scarce resources caused by the crowding."

Rini shrugged.

Mati took them through a large archway of bent metal and broken stone. Before they were all the way through, a loud thump filled the ship.

Rini looked up. "I th-think something hit the hull."

"Yes," Ilika said, working at the steward's console. "Many of these buildings were covered with stone, and now it's slowly falling off. No risk to the ship."

They gazed at their visual displays and saw piles of broken stone surrounding most of the buildings. At other places, broken glass glinted in the harsh yellow light. Where no rubble had piled up, the paving stones themselves jutted at odd angles.

"I suggest external audio, Kibi," Ilika said.

"Good idea."

Rini touched a control. "I don't hear a thing out there."

Mati guided the ship around a corner and they came face to face with the collapsed frame of a once-tall building.

"What was that?" Boro suddenly asked, looking up as if listening.

Everyone was silent as they strained to hear.

"I don't . . ." Sata began.

"Wait!" Kibi ordered, hand raised.

A few seconds later, a loud metallic creaking sound made them all shiver.

"I saw some metal move!" Rini yelled. "That building on the left!"

"Give us some distance, Mati," Kibi ordered with all the calmness she could muster while gripping the arms of her chair with white knuckles.

"It's coming down!" Rini shrieked at the same time that Sata yelled, Boro moaned, and they all heard a loud crashing sound. The entire metal frame of the tall building slowly collapsed onto itself, sending a huge cloud of brown dust outward in every direction.

Mati was still backing the ship away, and they appeared to be out of danger, when suddenly a loud clang was heard, the entire ship shuddered, and falling beams of rusty metal and chunks of broken stone came raining down, covering all the visual displays.

9

Falling debris continued to pound the hull of the Manessa Kwi for the next half minute, becoming softer and softer as the layer thickened. Then silence filled the ship as the crew-in-training realized what had happened. Ilika could almost taste the fear as five pairs of wide eyes looked around the bridge.

After swallowing several times, Mati found the courage to speak first. "Um . . . I'm . . . sorry . . ." she said through tears.

Kibi shook her head to clear her thoughts. "Ilika, I imagine you want to take . . ."

"No. It's good for people to clean up their own messes, whenever possible."

She bared her teeth at her captain and lover for a moment, then took a deep breath. "Status reports, all stations."

Mati was wiping her eyes on her sleeve. "I'm the worst pilot in Nebador, and I want to go off-duty and clean toilets or something."

"Denied," Kibi said firmly. "And I still need a report."

"Um . . . I think I backed into a building, and it fell on us."

"I guessed that much," Kibi said as Rini started chuckling.

Mati cracked a tiny smile. "Um . . . I'm okay and we're . . . um . . . on the ground, I think."

"Sata?"

The navigator turned, eyes still wide. "I thought we were going to be crushed! Um . . . like Mati said, we're on the ground. The map on channel five shows our exact location."

"Boro?"

"I'm fine. Engines are all green."

Kibi nodded and smiled at the engineer, always solid and reliable in any emergency. "You can shut them down, do diagnostics or whatever they need."

Boro turned back to his console.

"Rini?"

"Um . . . visual sensors in all directions are blocked, air outside is full of dust but otherwise the same. Mati doesn't have to clean toilets when she goes off-duty. Instead, she gets a neck massage."

Mati turned and smiled.

Kibi swiveled around. "Ilika?"

"Hopefully you are all a step closer to believing me when I say that very little in the physical universe can harm our ship in any way."

✳ ✳ ✳

Chapter 8: Out of a Trap

After everyone shut down their consoles, Kibi served a simple lunch and Ilika clarified his last statement.

"It's us, the delicate little creatures inside the ship, who can be hurt. This was good for Mati. She hasn't made a serious piloting mistake in a while. Situational awareness is more important for her than anyone else. Luckily the building she knocked down was uninhabited, and of no value to anyone."

The pilot grinned shyly.

"But the fact that Manessa is unharmed, and we're merely shaken, doesn't change the fact that we're buried under a huge pile of twisted metal and rubble. We have to find a way out. Kibi is still in command, but I'm limiting your options. Space thrusters will do the trick, but there's another way."

Kibi ate her reheated stew in silence for a moment. "Manessa, have you ever before been buried?"

"Yes," the ship's pleasant voice responded. "Two hundred and thirty-one years ago I had an avian crew who liked being nice and warm, so they chose an active lava flow for a landing site. I complained, but they shut off automatic warnings, as Ilika sometimes does for training purposes. By morning, we were covered by solidified lava. It took the crew four days to figure out how to get free. They never again shut off automatic warnings."

"How did they get you out?"

"Ilika asked me not to tell you."

Kibi flashed her captain an expression so sour, he burst out laughing. Rini and Boro both joined him. Mati smiled, but was still nursing too many guilty feelings to join in the laughter. Sata's eyes showed some fear, but after a moment she too smiled.

Kibi sighed. "Ideas, anyone?"

"I don't think I dare use atmospheric thrusters," Boro said. "Too much dirt and junk piled all around the ship."

Ilika nodded. "That's correct. They'd refuse to even warm up."

"Anti-mass?" Rini proposed.

"That's what I'm thinking," Mati agreed. "I don't know how much it'll take, but hopefully by level seven . . ." She looked at Boro.

He nodded, and took another spoonful of stew.

✳

The anti-mass drive at level one did nothing.

Level two caused a little bit of creaking and some dust to sift downward across their view screens.

Kibi ordered inertia straps before they tried level three. The ship quivered and shook, the metal above and around them groaned and creaked, but nothing moved.

As they tried level four, Rini started frowning and then doing something at his console. The ship moved up a small fraction of a meter, but could go no farther.

Once the screeching and thumping caused by level five ceased, Rini turned around. "We have a bigger problem."

Kibi looked at him.

"The metal frame of that building was all connected together. It's acting just like a net. The harder we push, the tighter it gets — I can tell from the pressure on Manessa's hull."

Kibi sighed. "So you mean . . . if we do get off the ground, we're going to take the whole pissing thing with us — metal, stone, everything?"

Rini nodded with a sad expression.

Kibi turned and looked at Ilika. He was careful to keep his eyes on the steward's console.

"Level six!" she said, turning back around. "We have to try."

The ship bucked and lurched, the metal all around them screamed like a frightened animal, and countless chunks of rock pounded on the hull before Kibi finally let Mati stop. Then she looked at Rini.

"Pressure's even greater. It's wrapped around us like a spider web."

"And we're the damned fly," she growled. "I don't really expect it to work, but no harm in trying seven, I guess."

Boro worked at his controls. "I'm bringing in more inertia canceling so we won't be jelly on the floor if we suddenly break free."

"Yeah, no jelly. Everyone ready?"

Sata's eyes were larger than before, even though she had pretty pictures on three-quarters of her display. Mati looked determined, and still nursing guilt. Kibi nodded for her to begin their last and final hope.

The tortured metal screeched and screamed so loudly that Kibi yelled for Rini to turn off the audio. One visual display cleared for a moment, allowing them to see twenty or more beams stretch tightly across that part of the ship. It was soon covered again by dust and grit.

After nearly a minute, which felt more like an hour, Kibi screamed, "STOP!" and doubled over in the command chair, crying her eyes out.

✳

Drawn faces sat around the large table nibbling on crackers without tasting them. Rini stood behind Mati, massaging her shoulders. Ilika tried to do the same for Kibi, but she just snapped at him.

Boro appeared unaffected. "I think we should all try to relax, maybe even get some sleep. We already know we can leave any time we want with space thrusters."

Kibi looked daggers at him. "That's easy for *you* to say. Some of us can *feel* in our bones that we're under a big pile of junk, even though we can't see it."

"Sorry," Boro mumbled.

Everyone remained silent for a minute. Mati had her eyes closed as Rini continued massaging her shoulders.

Ilika poked at a knowledge pad. "I think you need to teach Manessa how to dance."

Mati turned and glared at him. "How can a crippled slave teach a deep-space . . ." Their eyes met and suddenly her mouth opened.

"What?" Sata asked.

"What!" Kibi demanded.

"He's right," Mati said. "It's like a tangled ball of string. We've been using brute force. We have to untangle it, instead."

Rini smiled down at his dear friend.

"Boro!" Mati said in her flight-command voice, grabbing her crutch and standing up, "I want anti-mass one and maneuvering thrusters!"

Seconds later they were all at their stations. The pilot raised her flight control. "This could get a little bumpy. I want straps and seven-eighths inertia canceling."

Kibi nodded. "Whatever she wants, Boro."

"Warming up!"

Everyone pulled down their inertia straps.

"Anti-mass, maneuvering, seven-eighths canceling, all green."

Kibi looked around. "Sata?"

"Chart is still good, flight recorder on."

"Rini?"

"Sensors ready, as soon as there's something to see."

"Ilika?"

"The Manessa Kwi is ready for flight."

"Mati," the acting commander said, "you have flight command."

Mati started the process slowly, nudging the ship back and forth, getting a feel for how the metal web around her reacted.

"I'm getting seasick!" Sata moaned.

"Sorry," Mati said without looking at her friend. "I need to *feel* what the ship is doing."

Ilika delivered a bowl to Sata just as Mati began swinging the ship.

"Pressure is easing up on the hull!" Rini announced happily.

Kibi began to breath deeply.

"Boro," Mati began, "I don't want anti-mass, I want *more* mass. The way out is *under* this slimy thing."

"Can do. It's for underwater."

"Give me a little so I can see what it feels like."

Just then Sata gave up and lost her crackers.

"Sorry, Sata," the pilot said.

"It's okay, as long as I get to see the stars again."

The pilot concentrated for a few more seconds. "More mass, Boro."

"You've got it."

Ilika brought Sata a towel, holding onto things as he moved about the ship.

"Our cage is getting bigger!" Rini called out.

"I have an idea," Mati said. A moment later the ship began spinning slowly while still wobbling. Suddenly all the dirt and rock covering the visual sensors fell away.

"Whoopee!" Rini cheered.

Ilika grinned from the steward's station.

"Okay," Mati began, "I think we're getting somewhere. I want all maneuvering thrusters. Don't hold anything back, Boro."

"Okay, you've got the works."

"Let's see what happens if I take a swing at it right about . . . here."

The Manessa Kwi dove for a point in the tangle of metal where most of the beams were just hanging loosely. The impact make the ship quiver as beams gave up and bent away, or fell to the ground. Several more still blocked the way.

Mati didn't apply any more force, but began rocking and spinning the ship again, nudging at the remaining metal.

Without warning, Boro tucked his head between his knees and lost his last meal onto the floor. Rini was just a few moments behind.

"Sorry," both muttered.

Mati didn't let up her concentration. For another half minute, she tickled the few metal beams between the ship and freedom, then started the ship spinning. "Anti-mass one, Boro."

"Ready," he said, touching controls with one hand, holding a towel with the other.

As the Manessa Kwi began to float, Mati used all her maneuvering thrusters to slowly coax the spinning ship into the weakest point of the trap. The metal fingers slid around them on both sides until nothing stood between the little ship and the freedom of the debris-littered streets.

Kibi, Sata, Rini, and Boro all began cheering. Ilika grinned happily.

Mati paid absolutely no attention until she had the ship a hundred meters above the tallest metal ruins of the dead city.

* * *

Chapter 9: The Slow Way

"Is there anywhere ... nice ... on this planet?" Kibi asked from the command chair. "Somewhere we can relax?"

Sata began selecting charts. "The poles are a little cooler. No cities or people."

"Make a simple flight plan, Sata, to somewhere ... anywhere."

The navigator soon passed the new flight plan to the pilot. "Your highest elevation is two thousand meters."

Mati took a slow, deep breath, then shivered for a moment. "Boro, ion three. Going up to six thousand."

Boro shook his head to clear the cobwebs before reaching for his console.

Ilika watched his crew deal with the lingering stress, and smiled to himself.

A few minutes later, with the yellow vapors much thinner at the south pole of the planet, Mati was able to use her visual display to lower the ship onto flat, rocky ground.

Rini selected atmospheric tests. "Sorry everyone, it's cooler, but we still can't breath it."

Kibi turned around and looked at Ilika. "NOW will you take back command of your ship? *Please?*"

Ilika smiled and nodded.

*

For the next hour, Kibi selected music and dreamily swayed in the space between her station and the galley, where Ilika worked. He often glanced at his beautiful lover and smiled.

Both Boro and Rini were on their hands and knees, under their consoles, with cleaning supplies.

Eventually Ilika brought cups of cold, sweet tea to the table. Kibi sat down with him.

He looked into her dark eyes. "I'm glad you're not ... feeling any desire to open the hatch and run outside."

She frowned. "In that hot, yellow air? Actually . . ." She looked around to see who was on the upper deck. "I've been watching Mati. I think getting us out of that trap made her feel better about her mistake, but she's really looking forward to Satamia Star Station. My knee almost hurts in sympathy when I see the longing on her face."

"It's been a heavy burden for her."

"And I think Sata felt some of her old fear today."

"A bunch," Sata said, stepping out of the toilet room, drying her hair. "But I could see how bad Mati felt about what happened." The navigator sat down beside her captain and reached for a cup of tea.

"I was really proud of both of you," Ilika said.

"Both of . . . who?" Mati asked, appearing in the lift with wet hair.

"You and Sata," Kibi informed.

Ilika looked into the sparkling eyes of his handicapped pilot. "You were both great."

"I knew if I didn't get us out of there, I'd feel like . . . like a crippled slave!"

Everyone at the table laughed.

"Today you were able to work out your feelings by getting us out of that little trap," Ilika said. "At times in the future, you won't be able to do that. You'll just have to relax and let others help."

"I know," Mati said. "But it sure felt good to clean up my own mess!"

Boro and Rini both looked up from their cleaning work and smiled.

*

That evening, the five new crew members selected a video about ships in difficult situations, and how the crews overcame problems, and their own fears, to bring everyone safely home.

At first Ilika was surprised by their choice. Then he began to understand as he watched from the back of the passenger area and saw them beaming with pride any time a situation was similar to one they had experienced. He also observed them paying close attention when the danger was completely new to them.

*

After a good night's sleep and a hearty breakfast, the crew of the Manessa Kwi looked at their captain to know the next phase of their journey.

Ilika took the last swallow of his beverage, then pulled a knowledge pad close. "We've already explored Sonmatia Three . . ."

Everyone chuckled.

"The journey from here to the fourth planet will be slow, with lots of time for lessons along the way." He could see Mati frown slightly. "We will review a number of topics, bring Boro and Kibi up to speed on some mathematics, and study words and customs we'll need at the star station."

Mati's frown changed to a grin.

"The next leg of our journey will mostly fall to Sata and Boro as navigator and engineer, although I want all of you to understand the basics after they work out the details." He tapped at the knowledge pad, and a diagram appeared on the big screen.

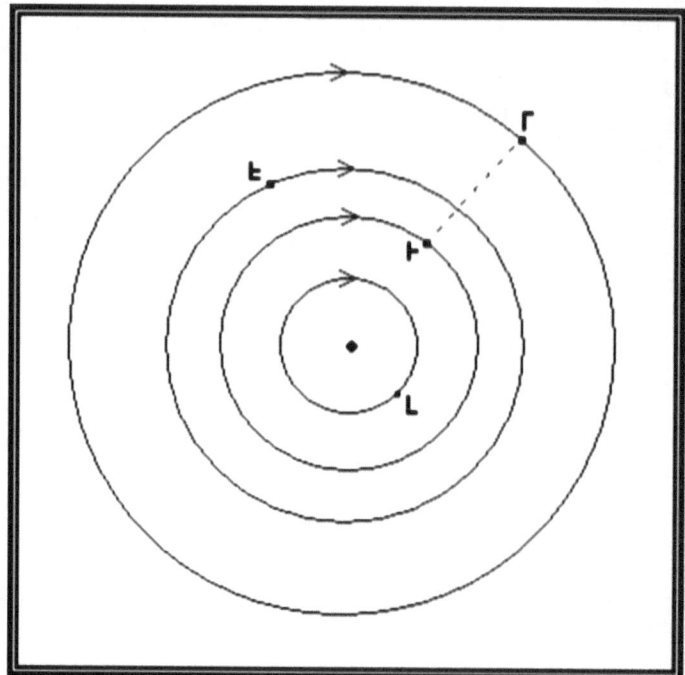

"Here are the current positions of the inner planets. Our location and our destination happen to be almost perfectly lined up. You might think that's a good thing. We'll see. Sata and Boro, you know how to use Manessa's orbit and transit simulation tools. Please calculate how much space thruster fuel we need for a direct route, orbit to orbit, no anti-mass, no ion drive."

Boro thought for a moment. "Depends on how fast you want to go."

"Start with minimum fuel usage."

Boro nodded. He and Sata headed toward her station, knowledge pads in hand.

※

Ilika began cooking in the galley, and the other crew members relaxed at the table. At first the sounds from the bridge were all calm and friendly. They heard Manessa's voice answering questions, and Sata or Boro chuckling with embarrassment.

As the first hour passed and the second began, the words and sounds from the front of the ship became more and more frustrated, sometimes almost angry. Kibi frowned as she fetched a game and sat down with Mati. Rini glanced at the bridge, didn't see any blood, so he stepped into the galley to help Ilika.

Near the end of the second hour, with the aroma of sweet biscuits filling the ship, those at the table became aware that no sound whatsoever was coming from the navigator's station. They looked and saw Boro and Sata standing side by side, holding hands and gazing at the display screen.

A few minutes later the navigator and engineer appeared at the table, looking happy but humble. Rini came out of the galley with a plate of sweet biscuits, and Ilika followed with cups of tea.

"I'm sure Ilika knew this was going to happen," Boro said with a half-suppressed grin.

"I'm not sure what you mean, Boro," the captain said, hiding his expression behind his cup.

"How did you put it, Sata?"

"There's no such thing as a straight line in space."

Ilika smiled. "Share with us what you learned."

Sata touched some keys on her knowledge pad. "Um, big screen, Kibi?"

The steward reached over to her console.

"Thanks."

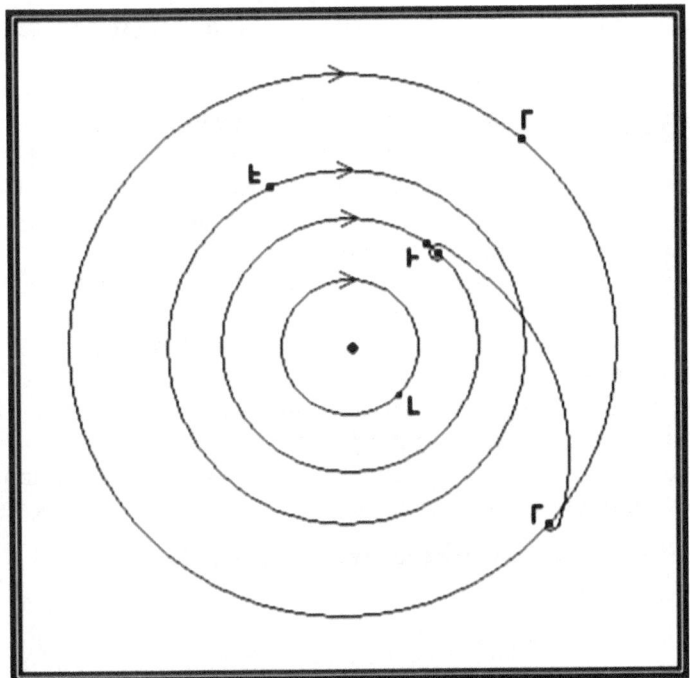

"First," Boro began, "Manessa reminded us that when we got free of this planet's gravity, it would be a little farther along in it's orbit of the sun. Okay, we could see that."

Sata nodded. "Then we tried to calculate flight path and time to that place where the fourth planet was supposed to be, and Manessa kept asking us why we would use that place as a navigation point."

Boro stepped in. "Manessa finally realized what was wrong when we said we wanted to go into orbit there. If a deep-space response ship could laugh, Manessa would have laughed."

Kibi chuckled, and everyone else was grinning.

Sata picked up the story. "Then Manessa explained that by the time we got there, the fourth planet wouldn't be there any more. In fact, by the time we could catch up with it, it would be almost a quarter of the way around the sun!"

"That means ..." Rini started to say.

Sata put a finger to her lips.

"As Rini guessed," Boro continued, "that means that from here to the fourth planet, with minimum fuel burn, would take about half a year."

Mati turned white. "Half a year!"

"Don't worry," Ilika jumped in. "We won't be using that plan. It was just for learning purposes."

The pilot struggled to regain her composure.

"So ..." Sata began again, "we learned that in space everything is always moving, nothing is as simple as we'd like it to be, and there's no such thing as a straight line."

"The funniest thing of all," Boro added, "is that Sonmatia Two will get to that part of the solar system way faster than we would!"

Ilika smiled and reached for a knowledge pad. "Well done, both of you, and thank you for sharing all your insights. Now let's see if we can whittle down that transit time. It just so happens that we have something handy that's a lot better than thruster fuel. We have a planet that's going our way."

Sata looked puzzled. "But if we just stayed on Sonmatia Two, we'd still have a big gap between the two orbits."

"I'm not thinking of this planet," Ilika replied. "I'm thinking of Sonmatia Three, your birthplace."

Expressions around the table varied from Rini's joy at anything that might be proposed, to Mati's dread at the slightest delay. No one, however, showed any sign of understanding what their captain could possibly be talking about.

Ilika sent another diagram to the big screen over the steward's station.

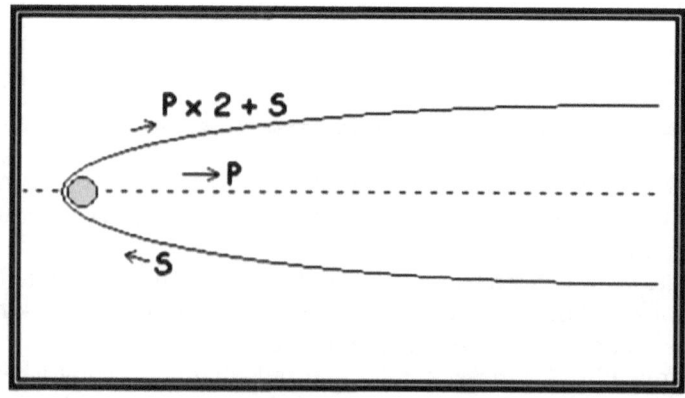

"If a ship, at speed S, swings around a planet orbiting the sun at speed P, the ship will add twice the speed of the planet to its own."

Boro sat with his mouth open. "Uh . . . that could really help."

Ilika nodded. "It's called planetary freeloading. All civilizations, who survive long enough to get into space, use it to get around their solar systems. By the way, how much fuel did your first plan use?"

Boro grabbed his knowledge pad. "Twelve point three kilograms, and that includes slowing down to enter orbit at Sonmatia Four."

"Use the same amount. With planetary freeloading off the third planet, you'll get a lot more speed."

Boro grinned at Sata, then they both drained their tea and headed for the bridge.

*

When Kibi saw that Mati and Rini were happily engrossed in a game, and Ilika was tending something in the galley, she wandered down to the lower deck.

After tossing some dirty clothes into the laundry machine, she stood gazing around at all the cabinets in the utility room, each one labeled with its contents. She smiled, remembering the first time she had stared at the strange writing, the language of Nebador, unable to read a word.

Now she could read the language quite well, was familiar with the contents of most of the cabinets, and responsible for them all. She opened several and saw things that would need restocking at Satamia Star Station.

Another cabinet caught her eye, *Sample and Display Containers*. Inside, she found the sample containers they had already used, lined with the same material as Manessa's hull and able to hold just about anything without harm to the sample or crew. She smiled, seeing that Ilika had already placed the stardust grains, and the rock from the daylight side, in a clear display container. Suddenly her eyes lit up with a memory, and she dashed to her cabin.

Deep in her old canvas pack, not used since the day Buna, Misa, Neti, Toli, and Tera walked down the trail and out of her life, she found what she remembered, a pine cone from the world of her birth, almost completely intact.

With mounting strips from another cabinet, she soon had a dozen display containers attached to the wall of the lower deck, just below the large display screen where the crew sometimes watched videos. The first held the pine cone, the second their samples from Sonmatia One, and the rest were empty. As she stepped into the lift to rejoin her friends, she wondered what the others would eventually contain.

*

"Amazing!" Boro said as he and Sata, glowing with pride, returned to the table less than an hour after going off to create a new flight plan using planetary freeloading. "I never would have guessed the best way to get somewhere was to go *backwards*."

Sata touched some controls on the steward's console and a new diagram appeared.

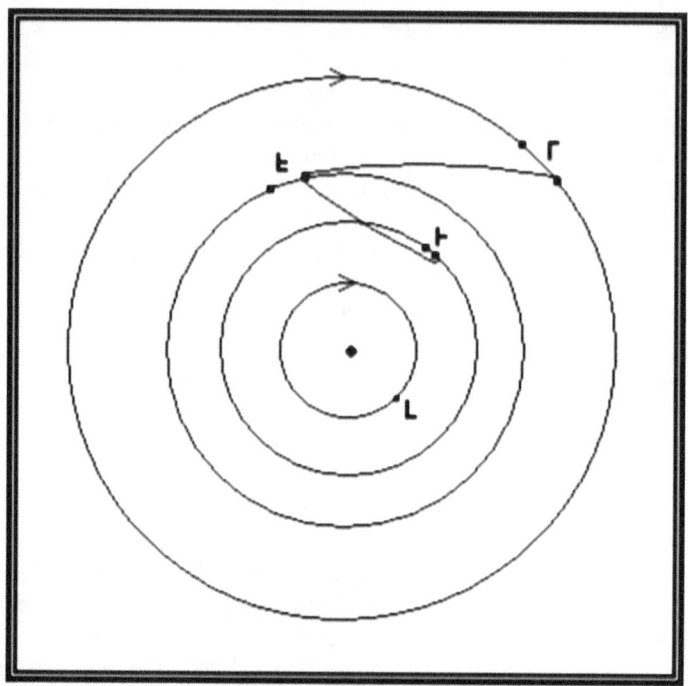

"Manessa says we should pass our planet at an altitude of fifty kilometers," the navigator explained. "That's almost close enough to pick berries in the mountains!"

Ilika smiled and nodded. "The closer you go, the more speed you pick up, as long as you don't get too much air friction."

"Or run into the mountains!" Mati added with wide eyes.

Everyone laughed, some a little nervously.

"So . . ." Ilika began after glancing at his handicapped pilot, "how long?"

"Just thirty days!" Boro answered, looking back and forth from captain to pilot. "That's . . . better . . . isn't it?"

Ilika watched as Mati took a deep breath, then cracked a little smile. "Yeah."

"Actually, we can do another trick," Ilika announced.

Mati's eyes widened with curiosity.

"Sata, your twelve point three kilograms of thruster fuel included both departure from this planet and orbit entry at the destination, right?"

"Of course. And most of it went to slowing down at Sonmatia Four."

"What would happen if you could use all of it for departure?"

"We could go *really* fast! But how? Are you going to let us use anti-mass at the fourth planet?"

"No. But that planet has an atmosphere. What happens if you go into orbit within an atmosphere?"

Both Sata and Boro were silent for half a minute, but the others could almost see the gears turning. A smile began to grow on Boro's face. "We'd . . . slow down from the friction."

"It's called atmospheric braking," Ilika explained. "Primitive space-faring civilizations rarely use it because it's so hard to build ships that can take the heat. Manessa's hull, as you know . . ."

"Can take just about anything!" Sata finished the thought.

Ilika smiled. "Manessa will show you how to calculate the braking orbits so you have just enough momentum left to get up to a stable orbit outside the atmosphere."

Boro and Sata looked at each other, grabbed knowledge pads, and headed for the navigator's station.

✳

As Mati descended in the lift, crutch under her arm, she wondered how much less than thirty days the flight would take with atmospheric braking. When she arrived alone on the lower deck, she reminded herself that even thirty, in base eight, was less than the thirty she used to know, a whole six days less.

She immediately spotted the new display containers on the wall under the large screen. Smiling, she gazed at the pine cone with fond memories, then entered her cabin.

After searching Buna's old rucksack and adding two dried maple seeds to the first display container, she looked at the third container, still empty. Suddenly a resolute expression came to her, and she hobbled toward the lift.

✳

A delicious savory aroma was coming from the galley when Boro and Sata plopped down at the big table and looked at Mati. "Eleven days!" they both said at once.

Mati grinned with thankfulness.

✳ ✳ ✳

Chapter 10: Presence of Mind and Memory

"Rini owes me an orbital excursion," Ilika said as they were finishing a tasty stew with a golden-brown biscuit crust.

Rini grinned. "I'm ready. I've been going over it in my head, remembering all the things I should have paid attention to . . . and didn't."

"Could you . . . um . . . do me a favor?" Mati asked with hesitation, looking at Rini.

"Anything," the freckled boy said with sparkling eyes. "After accidentally marrying the wrong girl . . ."

Mati turned bright red, and everyone else grinned.

"Actually . . ." she began, trying to find her voice, "it really is an excursion I want, back near a certain building that I . . . sort of . . . bumped into."

Ilika smiled with understanding. "Even though it's not the vacuum of space there, you can use the same suit, Rini, and then we'll go directly into orbit."

*

When they reentered the dead city, Mati kept a sharp eye on all her visual displays, especially to the rear. She set the ship down lightly not far from the collapsed building that had entrapped them.

Rini stepped through the airlock with a sample container, kept an eye on the metal skeletons looming above, and only went a few meters before he found a little piece of corroded metal, a small shard of broken glass, and a chunk of flat, smooth building stone. He looked around one last time, thought he heard the groan of twisting metal, and quickly returned to the ship.

Mati had the Manessa Kwi above the ghostly towers even before Rini could cycle the airlock.

*

Once they arrived in high orbit, everyone went down to the lower deck to see the new display.

"I know it's ugly stuff," Mati said, pointing at the collection of metal, glass, and stone from the dead city, "but it's part of our story, our new story, just us six, the crew of the Manessa Kwi."

The others nodded, then disappeared into their cabins for a few minutes. Soon the pine cone and maple seeds in the first container were joined by a feather, a small bone, a pretty rock, and a small dried mushroom.

✳

Rini floated through the airless void high above Sonmatia Two. This time, he had a plan. He set his bracelet to chime every minute. At each chime, he went down his checklist — air, thruster fuel, location, orientation, health status, mission status. It only took a few seconds, leaving him plenty of time for work or sightseeing.

On this occasion, he had no work to do. Ilika wanted him to practice presence of mind when he was most tempted to drift into an altered state of consciousness.

In one direction the sun blazed in a velvety black sky. The cloudy yellow planet turned slowly beneath him, causing him to wonder for a moment why he wasn't falling. Then he remembered that he was falling, just not straight down. He looked beyond the planet, and the stars seemed so close he could almost reach out and touch them.

Rini's minute-chime sounded, and his mind reluctantly returned from the stars. He took a few seconds to go through his checklist. "Sata, I'm down to five-eighths fuel, so I'm starting back."

"Great. I think Boro's making tea, and Manessa says a good orbital departure window is in about an hour."

Rini smiled and pointed himself back toward the little golden sphere orbiting not far away.

✳

Sata stayed at her station while Rini made his way back to the ship. She almost jumped when her communications display came to life with the image of the feathered navigator on the other ship. Sata smiled and touched a symbol.

"Hello, Sata, I noticed you were back in orbit, bok. Did you enjoy your visit to this sad little planet?"

"Hi, Drim-na. Well . . . we were in one of those old cities, and a building fell on us."

"Bok! Everyone okay?"

"Yeah, our pilot Mati is really good, and she got us out."

"Good. Our diplomats report that the people down here are looking at pictures of the planet we could relocate them to, bok, and are thinking about it."

"We're about to leave for Sonmatia Four, thrusters only."

"That will be slow and boring, bok."

"We have lots of things to study before we get to Satamia Star Station."

"The Tirilana Kril will be back there in a few days, bok, so maybe I will see you, and show you my favorite eating place."

Sata was silent for a moment. "That would be fun, Drim-na. You're the first friend I'm making who's not ... on my ship. Rini's coming in the airlock, so I should get ready."

"Be well, Sata. Tirilana Kril closing, bok."

"Um ... Manessa Kwi closing."

When the screen went dark, Sata turned around with a funny look on her face. "Ilika, what do Nebador birds eat?"

* * *

Chapter 11: Interplanetary Travel

"This kind of flight plan," Ilika explained from the command chair after everyone had completed basic pre-flight preparations, "is not possible manually. As Mati can see on her screen, all the timings are in thousandths of a second. Even so, Manessa will need to make further adjustments as we approach your home planet for freeloading, and the fourth planet for braking."

"So we just have to . . . trust Manessa?" Mati asked with a slightly worried look.

"Trust with knowledge. Sata and Boro have simulated the entire flight. With time, you'll be able to do that too, Mati. Manessa's contribution is the split-second timing, not the wisdom necessary to oversee the process. We're all on duty during the freeloading pass, and during braking orbits. Someone will be at or near the watch station for the next eleven days."

Rini sighed, but his eyes sparkled with a hint of pride.

"Orbital departure in four minutes," Sata announced.

"Even though you will not be handling the controls directly," Ilika continued, "you are still the pilot, Mati. You must approve each step before Manessa can carry it out. The first step is our orbital departure burn, then you have six days before the next step. But keep in mind that if you don't approve any part of the plan before its scheduled time, the entire plan is canceled."

"That would be terrible!" Boro complained.

"Remember, Boro, this is training. I'm going to do little things to force you and Sata to modify the plan at least once."

Boro moaned under his breath.

Sata rolled her eyes. "One minute."

Mati grinned, turned to her console, and approved the departure burn. "Up to three gravities of acceleration," she said, studying a graph on her screen. "We'll need inertia straps for a few minutes."

Everyone secured their straps.

"Watch station update?" Ilika requested.

"Nothing on the screen. Solar wind is on channel four, nothing unusual.

"Eight seconds," Sata said.

Remembering the space thruster burn that had saved them from falling into the sun, Boro, Sata, and Kibi gripped their chairs with white knuckles. As soon as the gentle departure burn was complete, they looked around sheepishly, hoping no one had noticed.

*

For the next few hours, everyone got comfortable with the new routine. Sata disappeared into the galley, and Kibi sat down with Mati to start a list of videos they wanted to watch during the slow transit to Sonmatia Four. Boro went down to the lower deck, one of his strange tools with blinking lights in hand.

Rini found himself alone on the bridge, the only crew member on-duty, so he selected one of the advanced lessons about his station and got comfortable in his chair. Most of his screen, however, contained the displays and graphs he had to keep an eye on, everything from magnetic fields to wandering chunks of rock and ice.

Ilika had his nose in a knowledge pad, pondering all the things he had to teach his crew before they arrived at Satamia Star Station. He wore a slight smile, remembering his own interplanetary training at age eleven.

Kibi and Mati wandered the ship, getting ideas from everyone about videos. Boro was on his back in the engineering ring, adjusting a mysterious glowing machine, when he asked for a video about old sea-going ships, the kind they once imagined Ilika having. Sata was spicing and tasting her soup when she requested a video about the birds in the Nebador Services.

Back at the big table in the passenger area, Ilika transferred a list of about a dozen videos from his knowledge pad to Kibi's. She and Mati looked at each other with knowing smiles — they were all about star stations.

*

The following morning, Ilika explained that a "day" on a ship in space was completely artificial, and always subject to change. If the crew felt plenty of energy, the steward could add a few hours. If they were exhausted from some trying mission, hours could just as easily be removed.

Kibi smiled for a moment, then took on a more serious look. "What do I do if some people have extra energy, but others are tired and want to go to bed?"

Ilika shrugged. "Life is full of tough choices. Of course, absolute Nebador time is the same everywhere in the local universe. Sometimes we'll have important things to do in the middle of our night."

Kibi yawned, but had a twinkle in her eyes.

After dishes were done, the captain began a series of advanced language lessons that focused on words needed at star stations. Every crew member received a list tailored to their jobs. Approach and docking terminology went to Sata and Mati. Rini and Boro learned the names of instruments and tools only available at a star station. Kibi received a short list about restocking supplies, and a much longer list related to passengers.

With plenty of breaks for meals, videos, and just plain fun, for the next two ship-days Ilika engaged each student in conversations when they least expected it, always emphasizing the new words they were supposed to know.

Rini noticed that something was bugging Kibi. Whenever she was not distracted by a tasty meal, an interesting video, or an intense lesson, she sat gazing at the walls and ceiling with a slight frown.

✳

With many new words at their fingertips, Ilika began to introduce them to the procedures and customs of star stations.

Rini would locate the artificial world, in its own orbit around a star. Sata would begin communicating with the station long before they could see it. Mati would use an assigned approach path to come to a complete stop near the station, then follow color-coded flight corridors both outside and inside. Manessa had simulations for each of them.

Boro, as always, was the crew member who would need to speak the least, but whose services would be absolutely essential. Kibi would have little to do until they arrived at the assigned space dock. At that point, Ilika assured her, she would wish for a twin sister.

Ilika shared one last thought. "As a deep-space response ship, we have an additional burden. We are the most maneuverable and flexible ship in space, so we have the lowest priority. If there is ever an overload, conflict, or emergency, we will be the ones to wait, move out of the way, or be called in to help."

Several crew members went off to try their simulations, and Boro entered the galley to work on the next meal. Ilika noticed Kibi staring at the main hatch for a long time.

✳

The following day, their fifth in space since leaving the second planet, everyone gathered for meals and videos, then went their separate ways for simulations and study. Ilika carefully watched all his crew members, looking for signs of cabin fever.

Boro seemed most happy spending time alone in the engineering ring, getting more familiar with all his engines. Ilika would occasionally wander through, and hear his student engineer asking the ship question after question about the pros and cons of the different fuels, or the difference between the electrical and magnetic fields of the anti-mass drive.

Sata liked to rerun the simulations of the freeloading pass and the braking orbits. She would try to guess what Ilika might do to make the trip to Sonmatia Four more challenging. None of her fellow crew members, nor the ship itself, cared to speculate.

Mati wasn't too concerned about the trip to Sonmatia Four, but her eyes sparkled every time she simulated the approach and docking at Satamia Star Station. She knew from the videos that student pilots could request automatic guidance through the color-coded maze, and if their piloting looked even a little dangerous, the station controller would require it. She intended to go from the outer system marker to space dock without giving them any reason to remember she was a student.

Rini discovered a new passion when he was on-duty at his station and not studying. While Sata's star charts were technical and not very pretty, Manessa also had countless pictures of planets, star clusters, nebulas, galaxies, and even stranger things Rini didn't yet understand. He would gaze at each one for a minute or more, and imagine himself flying among them like a creature of light who had no need of wings or a space suit.

Kibi dutifully studied her word lists and watched the videos that showed how busy a steward could be when passengers departed, supplies needed restocking, and new passengers came on board, sometimes all in just a few hours. She genuinely looked forward to those tasks, but right now she couldn't help but glance at the walls and ceiling every few minutes.

At one point late in the day, when Ilika was on the bridge talking to Mati, Kibi slipped away from her station, down the lift, and into the utility room. "Manessa, it seems to me the walls of the ship are getting closer, and the ceiling lower. I don't really understand all the stuff about dimensional shifting that lets the inside of the ship be a different size and shape from the outside, but is there any possibility the ship's getting smaller on the inside?"

"No, Kibi, the inside of the ship is always the exact same size and shape."

✻ ✻ ✻

Chapter 12: Knowledge

The following morning held an air of excitement, even though the approach adjustments for Sonmatia Three wouldn't happen until that evening. Rini and Sata made fried cakes with a sweet syrup on top, and Boro invited them all to see the video he chose.

The story began on an island that could have been Atorura. Brave men in hollowed-out logs dared to venture beyond the edge of the reef into the fury of the open ocean. Usually they returned to tell of other islands and good fishing waters, but sometimes they were never seen again.

Larger ships with a sail and a dozen or more rowers crept between mist-enshrouded islands seeking treasures and fertile lands. Those with crude compasses most often returned through the mists. Others left their broken hulls on the rocky beaches.

Huge wooden ships, driven by many sails, had crews of twenty or thirty, with two decks above the main deck, and three cargo decks below. A watchman, perched in a tiny basket on the tallest mast, scanned the horizon with a simple spy glass. Everyone smiled at Rini.

Enormous steel ships easily sliced through the waves as passengers lounged around swimming pools, or ate fine food in ornate dining rooms. Huge propellers churned the water as the engineer sat at a control panel with many lights and switches. Everyone looked at Boro, who instantly turned red.

✳

"I want to be honest with you," Kibi said to Ilika as they sat side by side in the passenger area about mid-afternoon. Boro was in the galley, and everyone else was busy with simulations.

Ilika leaned forward and kissed her lightly. "I'm all ears."

Kibi grinned for a moment. "My fear of . . . you know, tight spaces . . . is eating at me. The ship seems to be getting smaller every day."

"And we're still more than three days from Sonmatia Four . . ."

"Yeah, I know. I just wish I could go outside, take a walk or something."

"You can."

Kibi frowned with disbelief. "Really? But I thought the ship was going fast . . ."

"It is. So are you. If you were going at different speeds, you'd be a lump of goo on the wall."

Kibi smiled.

"The only problem is, you can't really go on a walk, you'll have to crawl because the repulsion field is only a meter outside the hull."

"I'll take it! Maybe it'll help me relax."

"We won't do slow trips like this very often, but it's just part of the basics that everyone needs to learn."

Kibi nodded with a smile and strode to the lift.

✳

"You in your suit, Kibi?" Sata asked from her station.

"Yeah, just doing my checklist. Pressure, air, cooling, thruster fuel . . . even though I won't need it. Okay, I'm in the airlock."

"The weather's nice," Rini said from his console, "just a gentle solar breeze. Your limit for x-ray exposure is four hours, but we'll be getting ready for the approach adjustments before then."

"Don't worry," Kibi said through her suit intercom as she opened the outer hatch, "I'll be in much sooner. What happens if I touch the repulsion field?"

"You can't," Ilika said. "It'll repel you, feels about like the detention cell door."

Kibi remembered Timod Gor. "Safety line attached. See you guys in an hour or so."

✳

Rini kept half an eye on Kibi with his visual sensors as she crawled around the hull of the Manessa Kwi, currently a long cylinder tapered to a point at both ends. She rolled onto her back and looked up at the stars, then chuckled when she tried to touch the repulsion field, but couldn't.

Sata left the intercom open and went back to studying the navigation beacons around star stations.

Mati lowered herself into a seat at the big table and waved to Boro in the galley. "What're you making?"

"I'm trying that stew with biscuit crust, like Ilika made."

Suddenly an alarm sounded and Rini's console lit up with flashing red symbols. His eyes were wide as he quickly scanned his graphs. "X-ray spike! A huge solar flare! It's still rising!"

Boro dropped what he was doing and leapt out of the galley, saw that Ilika was not on the upper deck, and remembered that Kibi was outside. "Manessa, maneuvering thrusters! Mati, roll the ship! Get Kibi in the shadow!"

Boro grabbed Mati as she stood up and quickly walked her down to the pilot's station.

Sata took a deep breath. "Kibi, grab the hull and stay right where you are. We've got an x-ray spike and we're rotating you into the shadow of the ship."

"Okay," Kibi's voice said. "I don't see anything. Oh, yeah, I forgot — you can't see x-rays. I'm almost in the shadow . . . there, that's about right. Hey, it's dark over here!"

Everyone on the bridge laughed nervously.

Ilika appeared in the lift and Boro quickly filled him in.

"Good work, everyone."

"Oh, no!" Rini yelled.

"What?" Ilika demanded, stepping that way.

"Asteroid shower from deeper in the system, impact in twenty seconds."

"Anything big?"

"No, just the grains of dust and sand we don't track. The repulsion field will protect Kibi, won't it?"

Everyone on the bridge looked at Ilika with worried eyes.

"Yes." Ilika stepped to the command chair and touched a symbol. "Kibi, in a few seconds you're going to see . . ."

His words were cut off by her first scream, but many screams followed as each tiny asteroid impacted the ship's repulsion field with a bright flash of light.

"Kibi, you're in no danger, just hold on and try not to look at them!" Ilika couldn't tell if Kibi heard him, as her screams and deep sobs were nearly continuous. "Rini, how's the x-ray storm progressing?"

"Um . . . worse than before."

"Kibi! Can you hear me?" Ilika asked loudly and firmly.

In between shrieks and whimpers, ". . . yeah . . ." was faintly heard.

"Kibi, listen! I want you to follow your safety line to the airlock. We'll rotate the ship as you go to keep you in the shadow. Do you understand?"

Mati's fingers were poised on her flight control, and her eyes glued to the visual display of her friend cowering in terror as thousands of asteroids burst into light just above her.

". . . yeah . . . I'll try . . ." they finally heard their steward say in a tiny, frightened voice.

Several tense minutes passed with no sign of either storm letting up. Finally Mati reported that Kibi was making some progress, and she was rotating the ship to match.

"You're doing well, Kibi," Ilika said. "You're in no danger, so take your time."

Kibi, screaming less but still crying, managed to choke out, ". . . hard to see safety line . . . so dark . . . asteroids don't help much . . ."

"I know, but the x-ray level is still high. Just go by feel."

"She's almost there," Mati said.

"Boro, you're in command here," Ilika said and dashed for the lift.

*

Tiny asteroids continued to sparkle when they hit the repulsion field as Kibi tumbled head first into the airlock, still crying. She screamed when she hit the floor, by which time Ilika had the outer door closed and the little room pressurizing. A moment later he was helping her remove the suit.

Drenched in sweat, she remained in his arms for several long minutes, crying with her eyes tightly closed, but still seeing clearly the countless flashes of light.

Slowly he guided her into the lift and up to the table, where Sata poured cups of tea. Rini remained on-duty at his station while everyone said comforting things to Kibi, and she slowly opened her eyes, ceased sobbing, and clutched her tea with shaking hands.

For the next half hour, while Kibi slowly collected herself, the others asked Ilika what they could have done differently.

Ilika reminded them that x-rays traveled at the speed of light, so prediction was not possible, and the tiny asteroids were not detectable until they were very close. He couldn't find any flaws in their response to the emergency.

Once the discussion was over, Kibi breathed a deep sigh. "I'd like to . . . get a bath and take a long nap."

Her fellow crew members smiled with understanding.

Ilika looked into her eyes. "Sorry, not right now."

She frowned.

"You saw something you've never seen before, and you were frightened. We understand. But you were in no danger, and no harm was done. So even though you have no important duties at the navigation point coming up, everyone needs to understand the process. And more importantly, I need to know, and your shipmates need to know, if you can recover from a little scare and do your job."

Kibi swallowed and slowly looked around. Boro nodded slightly, and a moment later Mati joined him. "Yes," came Rini's soft voice from the bridge. Finally Sata smiled at Kibi and nodded also.

With her eyes closed, Kibi took several slow, deep breaths. When she opened her eyes again, Ilika's smiling eyes looked back at her.

A tiny, nervous chuckle escaped her. "I . . . need to know that . . . too. Sata, how long before the approach adjustments?"

"About an hour, and Boro's gonna have dinner ready right after that."

Kibi looked into the eyes of her friends one more time. "Okay . . . I'm going back outside."

Rini focused on his display. "But both storms are still going, x-rays from one direction and asteroids from the other!"

"Good," Kibi said flatly. "You guys need to know if you have a steward . . . or if you should find a new one at Satamia Star Station."

Ilika looked at her. He would have been completely satisfied if she had simply stayed at her station and observed the approach adjustments. But he had seen that look before, and knew she was deeply determined to prove to herself, and everyone else, that a few measly asteroids were not going to stand in her way.

*

Kibi started by crawling a few meters from the airlock. By the flashes of light reflecting off Manessa's hull, she knew the asteroids were there, almost close enough to touch. But they couldn't get to her. "Good ship," she whispered.

"Thank you, Kibi," Manessa said.

Kibi chuckled, and while her courage lasted, she quickly rolled over and lay on her back, eyes closed. She could sense the flashes of light through her eyelids, and breathed through the feeling of panic that arose inside her.

After a few minutes, she felt completely relaxed, so she stretched out her arms as if to embrace the universe, but kept her eyes closed. *The last step, Kibi. They can't hurt you. Face them . . . or go home.*

She opened her eyes.

Breathe, Kibi. Breathe.

For the next quarter hour she struggled to keep her eyes open and her lungs working, slowly and steadily. Minute by minute the panic and tension became less, and the shaking in her body relaxed. The sparkling lights were not blinding, just completely outside her seventeen and a half years of worldly experience.

She thought of one more step she could take before going in. She reached up and tried to touch the flashes, knowing the repulsion field would keep girl and asteroids safely apart. After getting used to the tingly sensation, she began to feel a slight vibration every time an asteroid was repelled.

Kibi smiled, rolled back onto her knees, and crawled to the airlock.

* * *

Chapter 13: Planetary Approach

A new light showed in Kibi's eyes as she worked at her console, checking everything on the ship that was her responsibility, and at the same time listening to her captain.

"There are no mathematical solutions to the positions of the planets through time. We can make rough calculations, as Sata and Boro have done, but the universe is too complex for those calculations to remain good for very long. Rini, with Manessa's help, is about to find Sonmatia Three, compare it's position to where we thought it would be, and propose course adjustments for Mati's approval."

"No problem!" Rini announced. "It's right where it's supposed to be."

Kibi spotted the slight smile on Ilika's face as he turned to look at Rini. "Are you sure?" the captain asked. "Compare the numbers."

Rini worked silently for a moment. "Well ... it's not *exactly* where it's supposed to be. It's off by ... just forty kilometers."

"Not very far considering the planet is sixty thousand kilometers across ..." Ilika began.

Mati's eyes snapped open wide. "There's no way I'd approve a freeloading pass at fifty kilometers altitude if we could be off by forty! We'd be smashing into mountains!"

"Everyone see Mati's point?"

Boro nodded. "And we can't just miss the mountains. We have to miss most of the air. We're trying to speed up, not slow down!"

"Exactly, Boro."

"Now I see why Mati has to approve each thing Manessa does," Kibi said with a serious frown. "I didn't get that before."

Ilika nodded. "Now the process moves to Sata. Take the new position of the planet, and have Manessa do the math."

"Will I be able to do this kind of fancy math someday?" she asked as she selected the right function on her console.

"Yes, but when you see how tedious it is, you'll be very glad Manessa can do it for you."

"Okay," Sata began, studying the results on her screen, "our wonderful ship wants to do a tiny little thruster burn."

Mati looked it over when it flashed onto her screen. "It's in three minutes. Hardly any inertia. Any reason not to?" the pilot asked as she swiveled around in a complete circle.

"Wait!" Kibi said suddenly. "There's something I should practice." She touched a symbol on her console. "All passengers," she began, her voice slightly amplified, "please be seated for a minor course correction. Inertia straps are not necessary."

The rest of the crew looked at her and smiled, then glanced at the fourteen empty seats behind her.

"Okay," Ilika said, "Mati will approve the burn, and Boro will provide the engines."

The engineer tapped at his large flow-control panel. "Warming up. It looks like Manessa saved enough to squeeze the adjustment into those twelve point three kilograms. Thrusters are green."

"Burn is approved," Mati said.

They waited in silence. Less than a minute later, they all felt a slight lurch.

"Shall we run the numbers again?" Ilika suggested.

Rini checked the planet's position. Sata requested another calculation, then turned around with a grin. "No adjustment needed!"

✳

Boro's pot pie was not perfect, but with excitement high, no one complained.

Even though six hours separated the approach adjustments from the freeloading pass, no one could sleep. Ilika might have been tempted to try, but question after question came at him about what they would see and feel as they swished by their home planet.

With a defiant glance at Ilika, Kibi went to her console and announced she was adding six hours to that ship-day.

Ilika laughed. "We'll be close to the equator, and might see some places we've been, but they'll flash by very quickly. Kibi has command," he said, and slipped into the galley.

✳

About an hour later, two exciting things happened. With Rini magnifying the image, they began to see the continents and oceans of their home world. Also, the aroma of sweet biscuits started to fill the ship.

Boro dragged himself away from his display and made tea. Kibi, still in the command chair, asked Rini and Sata to double-check the approach. Again, no adjustment was needed.

As the image of the blue planet with white clouds grew larger on their screens, they gazed in longing, remembering their journey on foot and donkeyback.

As the third hour passed, Kibi mumbled something about another approach check, then turned red with embarrassment and cancelled the request.

"It's okay," Ilika said, appearing behind her and massaging her shoulders. "You can ask for as many checks as you want. Manessa has to earn your trust, just as I once did."

Kibi took a deep breath and made the request. Rini and Sata quickly announced that they were right on.

✳

During the hour before the scheduled freeloading pass, all five crew members were glued to their screens, searching for land shapes they recognized. Their own kingdom was hiding under a large cloud, far to the north of the flight path. From the command chair, Kibi gazed at the large display in front of her and spotted the tropical land where they had explored jungle, waterfall, and cave.

Sata smiled to herself, remembering her fear of deep, dark places. She reached over and touched Mati on the arm, a look of gratitude in her eyes.

Mati smiled.

As the white, blue, green, and brown planet began to completely fill their screens, Ilika sat down at the steward's station. "Sata should be able to project our course around the planet now. That will give us another check on the calculations."

Kibi looked at the navigator and nodded.

Sata quickly sent the course projection to all stations. "We're only going about three-eights of the way around, then we head off into space again."

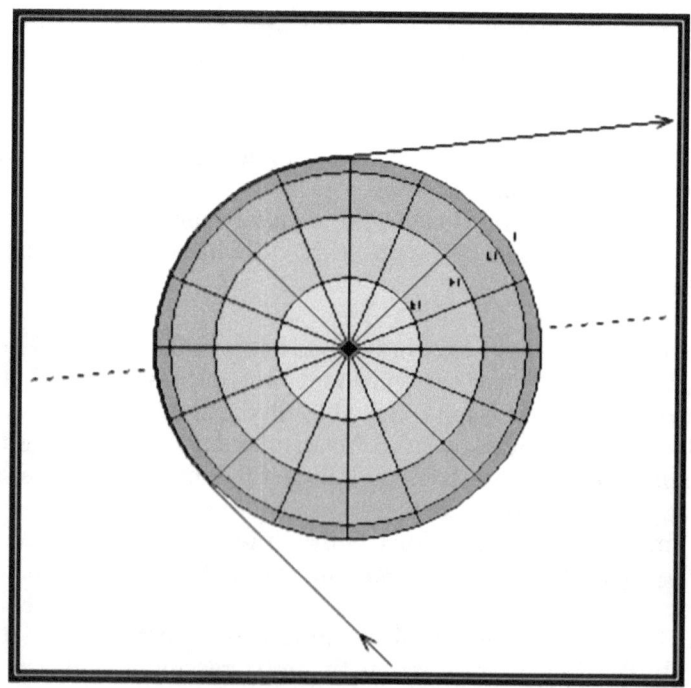

Boro stared at the projection. "That's . . . close! No wonder the course has to be exact."

"Freeloading in three minutes," Sata announced.

"Inertia straps," Mati said.

Kibi smiled, experiencing the joy of commanding crew members who knew what they were doing.

Ilika touched some controls on the steward's console, spoke a word softly, and all the display screens went blank.

✳   ✳   ✳

Chapter 14: Flying Blind

"Did you do that, Ilika?" Rini asked after touching several symbols, none of which worked.

"Of course he did," Kibi said with a slightly irritated voice. "I'm in command. He can't resist the temptation when I'm in command."

"So . . . what are we doing?" Mati asked with concern. "I don't have visual, flight plan, projection . . . anything."

Sata tapped at her console, searching for any navigation functions that still worked. "The calculations were right on. The freeloading pass doesn't need any more course adjustments."

"Yeah," Boro added, "we should sail right through and pop out the other side. This is probably just practice at trusting Manessa."

Several faces turned to look at their captain, but his lips remained sealed and his kindly expression told them nothing.

"I think you're right, Boro," Sata said. "Nothing works at my station, but nothing *needs* to work. Ilika even encouraged us to double and triple-check the approach. It was perfect."

Kibi wore a frown, and her mouth shifted from side to side.

"The freeloading pass begins in about two minutes," Mati said, "and is going to happen unless we do something to stop it."

Kibi turned to Rini. "What do you think?"

With nothing on his console working, he swiveled around. "I don't know. I'm willing to try it."

Kibi nodded, then turned back to the front. "Mati?"

"Um . . . I'm uneasy, but I think Rini has good instincts. We do need to trust Manessa, and after that last adjustment, our altitude should be exactly fifty kilometers. The highest mountain is only twenty-one kilometers, and it's not on our flight path."

Kibi's face scrunched with worry as the other four crew members all looked at her. "Manessa?"

"Ilika asked me not to . . ."

"Okay, okay."

"One minute," Mati said.

"I think we should do it," Boro said softly.

Sata nodded. "Me too."

Rini nodded.

Mati squinted for a moment, then nodded also.

Kibi took two more deep breaths, then opened her mouth to say something, but no sound came out. A moment later she frowned again. "No. Every bone is my body is screaming at me." She turned and looked at Ilika. "If you want this ship to do that freeloading pass blind, you'll have to take back command, or put someone else in this chair. I can't. I won't."

Ilika smiled slightly. "You're still in command."

With her heart pounding, Kibi turned back around. "Mati, get us out of here!"

Mati wasted no time turning to her console and raising her flight control. "Boro, I need anti-mass and ion drive seven."

Boro swallowed once, then moved his fingers on his control board. "Warming up."

"Where's the moon?" Mati demanded with a tinge of fear in her voice.

Rini tapped at his console frantically for a moment, then threw up his hands. "It wasn't near our entry or exit flight path . . . but I don't remember where . . ."

"We'll go a different way," the pilot declared, saw that her engines were green, and pulled her flight control back and slightly to the right.

Seconds before the beginning of the freeloading pass, the Manessa Kwi suddenly gained altitude and streaked away to the north, out of the flat plane of the solar system where most of the planets and moons moved in their slow, steady orbits.

*

"Kibi made the right call," Ilika said. His hands were the only ones not shaking as he held his mug of tea. "And I'm very proud of her for trusting her instincts and not giving in to the will of the majority."

Four faces around the table were riddled with guilt. "We're sorry, Kibi," Sata said.

Ilika continued. "There's no need to be sorry, Sata. Kibi asked for your honest opinions, and you gave them. That was the right thing to do, for Kibi, and for the rest of you. The commander needs honest opinions and uncensored options. Then, when she makes a decision, she needs skilled, coordinated action. You all did great. I have no complaints."

Everyone breathed easier as they sipped their tea.

"Very good call, Mati," Ilika went on, "taking the ship out of the plane of the solar system to avoid any chance of hitting the moon."

"Flying blind was the scariest thing I've ever done," the pilot responded.

"Fighting off a timber wolf sounds easier — at least I can *see* it. All I could do was remember how the ship was angled the last time we had visual, and hope it was still the same!"

After a moment of silence, Boro worked up his courage. "So ... doing a freeloading pass without sensors is ... not a good idea?"

"Flying blind, with the slightest possibility of hitting anything within a light-minute, is way too dangerous."

Boro swallowed.

"There could be other ships," Ilika pointed out, "or artificial satellites, like around Sonmatia Two. But the biggest danger on a freeloading pass is the planet itself. This was on my list to teach you, but teaching is always better with an example."

"We'll remember!" Rini said with wide eyes while nodding.

*

After sensors were restored, Sata created a new flight plan. Mati looped the ship back to the final approach, then let Boro shut down the anti-mass and ion drives. Kibi had them check the course twice before they began the freeloading pass.

They watched the planet race by beneath them, trying to spot more places they knew. Rini thought he recognized the tallest mountain, but couldn't be sure. Mere minutes later, they were released from the planet's grip and flew off into space toward Sonmatia Four.

Sata looked sad for a few minutes, but none of the others gave it a second thought.

* * *

Chapter 15: Slowing Down

After Ilika and Kibi said good-night and slipped into the lift, already kissing, Boro smiled to himself and swiveled in his chair. From the engineering station, he surveyed the entire bridge and passenger area, currently empty and silent.

Only a year before, he had been a slave in a little kingdom where people abused each other every chance they got. Now he was part of something else, something called Nebador that he didn't fully understand. He had seen many pictures of beautiful cities, gleaming star stations, sleek ships, and strange people. It had all come a step closer to reality when Sata chatted with another navigator, some kind of large bird. He cringed for a moment, remembering his first thought at the time, of plucking, gutting, and roasting the creature over a slow fire.

He turned to his console and selected some soft music as he pondered his new life. He felt a little confusion, and more than a little amazement. A few moments later, soft but strong hands began massaging his shoulders. He leaned his head back to look. "Hi, Sata. Couldn't sleep?"

She smiled. "Oh . . . I could, but I'd rather be with you."

After a slight flush of embarrassment, he swiveled around to face her. "Want to get a snack with me, sit in the passenger area?"

"Sure!"

Soon they had a plate with left-over biscuits, dried fruit, and cups of cold tea.

"This is only my second watch alone," he said. "I hope I remember what to do if Manessa starts screaming about an asteroid or something."

"You will, I know you. I think Ilika's gonna train me and Mati tomorrow. Then we'll all be doing it."

They nibbled in silence for a minute.

Sata cleared her throat. "Part of why I . . . um . . . came up here was because I couldn't quit . . . thinking about you."

Boro swallowed as he felt a wave of warm emotions flow through him.

She looked at him with dreamy eyes. "And . . . I want to make sure you know that I'm . . . ready to share a cabin with you . . . as soon as you want to . . ."

Boro's entire body suddenly became hot and sweaty, and he had to swallow several more times. He looked at Sata, and saw her sparkling eyes and happy smile, but his mouth was too dry to speak.

"Ilika tells me," she went on, "that in Nebador, girls ask boys just as often as boys ask girls."

She noticed his discomfort. "But . . . if you don't want to . . ."

"Um . . . no . . ." he stumbled, "it's not that. You're really . . . beautiful to me, and . . . um . . . I think about you too. It's just . . . you know . . . it's huge, and I want to . . . make sure it's just right, and . . . everyone feels good about it . . . you know. We have to think about Rini and Mati, and there's our training and work and everything . . ."

Sata grinned. "Mati and Rini aren't going to try anything until her knee is fixed, but I know they'd love to have some time to snuggle. And, you know, I wasn't asking you into my cabin while we're *on duty!*"

Boro chuckled nervously.

"Couldn't you just come over sometime so we could . . . play?" she asked with a smile of longing.

Boro's expression passed through several shades of smiles and two or three types of frowns as he sat wrestling with his emotions.

Sata slowly lost her smile, then looked down at her lap. "Okay, I get the message," she said as her voice started breaking. "I should have realized . . . why you've never even . . . kissed me." She started to get up.

Suddenly a strong hand grabbed her arm, and she froze.

"Please stay. I'm not as good as you at putting my feelings into words, but I still have . . . lots of feelings . . . and I want to be the only boy who ever . . . you know . . . touches you like that."

Sata settled herself back into the chair with a slight smile.

"And about kissing . . ." Boro continued, "I think I can fix that right now without any . . . complications."

Sata offered no resistance as she was pulled into Boro's strong arms. She felt the warmth of his lips on hers, timidly at first, then more firmly as he found his confidence.

It seemed like hours later when they finally parted and looked at each other shyly. Sata took a slow breath and smiled. "Yeah . . . slow is okay."

✳

Somewhat to the crew's surprise, they received a complete trigonometry review the following day covering all the functions, along with the inverse functions that would give them the angle. With knowledge pads at their fingertips, they only had to remember which function to use for each problem. As Ilika clearly wanted them all to get it, Sata and Rini worked with

Boro and Kibi. Mati worked slowly and carefully, and Ilika was ready to assist, but she held her own.

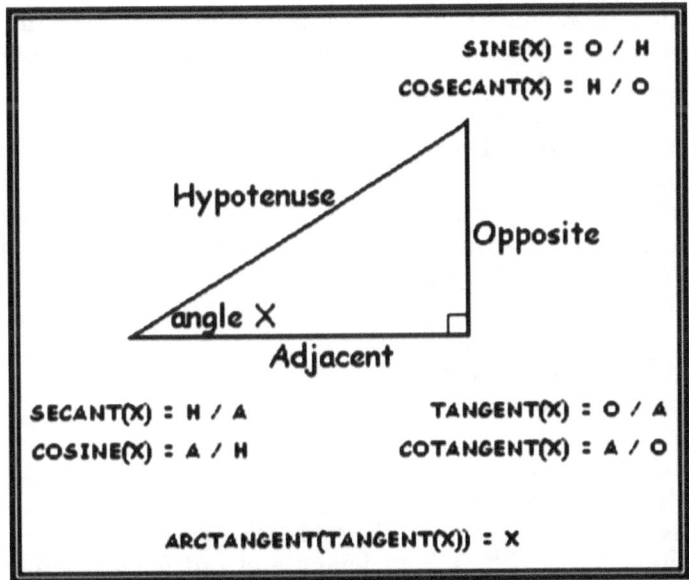

On the second day of their transit from Sonmatia Three to Four, they took turns presenting the new words they were studying. Sata and Mati could hardly stop giggling as they stood before the others, trying to explain star station approach procedures.

Boro, still a little clumsy with the language of Nebador, had trouble describing the new tools he was learning about, so he grabbed a knowledge pad and found pictures. Ilika, of course, made him do his best to describe them in words also.

Rini bubbled with excitement as he talked about the hundreds of instrument checks and calibrations the star station could do as soon as the ship was docked. Suddenly he stopped in mid-thought and looked at Ilika. "The star station . . . it's sentient too, with feelings and everything, right?"

Ilika smiled and nodded.

Kibi went through the entire passenger receiving process, using her shipmates as guinea pigs, and pretending they had never been on a deep-space response ship before. They were all soon tucked under soft blankets, in their reclined seats, with cold drinks at hand and a video on the big screen.

On the day they were scheduled to arrive at Sonmatia Four, Ilika emerged from a relaxing bath to find his entire crew at their stations, ready for approach adjustments an entire hour early. "Hmm. I need to find something for you guys to do. Let me think . . . we don't need to collect firewood or brush donkeys . . ."

Everyone laughed. A gleam of sadness crept into Mati's eyes.

After drying his hair and shooing Kibi away from her console, Ilika sent math and logic problems to all stations to pass the time. Finally, with the scheduled adjustments minutes away and his crew unable to concentrate on anything else, he gave in.

"You guys are tired of slow space flight, aren't you?"

Mati turned and nodded vigorously. "*Really* tired of it."

All the others agreed.

"Rini, any sign of Sonmatia Four?"

He smiled. "I've been watching it for an hour and a half! It's just a few kilometers from where it should be."

"Sata?"

"Approach adjustment calculated!"

"I should have known. Mati?"

"Burn approved, one minute."

"Boro?"

"Thrusters are green."

"Kibi?" Ilika asked, turning his head.

"The passengers are all seated," she said with a grin.

Ilika grinned back. "It is both happy and sad for a captain when he realizes his crew no longer needs him."

✳

Three anxious hours later, as Sonmatia Four began to loom large on their screens, the crew gathered around the galley with worried faces. Ilika was busy making potato cakes. Kibi put into words what they were all thinking. "We need you, Ilika. We may have approach adjustments memorized, but we have no idea how to do atmospheric braking."

Ilika took a minute to secure the galley and wipe his hands. As soon as he took the command chair, his entire crew, back at their stations, looked happy again.

"The freeloading pass was too close to do without sensors, and this is far closer. Sata, what's our highest elevation on the equator?"

The navigator took a moment to enter the question at her console in the precise mathematical language that would allow the ship to search hundreds of charts in an instant. "Six thousand three hundred meters."

Ilika nodded. "If we tried to orbit at our current speed, what would our altitude be?"

Sata selected the proper function. "Eight thousand one hundred. Isn't that . . . too close?"

"No, it's just right. The atmosphere of this planet is thin, so we have to go as deep as we can. The safe lower limit is one thousand meters above terrain, but I've heard of ships going down to a hundred in an emergency."

"Whew," Boro breathed. "They'd almost scrape the hull!"

Mati peered at her display. "I'll have to do a slight adjustment to nail that eight thousand one hundred."

"Then, as we slow down," Ilika continued, "you'll raise the orbit, Mati. Sata will give you an orbital velocity graph. As soon as the line on the graph becomes flat, you'll know we're out of the atmosphere and in a stable orbit. Boro, Mati will need maneuvering thrusters and anti-mass on standby. Ready an alternate fuel for both."

Boro's eyes grew wide at the implied danger. "Engines warming," he said, turning to his console. "Alternate fuels . . . selected and ready."

Mati's heart pounded as the little ship streaked toward the barren brown horizon of the fourth planet, lower and lower with each passing second. She watched the altitude constantly, ready to bring in the anti-mass drive if they went below eight thousand one hundred meters.

At first, the rocky surface appeared airless, but she soon glimpsed haze in the distance. "Eleven thousand four hundred and dropping." Barren mountains reminded her of those in the deserts of her own planet.

A thick reddish-brown cloud appeared on the horizon directly in front of them. "Dust storm," Ilika said. "Not a problem."

The ship, still moving at interplanetary speed, covered the distance in seconds. Mati frowned as they plunged into the brown haze, but gritted her teeth and kept her eyes on her display.

Sata's eyes snapped shut, and didn't open until the dust was far behind them.

"Eight thousand two hundred," the pilot said. A deep valley sliced the surface of the planet just before they streaked into the darkness of the night side.

"Trust your instruments," the captain reminded.

Mati smiled when she noticed the first bit of speed reduction. A glance at her altimeter showed eight thousand one hundred and five meters. She settled her hand on her flight control and nudged the ship up slightly to begin following the orbital velocity graph.

Back in the brilliant daylight, a cone-shaped mountain raced toward them.

"Volcano?" Boro wondered aloud.

"Yes, completely dormant now," Ilika said.

"That's the high point," Sata added, squinting at the sudden brightness.

"Eight thousand five hundred and climbing," Mati reported. "Another dust storm."

They streaked into and through the brown haze before Mati could finish speaking, then plunged back into darkness.

"Actually, same dust storm," Rini informed.

Sata swallowed. "Every time I see it coming, I worry there's a mountain hiding in it."

Mati glanced at her friend. "I'm watching the topographics. If there's *anything* hiding in it, I'll have us out of there in a heartbeat."

Ilika smiled as the volcano flew by beneath them again.

Sata breathed easier, but couldn't keep from closing her eyes on the next pass.

"Eleven thousand," Mati said as they punched another hole in the dust storm and entered the night-side once more.

* * *

Chapter 16: The Monuments of Zolko

Seven laps later, the Manessa Kwi had risen high above the dust storm and the volcano. The pilot announced they were almost in a stable circular orbit, but she wanted to go around once or twice more.

Rini reported nothing in orbit with them.

"If it's okay with all of you," Ilika began, "I think we are done with slow, old-fashioned space travel."

"Yay!" several crew members cheered at once. Mati grinned from ear to ear, while keeping an eye on their last climbing orbit.

"There's a small emergency shelter at the coordinates on your flight list, Sata. Please make Mati a flight plan. I'm going to give Kibi a tour while the rest of you solve a little puzzle."

Rini sparkled with curiosity.

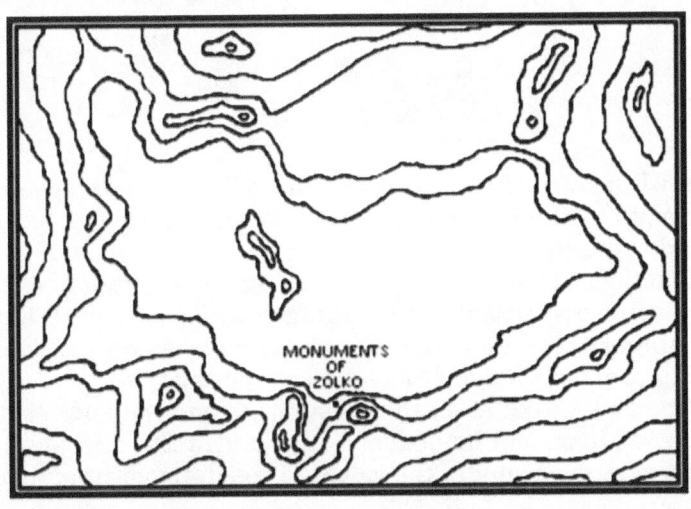

Sata studied a chart on her display. "It's in some hills beside an old dried-up sea or lake. What's a mon . . . u . . . ment?"

"Anything to remember someone or something important, usually made to last a long time."

"Like a statue?" Mati asked, letting Manessa take over the orbit and swiveling around in her chair.

"Yes. A story took place here almost twenty thousand years ago, and it's still told and retold all over Satamia. A plaque at the landing site will tell you about Zolko, the builder of the monuments, and you'll learn the rest of the story as you solve the puzzle."

Boro grinned, remembering the pride he felt after solving the puzzle of the Atorura tribe.

Sata picked a point on their orbital path and drew an elliptical curve from there to the destination. "You can de-orbit in about twenty seconds."

Mati looked over the route when it appeared on her screen. "Boro, anti-mass two, ion three, please."

Dozens of deeply-weathered stone monuments bristled all over the little valley surrounded on three sides by barren brown hills. The yellow and red stone columns were nearly devoid of features, but every once in a while, part of an ancient face would stare at them, or a few letters could be seen of a long-forgotten language.

Mati slowly piloted the ship among the pillars. Some appeared to be whole at twenty or thirty meters tall. Others were obviously broken, stone shards littering the ground.

The remaining side of the valley was just an ancient coastline that sloped down quickly into depths that once might have held sparkling water, but now contained only dust. A thin wind occasionally picked up the powdery dirt and spun it into ghostly funnels that lasted a minute or two.

Once they had looked at all the monuments and the ancient dry shore, Mati glanced at Ilika, and he nodded. She guided the ship toward a large stone platform in the center of the valley. Though rough from thousands of years of wind and sand, it was still almost perfectly flat on top, and large enough for several deep-space response ships. Obviously of about the same age as the monuments, two things upon it appeared much newer.

A small monument and plaque, of some smooth black material, perched on one side.

On the opposite side sat a brilliant-white dome, slightly larger than the ship.

"The plaque is part of your puzzle, so you can look at it after you drop us off. Mati, see the hatch on the right side of the shelter? It will mate with our airlock."

Hovering just a meter above the ancient stone, Mati guided the ship in that direction. Ilika stepped to the pilot's station and showed her several new controls. Mati lowered the struts and settled the ship when the diagram on her screen showed proper alignment. Touching another control, the shiny golden ship extended its hull and connected with the hatch of the emergency shelter.

"We now have a passageway from the ship to the shelter, so we don't have to mess with space suits. The rest of you can have a tour of the place after finishing the puzzle. Kibi, all we need are mission bracelets."

Ilika and Kibi quickly grabbed bracelets and disappeared into the lift.

Boro raised his eyebrows. "Why do I get the feeling this puzzle is going to make Atorura seem easy?"

✳

"What's going on, Ilika?" Kibi asked as soon as they stepped through the airlock tunnel into the domed shelter. A larger version of the ship's entryway surrounded them, with shelves for equipment and clothing, a shower, and soft light coming from the curved ceiling.

Ilika touched some controls on the wall and the hatch closed. "A number of things, most of them challenging, all very good for the crew."

"Where do you get these puzzles?"

"We've got millions of them, all over the universe, just waiting for students who need to sharpen their wits. Remember, Nebador is a huge college. As soon as you guys learn the basics, there's plenty of advanced training waiting for you ... and for me. You're familiar with all these emergency kits — they're the same as on Manessa, just larger."

Kibi looked over the kits and didn't see anything new. "But why don't I have to do the puzzle along with the others?"

"Oh, that. The head of the Transport Service has learned, from long experience, that new crews tend to get too dependant on their usual commanders at about this point in training. That's not good, so the training manual suggests they do a puzzle or two without us. They know everything they need to know, or, with Manessa's help, they can learn it."

"How long will they be gone?"

"This puzzle ... two or three days."

"Serious puzzle! What's this machine do?"

"Gas separator. It takes apart the thin atmosphere of this planet . . ."

　　　　　　　　　　*

The remaining four members of the crew swiveled their station chairs and looked at each other.

"Who's in command?" Mati asked.

"While we were traveling," Rini said, "Boro was usually in charge after Kibi."

Sata smiled and nodded.

Boro turned slightly red. "But Mati has more experience than I do on the ship . . ."

The pilot squirmed. "That's just flight command, engines and straps and stuff. I always have to do that. We need someone who can organize this puzzle thing."

Boro looked around. The other three were grinning and looking at him. "Okay, but I'm handing it off if I get tired, or start screwing up." With an uncomfortable expression he took the command chair. "What do we know about this puzzle?"

"Nothing," Sata said flatly.

"The plaque on the little black monument is supposed to tell us something," Rini said.

Boro scrunched his face for a moment. "Mati, is the shelter hatch closed?"

"Um . . . yes."

"Okay, let's disconnect the airlock and go look at the plaque."

A minute later, the Manessa Kwi sat a meter from the little monument. Rini magnified the image. With a nod from Boro, he read.

"Satamia one-one-three-six, Sonmatia Four, marker four-seven. The Monuments of Zolko."

Boro frowned. "Is that all it says?"

"That's all we can read," Sata said, looking at her display, "but Manessa just received a transmission from the monument. It's the story of what happened here twenty thousand years ago!"

　　　　　　　　　　*

King Zolko struggled to pull enough air into his lungs as he sat on his throne and looked over the shriveled fruit and hard bread on the silver platter close at hand. For a moment he bristled, then relaxed as he remembered the even-poorer food in the marketplace these days. Several councilors sat in lesser chairs, also struggling to breathe while keeping their gaze respectfully low. Servants stood, hands behind their backs, trying to hide their discomfort.

The great doors at the far end of the hall opened, and a well-dressed man strode in. For a moment, harsh sunlight entered, along with some reddish-brown dust. The door guards quickly closed the doors and tried to muffle their coughing.

"Councilor Ganlo!" the king said with both a friendly greeting and frustration. "Why is the air so thin today? Did you speak to the priests and scholars?"

Ganlo stopped the proper distance from the throne and bowed. "I did, Your Majesty, as many as I could find. Some have abandoned their duties and left the city. The priests have been praying day and night, they say, and the scholars have searched every book. No one knows what else can be done to appease the gods."

The king suddenly stood, his chin thrust forward. "The scholars have repeatedly stood before me and proclaimed that all important knowledge is in their books! I want all of you on the streets, searching for answers! I will not let this be the end of our great kingdom!"

The other councilors, most of them old men, started to rise.

"Sire, there is one other possibility," Ganlo said, head half-bowed.

"Speak!"

"There is a woman in the marketplace. She calls herself a prophet, but the priests deny it. She says we need not fear, that the gods will save our kingdom by taking a few to a new land flowing with nut milk and honey. She gathers people around her to listen, and children sit in her lap and are comforted."

The king stood thoughtfully, rubbing his chin. "How does she say the chosen few will be selected?"

"I do not know, Sire."

"Go! All of you! Sit at her feet and listen, and come back in three days with what you learn!"

✳

"Sounds like the atmosphere was getting thin twenty thousand years ago," Sata speculated.

Boro nodded. "I wonder what the puzzle is."

"It's probably like the story problem about Poki and his cows," Mati proposed with a furrowed brow. "We won't know until we hear the whole thing."

✳

The councilors of King Zolko listened to the prophet for two days, and when she was at table eating, or asleep, they questioned the priests and scholars further. Some of the councilors became convinced that the wrath of the gods could be appeased by great works. Others were not so optimistic, and tried to discover how the chosen few would be selected, as the king had ordered.

On the third day, Councilor Sarto crept away and sold all his property to hire a ship and many strong men. He believed the gods would look favorably on them if they found the most beautiful gemstone in the world and placed it in the temple. He carried books and maps from the great library, all telling him that such a gemstone could only be found across the sea, in the Desert of Bakka, somewhere along the eight degree line, for that was the number most sacred to the gods.

Also on the third day, Councilor Memna, the greatest politician in the kingdom and the king's official speaker, slipped away from the group to sell all her property and hire a ship. "I shall create a city in the wilderness, seventy-six kilometers west by northwest of here. All who love the gods may come, bring their children, and help make a society of peace and harmony. The gods will see our creation of love, smile upon us, and make the wind to blow and the rain to fall."

Word spread rapidly, and when she arrived at the dock to board the ship, hundreds of people were already assembled and ready to follow, in rowboats if necessary.

✳

"Yeah!" Boro cheered. "We've finally got some numbers we can use to find things! But there's something Ilika or Kibi usually did that we need to do."

Sata looked puzzled. "I don't think we know enough yet."

"Not enough to do the puzzle. But my stomach is telling me all I need to know about something else."

Rini grinned. "Lunchtime!" he said and dashed for the galley.

✳

On the evening of the third day, Ganlo and the few other remaining councilors entered the king's hall.

"Your Majesty, we are divided on how the gods might be appeased. Sarto seeks the most beautiful gemstone. Memna plans to create a city of peace and harmony. The priests, however, are convinced that only great monuments would be pleasing to the gods, monuments bearing the likeness of the high kings, such as yourself, and the high priests . . ."

"But I sent you to learn how the chosen few will be selected!"

"We were able to discover little, Sire. The prophet only babbles about children and their pure hearts. I don't think she knows."

The king questioned the other councilors. They were all in agreement with Ganlo, and could add little else. Silence prevailed in the great hall as the king rubbed his chin. Finally, he spoke. "So be it. Scribes!"

Two old men emerged from nearby rooms and sat down at writing desks.

"Let it be known that all men, and all women not with child, must report to the palace at sunrise every morning until suitable monuments have been raised to let the gods see the faces of all the high kings and high priests of the land."

"But Sire," Ganlo interrupted, "bringing that much stone from beyond the sea will take years."

The king took a breath of the thin air. "Then we shall not use new stone. We shall take down the buildings of the city, one by one. If necessary, only the foundation of the palace will be spared, a place for the gods to rest as they admire the beauty and grandeur of the Monuments of Zolko!"

✳

"Talk about full of himself!" Sata sputtered.

"About the same as kings and priests on our world," Rini observed.

Boro nodded. "I think . . . we're sitting on the foundation of the palace. It seems . . . somehow wrong to park our ship where the gods were supposed to rest."

Mati swiveled around. "Boro! Who do you think would have saved the children with pure hearts and taken them to a land of milk and honey?"

The bridge was completely silent for a long moment.

Rini swallowed before speaking. "Probably . . . the Nebador Transport Service."

* * *

Chapter 17: The City of Memna

Searching their memories for old measurement systems they thought they'd never use again, the partial crew managed to convert "west by northwest" into something Sata could use for a flight plan. The seventy-six kilometer trip took almost three seconds.

"I *love* ion drive!" the pilot declared.

Boro chuckled as he stepped to the engineer's console.

Mati raised her flight control. "Give me ... anti-mass one and maneuvering thrusters."

"All green," Boro said, then returned to the command chair.

The City of Memna, on a level plain near the old shoreline, had no monuments or massive palace foundations. All that remained were small blocks of rough stone, piled no more than a meter high, that outlined former houses and a few larger buildings. As Mati lowered the ship from two thousand meters, they could see the circular layout of the ancient city, with an open plaza in the center, and avenues radiating out in eight directions.

"The number most sacred to their gods," Rini whispered.

Mati guided the ship slowly along the avenues and among the ruined buildings for several minutes. "It looks like . . . this city didn't grow, bit by bit, like the capital of our kingdom. It was planned and built all at once."

"I hope there's a Nebador marker somewhere . . ." Boro mumbled.

"It's in the middle," Sata said. "Manessa spotted it as soon as we arrived."

Boro nodded to Mati, and she guided the ship along one of the main avenues, then landed in a clear space near the black marker.

"Marker five-zero," Rini read. "The City of Memna."

✳

Councilor Memna worked side by side with her people, never asking them to do anything she wasn't willing to do. So it was that they worked with glad hearts, and within a year they all had houses and the new city was functioning well.

The air seemed to get no worse, and some even said it was a little better. The drought continued and the crops were poor, but they shared alike in what they had, and Memna made sure no one hoarded more than their share of anything. She dispensed justice as cases were brought to her, barely pausing in her work with stone chisel or garden hoe in hand. The people around her listened to her wise words as they worked, and knew in their hearts they had chosen the right path and their city would be pleasing to the gods.

"Why do you not take the best food and live a life of leisure, like King Zolko?" a young woman asked, pausing in her work to comfort her baby.

Memna smiled. "The gods are pleased when each citizen gives what she is able, and only takes what she needs. That is the essence of civilized life. King Zolko's way is the way of the animals in the jungle of Torku."

The girl smiled and returned to her work.

✳

Sata was grinning. "That is so wonderful! I wish our kingdom was like that. Could you imagine our king helping to rebuild the houses at Lumber Town, listening to petitions while he pounded nails?"

Boro howled with laughter. "No, I can't! I don't even think the soldiers will help. The people will do it all."

"I think . . . Nebador's sort of like that," Rini said with a smile and sparkling eyes, "like Memna's city."

Mati wore a slight frown. "I think you're partly right — about giving and taking. But I'm worried that in Memna's city, they did it for all the wrong reasons."

The others shrugged, and Rini continued reading.

✳

As the months of the second year began to pass, some of the people of the City of Memna became unhappy. Memna's judgments always favored social harmony, and whenever that goal was in conflict with the needs of an individual, the group won and the person lost.

Those who saw the city as a hive, whose purpose was to function as efficiently as possible, were happy. Artists and other sorts of free-thinkers did not feel the same.

Also, travelers occasionally arrived from the old capital city, now being quickly dismantled to create the monuments King Zolko had ordered. They hoped to find better air, less dust, and perhaps a little rain, but were disappointed. Memna tried to silence them and brand them as heretics, but the truth crept throughout the city like a disease.

Some people gathered in houses late in the evenings to carry on the traditions of their previous guilds and orders. One such order contained a couple of old masters and several young students, all dedicated to mental discipline and psychic abilities. After doing her share of the work of the city for more than a year and a half, Nosta, a young woman of the order, decided it was time to act. She knelt before her masters one evening.

"I believe the City of Memna is pleasing to many of the people, those who never have an original thought in their heads. I do not believe the gods are so small-minded. I have repaired a little boat that no one wanted, and I plan to depart tonight. I will find the fabled Arch on the Island of Glimpa, where I will sit in meditation until the gods receive my offering of mind and spirit, or until I die."

✳

"I thought so," Mati said. "If something is good just because it pleases the gods, that leaves you at the mercy of the priests to know what is good."

"Or . . ." Rini began, hands behind his head while looking up at the ceiling, "or other people acting as priests, like King Zolko, and Memna."

Mati nodded. "Nosta figured that out. She must have had good teachers."

Boro's face scrunched as he tried to follow the discussion. "So . . . by priests you mean people telling you what the gods think?"

Mati nodded.

"There's just a little more," Sata said.

✳

The masters and the other students of the order quickly gathered as much bread and dried fruit as they could find, and went down to the shore to see their brave friend off in the darkness. Nosta was never seen again by mortal eyes.

After that time, the air became thinner and thinner, and no more clouds appeared in the yellowing sky. The crops failed at both the Monuments of Zolko and the City of Memna. By the end of the second year, the people were dying and had forgotten all about the joys of peace and harmony. No one in either city claimed to know what might be pleasing to the gods.

✳

Boro growled. "But what's the puzzle?"

Sata swiveled in her chair and looked at him with sympathy.

"Maybe that's part of the puzzle," Rini suggested with a coy smile.

Boro growled again. "A puzzle in a puzzle. Let's see if we can find that arch."

Sata turned to her console and selected the chart. "Hmm. There's only one group of hills that would have been an island when this was a sea. Must be Nosta's island."

"Glimpa," Mati remembered.

"Thanks. It was big, about thirty-five kilometers from here, spanning the horizon from east to northeast. You don't need a flight plan for that!"

"Nope. I'll just use atmospheric thrusters, if Boro doesn't mind," the pilot said, placing one hand on her flight control.

Stepping to his console, Boro touched a symbol. "I think we can spare a few minutes."

Mati lifted the Manessa Kwi a hundred meters into the thin atmosphere, then pointed the ship eastward over the empty, dry seabed, the same way young Nosta went, alone in her little rowboat, twenty thousand years before.

※　※　※

Chapter 18: The Fabled Arch of Glimpa

They could easily see the dark stain on the crumbling rocks where the ancient sea had lapped at the shores of the island. Mati took the ship a little higher and they began searching for an arch, or a twenty-thousand-year-old rowboat. No one held their breath about the rowboat.

About a quarter hour into the search, Boro grumbled. "There's probably a Nebador marker. Can't Manessa follow the transmission from it?"

"No," Rini said. "The markers don't start transmitting until the ship is near."

"Damn . . ." Boro whispered, and went back to staring at the visual on the large bridge display.

"You okay?" Sata asked, turning to look at him.

"Yeah. Just . . . learning patience."

"I know what we need!" she said, hopping up and dashing to the galley. Soon each person received a cup of cold tea in their drink holder. "We've been forgetting the things Kibi usually does."

"Bull's eye!" Boro suddenly shouted, bouncing up and down in the command chair and spilling his tea. "The Arch of Glimpa, or I'm a purple donkey!"

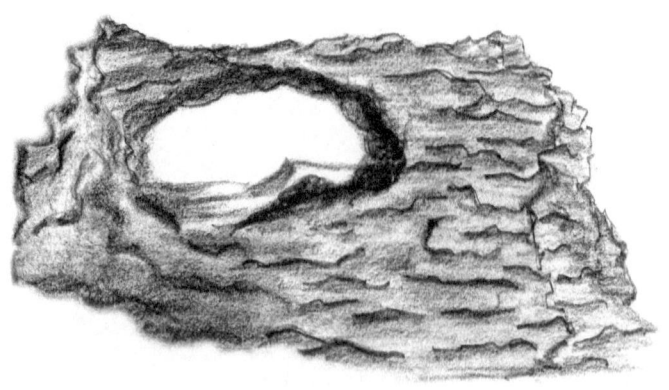

Mati grinned as the natural rock arch came into view, spanning fifty meters or more with stone of yellow, orange, and deep rusty red. She gained a little altitude and guided the ship in that direction.

"There's the Nebador marker!" Rini announced as they cleared a low ridge of boulders between the ancient coastline and the arch.

As Mati lowered the ship into the sandy open space near the little black monument, Boro frowned and looked askance at the huge rock arch that seemed to tower over them.

Sata noticed his worry. "We're uphill from it, and more than a hundred meters away. It's only about forty meters high, so it can't fall on us."

Boro relaxed, but his frown didn't completely disappear. "No closer!"

Mati nodded.

"Sonmatia Four, marker five-one," Sata read. "The Arch of Glimpa."

✳

Day one. I rowed all night long. As the sun rose, my arms felt like lead, but I dared not stop or I would drift south. I entered a second-level walking meditation, but willed my arms to move instead of my feet. In a clear sky, the sun seemed bent on cooking me. Somehow, as the blessed evening finally arrived, I crawled onto the rocks at the south end of Glimpa.

Day four. The sun-blisters on my hands and arms are beginning to harden. The air is so thin, I drag myself along slowly, ever searching for the Arch. I found one spring with water, but many others are dry.

Day seven. The fabled Arch stretches itself before me, silent as a . . . tomb. My tomb, I guess. Whether the gods accept my humble gift or not, I know my mortal body is done. I shall never know the touch of a mate, nor bear a child. Perhaps, if my offering is accepted, the wind will blow again, the rain will fall, and my friend Kelsa will ask Regno to join with her, and they will have a daughter and name her Nosta.

Day eleven. At sunrise I sit on the Arch to salute the new day and summon courage and joy into my heart where dread and fear lurk in waiting. I can see smoke rising from the City of Memna, and in the exact opposite direction, somewhere in the Desert of Bakka, more smoke from the Mines of Sarto. By mid-morning I seek the shade beneath the Arch, and descend into the deepest levels of meditation. Slowly, without any act of will, I allow my spirit to rise up to Heaven.

Day fifteen. I am completely out of food. I am too weak to travel far, and the only things growing here are bitter and make me lose more than they give me. Even if I had the will to return to the boat, I know I would die on the way. No, I will finish what I started, here, at Glimpa's Arch. The act belongs to me, the consequence, pleasing or not, belongs to the gods.

Day seventeen. I can no longer climb the Arch to see the sunrise. My world has shrunk to the little strip of shade beneath the Arch as it moves from hour to hour.

Day twenty-one. Yesterday I sat in the most joyful awareness of the gods for half the day and all the night. The morning glow in the sky was like a gift to me, a little private celebration, for I no longer have the strength to follow the shade. After I write this, I will prop myself against the base of my beloved Arch, giving everything in my mind and heart and spirit to the gods. As the sun climbs into the sky, I will die.

My hand shakes and I can write no more.

✳ ✳ ✳

Chapter 19: The Sonmatia Four Puzzle

The bridge of the deep-space response ship was deathly quiet, save for a slight sniffling sound coming from the navigator's station. Tears ran silently down the pilot's face. Rini had his knees up in his chair and was hiding his face in his arms. In the command chair, Boro's unfocused eyes glistened with moisture.

A quarter hour later, Sata silently made her way to the galley and reheated some left-over soup. They gathered like zombies and poked at their bowls, but ate little.

"I think . . ." Mati finally said in barely more than a whisper, "I think it doesn't really matter what the puzzle is. We're here to . . . you know . . . feel what happened to these people, twenty thousand years ago."

A few minutes later, Rini collected his thoughts. "Yeah. We should do the puzzle, which is to learn everything we can about what happened, but the puzzle's not the important thing."

Boro nodded. "I think Nosta said something in her journal, near the end, that will let us find the Mines of Sarto."

"She said she saw smoke at Memna in one direction," Sata remembered, "and smoke at the mines exactly opposite. Calculating reciprocal compass directions is easy. The only problem is . . . I forgot to mark the city on my chart. I didn't think we'd be going back, or needing to know where it was."

"I can find it," Mati said, examining a spoonful of soup before slipping it into her mouth.

"Good," Boro began, "because I need to stretch my legs . . . in the City of Memna. Something about the place calls to me, and I think I would have liked it there. I want to walk the streets and see what the stones whisper to me. Rini, you're in command."

✳

By following their flight path in reverse, Mati brought them to the old mainland shore within a few kilometers of the City of Memna, and a minute later lowered the ship near the Nebador marker.

After leaving through the airlock, Boro stood beside the marker as the Manessa Kwi retracted its landing struts and floated away.

"You guys have fun," Boro said through the intercom. "If you find the mines, look for something for our display containers."

"We will," Sata replied. "Remember to watch your air supply!"

"I've got two hours. I'll either find my ghosts by then, or get bored. Manessa will yell if I start turning blue."

"I *guarantee* we'll be back before then!"

"Thanks!" Boro waved one last time to the departing ship, then started walking down one of the streets where people worked and children played twenty thousand years before.

✳

Rini looked very uncomfortable perched on the edge of the command chair on the trip back to the island. "I can almost *see* Nosta when I close my eyes, meditating under the Arch of Glimpa."

Mati turned her head slightly, a gleam of jealousy in her eyes for a second. "You want to walk around there?"

"Um . . . yeah."

Mati lowered the ship near the Nebador marker.

Sata went to work. "I marked the City of Memna on the chart when we dropped off Boro, and it matches his tracer molecule. All I have to do is draw a straight line, and we should be able to find the Mines of Sarto."

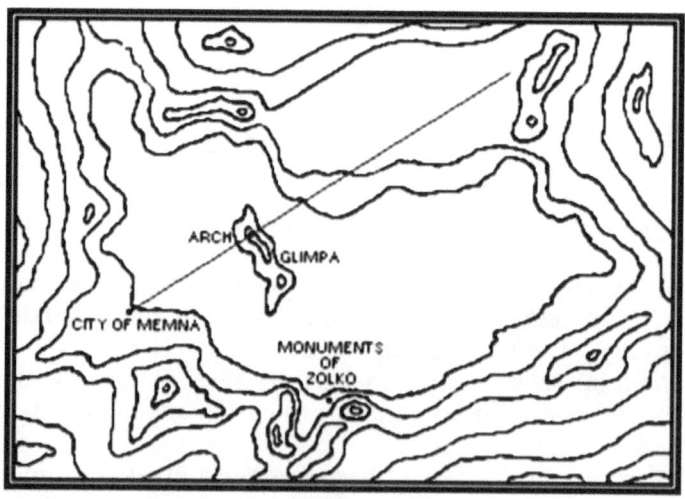

Rini hopped up. "I'll pay my respects to Nosta while you guys go find the most beautiful gemstone in the world! I guess . . . Sata, you want to be in command?"

"Um . . . sure. It doesn't really matter. Me and Mati are a team — we'll make decisions together."

Mati swiveled around and smiled. "This'll be fun, just two girls and our space ship!"

Rini smiled and stepped into the lift.

✳

As Rini walked down the sandy hill toward the Arch of Glimpa, a noticeable spring in his step even in a space suit, Mati prepared to lift the ship back into the air.

"We could just sit here awhile," Sata said from her station. "I have to do some trigonometry."

"I want to give Rini some space. He's got a thing for Nosta, and I don't want to come between them."

Sata glanced at her friend, but didn't say anything.

"Why trigonometry?" Mati asked as she piloted.

"We just had a review of all the trig functions. If that isn't a hint, I don't know what is!"

"I trust you. If you can't figure it out, I sure can't! I'll just pilot the ship wherever you tell me to go. I hope we can find it before we have to get Boro and Rini."

A minute later, Mati lowered the ship onto an ancient beach somewhere on the edge of the Desert of Bakka.

✳

Rini slowly climbed the surrounding rocks, then stepped carefully onto the rock arch, about three meters wide at that point. His bracelet chimed the four-minute reminder he had programmed. He paused to glance at his air supply, then looked around.

The yellow sky almost completely surrounded him, broken only by a small cloud of dust somewhere in the desert to the northeast. Directly overhead, the sky was nearly black. The sun hung in the west, over the City of Memna. Rini thought of Boro, opened his bracelet, and tapped at the tiny keys.

"Boro, this is Rini. Can you hear me?"

"Hi, Rini! Are you outside too?"

"Yeah. I'm on the arch. The girls are looking for the mines."

"Nosta really spoke to you, didn't she?"

"Yeah. I could see myself in her shoes. You find anything interesting?"

"The more I wander around, the more I can understand how deeply the people believed they were doing the right things to make their gods happy and reverse the climate change. I guess Zolko believed it too. And Sarto."

"And Nosta," Rini added.

"Yeah. I think they were all off the mark."

"Ilika can help us understand it when we get back. I'm almost to the middle of the arch, about two meters wide here. No cracks that worry me."

"I'm on the northern edge of the city. Just a large village, really. Nothing left but stone and dust, but every time I sit down, I can almost hear the people talking . . ."

✳

Sata cocked her head. "Manessa, how much air does Boro have left?"

"Assuming normal activity, one hour and seventeen minutes."

"Okay, let's see if I can figure this thing out," Sata said, moving her hands on the console. "Zolko to Memna was west by northwest, and I've got those points on the chart. Manessa, please playback the story of the Monuments of Zolko where it mentioned the Desert of Bakka."

"On the third day, Councilor Sarto crept away and sold all his property to hire a ship and many strong men. He believed the gods would look favorably on them if they found the most beautiful gemstone in the world and placed it in the temple. He carried books and maps from the great library, all telling him that such a gemstone could only be found across the sea, in the Desert of Bakka, somewhere along the eight degree line, for that was the number most sacred to the gods."

"Eight degrees ... eight degrees ... I hope it really was on the eight-degree line," Sata mumbled as she worked. "Okay, there it is! And we've got a nice, pretty triangle. I just have to figure out which trig function to use."

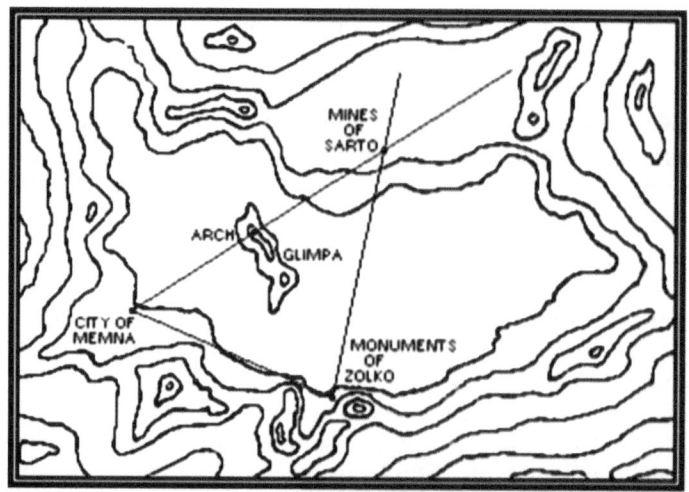

While Sata worked, Mati got her crutch and hobbled to the galley. As she slowly put together a snack for the two of them, she heard mumbled trigonometry functions, intermixed with curses, coming from the navigator's station. The words and other noises started out sounding a little annoyed, soon became frustrated, and eventually seethed with anger. Mati left the tray and hobbled down to the bridge.

Sata burst into tears when Mati put her free arm around her friend.

✳

"Rini, this is Boro."

"I'm under the arch now, probably about where Nosta died."

Boro was silent for a moment. "Any bones?"

"No, they would have turned to dust a long time ago. Any more ghosts there?"

"I think I found the place where they built the smoky fire. It's a pit in the middle of a small plaza. I scooped out some of the dust, and can see blackened sides, maybe even some charcoal."

"The smoke Nosta saw."

"Yeah. As things got worse and worse, I bet the people became frustrated and angry, so they burned stuff." Boro was silent for a long moment as he gathered his courage. "Rini?"

"Yeah?"

"I'm worried about something. I'm down to about half an hour of air. I was hoping I could let the girls finish what they were doing, but I'm starting to get a little scared."

"Want me to teach you how to change that half hour into an hour?"

"Could you?"

"First you have to let go of that fear — it will only make you breathe faster and waste air . . ."

✳

"I've tried *everything!*" Sata nearly screamed, red-faced. "It's not sine or cosine, tangent doesn't work, and *forget* the reciprocal functions!"

"Secant or cosecant?" Mati asked in a timid voice.

"No! Nothing!"

"You're worried about Boro, aren't you?"

Sata burst into tears again. "He's down to . . . about a quarter hour of air . . . and I wanted to have some beautiful crystals to show him. And I wanted to show him . . . that I could be in command and not mess up!"

Mati wrapped her arms around her friend as best she could. Eventually, Sata relaxed and started wiping her tears on her sleeve.

Mati sat down at her own station. "Why don't you ask Manessa for help?"

Sata sniffled and pursed her lips in thought for a long moment. "I wanted to do it myself . . . but I guess I should. Manessa, please analyze the problem on my screen and tell me which trigonometry function to use."

"Ilika asked me not to tell you."

Sata didn't start crying again. Instead, she became beet-red and looked ready to explode. "Manessa! Who is in command of this ship?"

"You are, Sata. Rini transferred command to you before leaving the ship."

"Am I in *complete* command of this ship?"

"Yes, Sata."

"Then why won't you answer my question!"

"I will answer your question, if you wish. All you have to do is override Ilika's request."

Sata's mouth opened, but no sound came out.

Mati was trying very hard to hold in a snicker, but a little bit escaped.

"What?" Sata snapped.

"Manessa never said she wouldn't answer your question. It's happened to Kibi too. Manessa just said, 'Ilika asked,' not 'I can't' or 'I won't.' No one's ever tried overriding Ilika's request."

Sata was silent for a long moment, dumbfounded but thoughtful. Finally she took a deep breath. "Manessa, override any requests Ilika made about not helping with this problem."

"No trigonometry function works in this situation because it is not a trigonometry problem. The triangle on your screen is not a right triangle, nor are you attempting to find an unknown angle or length. It is a position problem defined by the intersection of two lines, and is best solved by creating two directional functions, one in which the direction to Boro's tracer equals the direction to Rini's tracer, and another in which the direction to Ilika's tracer equals the reciprocal of eight degrees. Then the pilot can use the functions, just as she would a navigation beacon, to adjust the flight path until both functions have a value of zero. We would then be right over the target. Altitude is not an issue because the target is, by definition, on the surface."

Sata remained silent for a moment, swallowing and breathing. Mati watched her friend, but said nothing.

"Boro should be out of air in eight minutes," the ship suddenly said.

Sata sat bolt-upright, moving her hands on her console, all hints of earlier emotions gone. "Boro, this is Sata! We're coming!"

Mati quickly raised her flight control.

"What's the hurry?" Boro asked through the intercom. "I've got forty minutes of air, several more stones to photograph, and a few more ghosts to talk to."

"Are you sure?" Sata asked with a wrinkled brow. "Manessa said you should be almost out."

"Rini taught me how to relax, turn down my suit temperature, and sort of meditate while I walk. I've almost doubled my suit time!"

"Um . . . okay. We're about to go find the Mines of Sarto. See you in half an hour or less!" She made another selection. "Rini? How much air do you have."

"More than an hour. I'm sitting under the arch, and sometimes I think I can almost feel Nosta's presence."

"Okay. See you in an hour or less."

Mati, following the conversations closely, let go of her flight control.

"Manessa," Sata began, "give me those directional functions again . . ."

✳   ✳   ✳

Chapter 20: The Mines of Sarto

Minutes later, Mati watched the two directional functions on her display as she guided the Manessa Kwi over the Desert of Bakka. Sometimes the indicator line of the Boro and Rini function would move slightly to the left or right, and she would correct the ship's course until the line was again centered. The line on the Ilika and Kibi function was still quite a ways off, but slowly approaching center.

"If we find it in the next few minutes," Sata thought aloud, "we'll have about a quarter hour for exploring."

"I think we'll be there soon," Mati said, "and ion drive can get us back to the City of Memna in seconds, although we might scare Rini as we pass."

Sata snickered. "You're a little miffed at him, aren't you?"

Mati was silent for a moment. "I guess it's a little silly to be jealous of someone who died twenty thousand years ago."

"Anyway, they probably weren't human."

Mati's eyes opened wide. "What were they?"

"I don't know. Manessa, what kind of creatures were the people who used to live here?"

"Ilika asked me not to . . ."

"Override."

"All of the sapient inhabitants of the places we have visited on this planet were reptilian bipeds."

Sata burst out laughing.

"No," Mati said, grinning and laughing, "I don't think I'll be jealous of long-dead lizards! We're getting close, and I'm taking us down to one hundred meters. Help me look for it."

Suddenly Sata received a transmission, and a symbol appeared on her chart. "No need. The Nebador marker just came to life, and it's off to the left a little."

*

"Marker five-two," Mati read. "The Mines of Sarto."

"No writings or recordings have been discovered that detail the lives of the people who worked these mines. Apparently all of the people who labored here were driven by an intense desire to find a gemstone worthy of offering to their gods. There is no evidence of slavery.

"Nor were there any class or status differences. Councilor Sarto appears to have worked right alongside the other miners, day after day, until the very end. Judging by the positions of bodies, tools, and gemstones, the following reconstruction of events seems most likely:

"Sarto and his followers decided on this location about half a year after crossing the sea. With shovels and blasting powder, they dug shafts into the bedrock until they found veins of crystals that angled deep into the planet. These they followed as far as they could, bringing every find to the surface to be cleaned and inspected.

"About a year into their work, they could go no deeper as carbon dioxide began to fill the lower tunnels. Many miners died from the bad air or sheer exhaustion. Sarto and a few hearty followers pressed on, taking turns working for just a few minutes each in the deep places.

"Those who could no longer work in the mines helped to clean and sort the crystals, each hoping to find the object of their quest. When nothing else could be done, they burned whatever they could find to send their prayers up to the gods.

"The day came when only Sarto and one other miner remained alive. The miner was large and strong, but his name is not known. He struggled up from one of the deep tunnels, placed a dirt-filled box at Sarto's feet, and died.

Mati paused to wipe her eyes. "You can finish. I can't see very well right now."

Sata waited until her friend was ready. "After honoring the fallen man with tools in his hands and gemstones over his eyes, Sarto was amazed to find, in the box of dirt, the most beautiful cluster of crystals he had ever seen. Alone, he lovingly cleaned the precious object. With his last bit of strength, Sarto placed it on a boulder for the gods to see, cried himself to sleep, and never woke up.

"The mine tunnels collapsed long ago. The boulder where Sarto placed the offering still sits forty meters east of this marker. The crystal cluster resides in the museum at Satamia Star Station, and the gods often come to admire it and remember Sarto and his people, just as they do the Monuments of Zolko, the City of Memna, and the Arch of Glimpa. Visitors may find souvenir crystals among the mine tailings north of this marker."

*

Boro had only twenty minutes of air, even with all the tricks Rini could teach him, so Mati and Sata agreed on a plan that would shave minutes off the last two things they wanted to do.

While Sata climbed into a space suit, Mati moved the ship to the boulder where the crystals had been offered up. About a meter high, it showed signs of braving dust and sand storms for at least twenty thousand years.

Sata opened the outer airlock door but didn't step outside. As soon as she had taken a photograph and glanced around, Mati moved the ship to the ancient piles of rock and dirt that had come from the mine. With sample container in hand, Sata was quickly on the ground.

"This'll be easy!" Sata announced after walking a few meters from the ship. "Crystals all over the place. I just have to pick out a nice one that'll fit in our containers ... like this one!" She held up a small cluster of purple spikes for Mati to see.

"Looks perfect. Now let's go get our boys. It's been nice taking a break, but I'm starting to miss them."

Sata grabbed two more small crystals and added them to the sample container. "Me too."

* * *

Chapter 21: Picking Up the Puzzle Pieces

Mati took a deep breath. For the first time, she was about to move the ship a long distance with no one else on the bridge. Her heart beat faster as she gave the ship voice commands to warm up the ion drive.

Sata, by agreement, waited in the airlock in case anyone needed help getting into the ship.

"The City of Memna," Mati announced through the intercom a minute later as she extended landing struts. Long shadows reached out across the central plaza from the surrounding ruins as the sun approached the horizon.

Sata opened the outer door. "Boro? Are you nearby?"

"Sata, you in a suit? You gotta see this!"

Sata stepped outside to see Boro, not far from the Nebador marker, waving and pointing downward. She walked in his direction. "We can't forget Rini."

"He has about twenty minutes more than me, and I have at least eight, maybe twelve minutes. It's amazing how much air you save just by breathing through your nose."

She self-consciously closed her mouth and followed him down an old dusty stairway into the ground. He activated his bracelet light and she did the same.

"I found this just a little while ago."

Sata gazed around with wide eyes, taking in the faded mural paintings covering all four walls. Lizard-like people in ornate robes, sometimes with elaborate jewelry, stood or walked in ritual formation, carrying offerings of fruit, gemstones, or scrolls.

"They were reptiles," Boro said.

"Manessa told us, but we had no idea what they looked like."

The back wall, never touched by sunlight, was the least faded, and one figure stood foremost, reaching up with her offering of a large double-rolled scroll while searching the cloudless yellow sky with desperate eyes.

"Memna, probably," Boro whispered.

Sata nodded, then something caught her eye in one corner of the mural. She moved closer and aimed her light.

"I was hoping you'd see that," Boro said.

A small golden sphere perched on three legs, ramp extended and hatch open, and a reptilian in a blue robe stood at the top of the ramp, talking to a group of children who had gathered around.

✳

"Manessa says she has photographs of all the mural paintings," Mati said over the intercom, "including a bunch you haven't seen yet. Aren't you about out of air, Boro?"

"Yeah. I just got my four-minute alarm. We're coming."

The pilot made sure her engines were ready while Boro and Sata entered the airlock, then made quick-work of the journey back to the Arch of Glimpa.

Rini sat cross-legged on the arch, facing the sunset, as the Manessa Kwi settled onto the sand near the marker. He waved, and Mati's heart beat a little faster.

"Did you get Boro first?" he asked with concern, standing up.

"I'm right here!" Boro announced, touching the intercom symbol at his console. "Did you know they were reptiles?"

Rini was silent for a moment as he stopped dead in his tracks near one side of the arch, then burst out laughing. "I pictured Nosta having tangled black hair, like Kibi."

"Sorry, just scales and spikes," Mati said. "Aren't you almost out of air, or should we come back after dinner, maybe a video?"

Rini whimpered. "I'll make it to the airlock, but not by much. It takes a few minutes just to climb down from here."

Just then the sun sank below the horizon, and suddenly the land became pitch-dark.

"Uh oh," Rini said with a trembling voice.

"Thin atmosphere, no twilight," Boro explained.

"Rini, stay right where you are," Mati asserted, "that's an order." The ship's external lights came on and lit the area brilliantly. "Sata, you still in the airlock?"

"Yep!"

"Good. Boro, anti-mass one, maneuvering thrusters."

"Blue-green . . . green."

Mati carefully lifted the Manessa Kwi to the height of the arch.

"I just got my four-minute alarm!" Rini squeaked. "I guess I'm scared and breathing faster."

"That fear has to go . . ." Boro began in his deep voice.

Rini chuckled, remembering his own words. "Yes, master. It's harder when it's *your* air that's almost out!"

Boro smiled as Mati maneuvered to the top of the huge rock outcropping.

"Sata, I don't know how stable this rock is," Mati said, "so I'm just going to hover. Open the outer door, then tell me if I'm close enough."

"A meter lower . . . that's good. Rini's coming with his bracelet light . . . he's in Manessa's lights now . . . he's climbing in."

As soon as Rini was inside, Sata closed the outer door and pressurized the airlock.   Rini opened his faceplate, and both he and Sata heard his one-minute air alarm. They both grinned and slapped hands before opening the inner door.

*

The four members of the crew who were not usually in command, but who had all experienced the responsibilities of command that day, agreed they needed some time to talk. By Manessa's external lights, Mati lowered the ship back onto the sand near the Nebador marker.

Sata, with Rini's help, quickly put together a hearty dinner of reheated left-overs from the refrigerator.

Boro transferred his photographs from bracelet to ship, then shared all his discoveries of strange symbols etched in stone, mural paintings, and pits where the people had once burned their belongings.   With some embarrassment, he also talked about the voices he thought he heard in many of the ruins.

Rini had begun his stay on the Island of Glimpa thinking he was there to remember an apprentice wizard named Nosta, a girl about his age. He soon discovered she had friends, and the longer and deeper he meditated, the more presences he felt. He speculated that she was only the last of many who had come to the Arch for solitude and enlightenment.

Sata showed the boulder where Sarto had made his best and final offering, and described the mine tailings littered with beautiful crystals. She opened the sample container, and the shimmering pink and purple gems were passed around.   Then she shared her deep embarrassment at trying to find the intersection of two lines using trigonometry.

Rini grinned with sparkling eyes. Boro's face twisted in thought.

In Mati's opinion, Sata had left out the most important lesson they learned. With a nod from Sata, she explained how any previous order from Ilika could be overridden by the commander.

"But we should only do that if we really need to," Boro said with a worried look.

"True," Rini agreed, "but I think Ilika *wants* us to know how."

Mati nodded. "It should be up to whoever's in command."

Boro thought for a moment. "That sounds right."

After talking for hours, the four crew members of the Manessa Kwi began yawning, and decided that Ilika and Kibi would find something to do without them for one night.

* * *

Chapter 22: Farewell to Sonmatia Four

In the emergency shelter, Kibi pulled a warm robe closely around her and gazed at the display screen at the end of the table where six people could eat or work. On the screen, the rising sun lit up the tallest of the Monuments of Zolko, but the palace foundation was still in shadow.

Behind her, Ilika worked in a tiny galley sandwiched between shelves of supplies, racks of fuel canisters, and bunk beds.

"What smells so good?" Kibi asked, putting her bare feet up on the seat across from her.

"Eggs, mushrooms, and onions . . . cooked in a little bit of tasty nut oil."

"Yum! We'd better finish before the others get back, so we don't have to share!"

Ilika grinned, and carried two trays to the table.

☀

The Manessa Kwi arrived about an hour later, rotated until the airlock aligned with the shelter's hatch, and settled onto its struts. Rini poked his head in. "Are we interrupting?"

The four from the ship received a complete tour of the emergency shelter. Ilika noticed Boro's eyes sparkling when the engineer saw the rack of fuel canisters. "Boro, we should get some liquid number five. Kibi will show you how to log it."

"Yeah! Space thruster fuel!"

"I've already picked out a case of pinkfruit juice," Kibi announced. "Just use this knowledge processor, open the shelter transaction list, and add a new record."

"How much does it cost?" Boro asked with a slight frown, remembering Ilika didn't have much gold or silver left after Rini's marriage ceremony.

Ilika smiled. "Nebador doesn't use money. We keep different kinds for visiting planets like yours. There, I had to take metal coins. Sometimes it's seashells, sometimes just numbers stored in a machine."

Boro looked confused. Mati and Sata both shrugged.

"You'll learn more about that at Satamia Star Station. So . . . what did you learn on your adventure without Kibi and me?"

"Well . . ." Boro began with hesitation, "most of it we want to show you. But there is one thing . . . at first we weren't sure we should even tell you . . . but we decided to, and since Sata discovered it . . ."

All eyes turned to the navigator. She took a slow, deep breath. "We discovered . . . how to override . . . any commands you've given Manessa . . . that would keep her from helping us with something."

Kibi's eyes snapped open wide. "Teach me!"

Everyone else glanced at Ilika. He was trying to hold in a smile.

"I thought so!" Rini said. "He wanted us to know."

"It's a time-honored rule," Ilika began, "that a commander must have *complete* command to deal with unexpected situations, the ability to change any previous command or break any rule. Every emergency is different. No one can anticipate what will be needed. That is one reason Manessa, who is only sentient, must have a sapient crew."

Boro's mouth twisted back and forth for a moment. "But only in an emergency, right?"

"That's a little harsh," Ilika replied. "I think it would be better to say, only in need. Let's say we're doing a training flight, and I've restricted your engine power. The exercise may be hard, but you're learning things, and I'm watching for dangers. Then, during the exercise, I have to step into the toilet room, and while I'm in there, your flight conditions change. You have to be willing to override my previous limits because you know the current conditions, and sitting on the toilet, I don't."

Several cheesy grins greeted Ilika as he looked around at his crew members.

✳

Ilika and Kibi took the front two seats in the passenger area.

Mati read the story of the Monuments of Zolko as she slowly moved the ship from pillar to pillar. Each ancient face gazed at them from the large screen over the steward's station, etched by dust and sand until the species could only be guessed, human or ursine, avian or reptile.

Boro read the story of the City of Memna, then continued with his own discoveries of charcoal pits, mural paintings, and whispering stones. The screen alternated between views of the city below and photographs selected by the engineer.

Rini told the story of Nosta and the Arch of Glimpa, while Mati slowly gave them a view from every angle. He described his own meditations on and under the Arch, and finished by telling of his rescue in the dark with one minute of air remaining.

Sata began with her embarrassing assumption that trigonometry could solve her navigation problem. Kibi admitted she would have made the same mistake. Ilika only smiled.

The navigator read the story of the Mines of Sarto while Mati hovered near the boulder and mine tailings, all that remained of a once proud and determined community. Sata finished by presenting the souvenir crystals.

"It's time for another display container!" Kibi asserted. "Do we have anything else from the fourth planet?"

Rini brought out a cup containing a handful of sand he had pocketed from beneath the Arch of Glimpa, about where Nosta had probably turned to dust twenty thousand years before.

✳

Over soup and freshly-baked biscuits, Ilika looked around the table at his crew, more confidence showing in their eyes and bearing than ever before. He noticed that Kibi wore a thoughtful expression.

"If these Nebador markers are numbers forty-seven through fifty-two," she pondered, "there must be others all over the planet."

"There are," Ilika confirmed with a nod. "Several hundred. We could spend weeks studying the history of this planet, going from marker to marker, reading text and looking at pictures."

Mati looked up from her soup bowl with cold, flashing eyes.

"But we have important things ahead," Ilika said, smiling at his pilot, "and few of the markers make good puzzles, like these do. Want to take us out, Kibi?"

The steward of the Manessa Kwi grinned. "Flight objective?"

"Let's start with a stationary orbit."

Mati smiled. "Easy!"

"Then we'll put Sata and Boro to work figuring out how to get us to Sonmatia Five."

"No problem!" the engineer declared. "I've got fuel out my ears, *including* space-thruster!"

They quickly scraped their bowls, and Rini dashed for the galley to do the dishes.

✳

"A stationary orbit ..." Kibi pondered aloud from the command chair. "How high is that on this planet, Sata?"

The navigator began working at her console. "About a hundred thousand kilometers. Chart on channel five."

"Got it," Mati said.

"Rini, anything up there?" Kibi asked.

He looked over his displays. "Just two little moons. I'll add them to the chart."

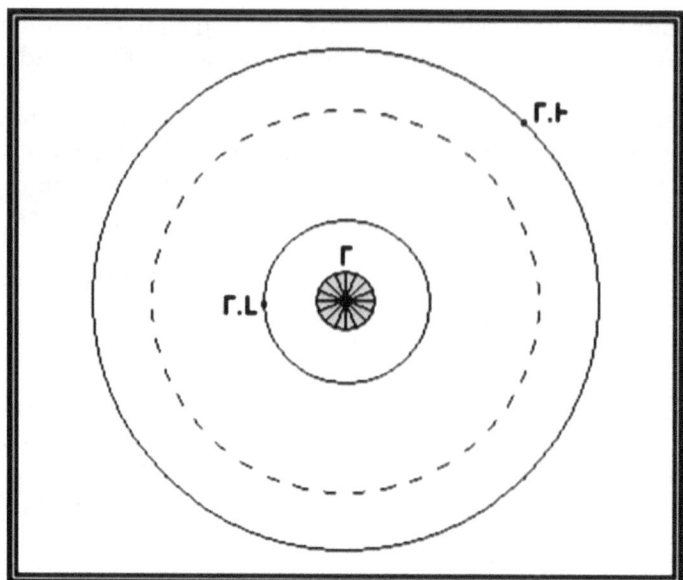

"Ilika!" Mati shrieked. "The orbit you want is *between* the two moons!"

The captain grinned from the steward's station. "Those orbits are more than a hundred thousand kilometers apart. Do you think you can squeeze Manessa in?"

Mati growled under her breath, leaned back in her chair, and stared at the graph. "I just don't want to get whacked by a big rock."

"Think in *three* dimensions, Mati. Remember, almost everything in the solar system is in one flat plane. You already made use of that, instinctively, back at Sonmatia Three."

Mati sat up straight and tapped at her display selector.

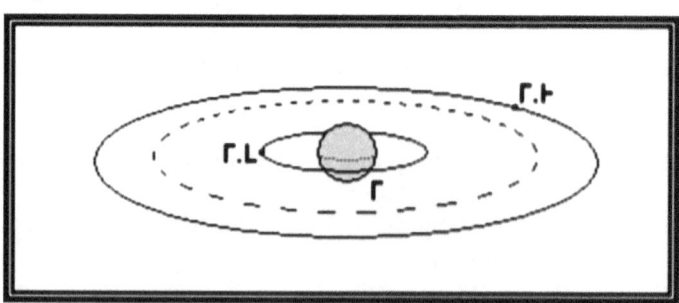

"Okay, I get it. Don't worry about the moons, just go over or under."

"Pay attention, Sata and Boro. You're going to need this technique to get us to Sonmatia Five."

Sata and Boro looked at each other.

"I need anti-mass and ion five," Mati said.

Kibi checked the status of all stations, and Rini produced a weather map showing a dust storm to the east. Mati slowly lifted the ship to a thousand meters, and with a nod from Kibi, the Manessa Kwi streaked away toward Sonmatia Four's north pole.

* * *

Chapter 23: Lots of Rocks

"Ilika!" Sata called from her station where she and Boro had been peering at solar system charts ever since they entered stationary orbit. "What's this nonsense about Sonmatia Five? There's nothing there but a bunch of rocks spread out in a wide band all along the planet's orbital path!"

Ilika looked up from the steward's console where he was working with Kibi. Rini stepped out of the galley to listen, and Mati looked up from her knowledge pad at the table.

"It was a nice little rock and ice planet once, I hear," the captain said, "about four billion years ago. Even had a bit of primitive life. Then it got too close to Sonmatia Six, the big gas giant. When gravity from another source interferes with the internal gravity of a planet, it usually falls apart."

"There are more than a million fragments," Boro noted, studying Sata's display. "You want to visit them all?"

Mati frowned from the table.

"One will do," Ilika said as he began tapping at Kibi's console. "Let's visit . . . five-three-three. It's a metallic core fragment."

Sata and Boro went back to work.

Mati looked happy again.

✳

"Ilika was serious about going over or under, instead of through," Sata explained as she stood at the end of the big table near the steward's station. She touched some symbols on a knowledge pad and their next flight plan appeared on the large display. "If we went straight along the plane of the solar system, we'd have to worm our way through thousands of rocks. If we go in from the north or south, there are only six or eight rocks between clear space and fragment five-three-three."

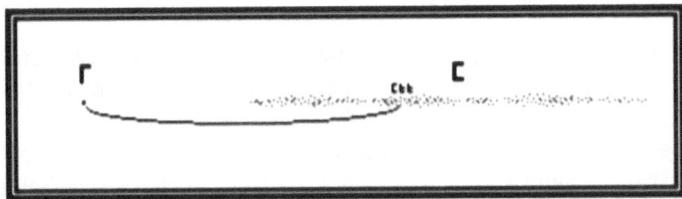

Mati gazed at the display. "Why did you pick going in from the bottom . . . I mean the south?"

"Ilika's idea. He wanted us to get used to the fact that over and under are exactly the same in space."

The pilot nodded.

Boro stood up, touched his knowledge pad, and a photograph appeared on the screen. "Five-three-three is a very irregular metal thing, two kilometers across, big pointy spikes sticking out all over it, gravity about one-thousandth of what we're used to. It's not just floating peacefully in space, it's tumbling. Ilika says if we can land on it, we can land on *anything*."

Nervous chuckles came from all around the table.

Ilika smiled. "It will require canceling Manessa's proximity responses, and good teamwork from watch, navigator, pilot, engineer, and steward. Are you up to it?"

Mati grinned and nodded, with Rini only a heartbeat behind. Sata and Boro joined a little more slowly.

Ilika looked at Kibi.

"This wouldn't be a good time to go back to the desert and eat lizards, would it?"

"No," Boro and Sata both said with stern looks. Ilika kept his mouth shut.

"Then . . . count me in!" she said, cocked her head, and smiled.

*

The departure from Sonmatia Four was completed with hardly a word from Ilika. Mati engaged her ion drive at its highest power level, and the Manessa Kwi followed an elliptical course that avoided the outer moon's orbit. The flight leg ended a little more than an hour later, after traversing almost fifteen light-minutes of interplanetary space, on the southern edge of Sonmatia Five's asteroid belt.

A black sky full of shimmering rocks greeted them, some large enough to reveal the crescent shape created by the harsh light from the sun, most so small they were no more than points of brilliance.

"I thought you said six or eight rocks in the way," Mati said as she touched symbols to transfer helm control to the ship.

"Er . . . um . . ." Boro mumbled from his station, gazing at his display while moving his hands to shut down the ion drive.

"I can explain," Ilika said from the command chair. "There are so many fragments in an asteroid belt, all the way down to dust particles, and all in constant motion, that it would be impossible to chart them all. We only attempt to keep track of those one-meter across and larger. There may be six or eight of those between us and fragment five-three-three, and millions of smaller fragments."

"We don't need engines for this," Boro began, "we need a shovel!"

The bridge erupted with laughter.

"There's one in the utility room," Kibi said, grinning from ear to ear.

Rini doubled over with laughter and almost fell out of his chair.

When everyone finally collected themselves, Ilika cleared his throat. "As you know, in space we have to avoid asteroids down to about a millimeter because they can be moving at very high speeds in relation to the ship. Here, there are too many to avoid, so we use a different solution. We go in slowly, with Manessa in her minimum profile, and the repulsion field at maximum . . ."

"Shape selected," Mati said, moving her hands on her console.

"Repulsion field three," Boro confirmed.

". . . and Rini will give us a real-time, color-coded, three-D view that will be much more useful than the sparkling visual scene before us."

Rini started making selections at his console.

"Sata will not plot an exact course," Ilika continued, "but instead will map out corridors that avoid the large fragments. Mati's job will be to fly the corridors, avoid rocks one-eighth of a meter and up whenever possible, and ignore everything smaller. We'll feel some reaction when we bump into things. Kibi may need a bowl."

The steward pouted silently for a moment, but when she saw that everyone else was too busy to notice, she sighed and stepped into the galley.

"Okay," Mati said, "I have the color-coded three-D, the big rocks on the chart are red, I avoid yellows, greens are little. What's the big purple thing?"

"That's our destination," Rini explained.

Ilika took a few minutes to help Sata plot the corridors, then went from station to station to see if everyone was ready. "Inertia straps," he commanded as he returned to his chair. "Maneuvering thrusters. Manessa, cancel all proximity responses."

Mati turned and looked at her captain. "No bolting allowed in that mess!"

"That's right. If in doubt, stop and be still. These rocks all orbit together, and rarely collide."

✳

For the next quarter hour, the bridge was very quiet as Mati concentrated on guiding the little ship through the asteroids, following Sata's corridors to miss the worst. The pilot did her best to avoid the medium-size rocks, but was not always successful. None of the bumps caused Kibi to lose her lunch.

It was the sight of fragment five-three-three, slowly spinning and tumbling directly in front of the ship, that did the trick.

✳ ✳ ✳

Chapter 24: Hard Landing

Ilika declared a break so Kibi could clean up and everyone could munch on dry crackers. He promised a tasty meal once they landed.

"Manessa, general analysis of the motion of fragment five-three-three, please."

"An extreme negative pitch and a slight left yaw."

Several crew members frowned at the new words they were hearing.

"What's yaw?" Sata asked.

"Movement around the vertical axis," Ilika explained as he turned his head from side to side. He grabbed a knowledge pad, and a moment later a diagram appeared on the large screen. "Everyone needs to memorize these words."

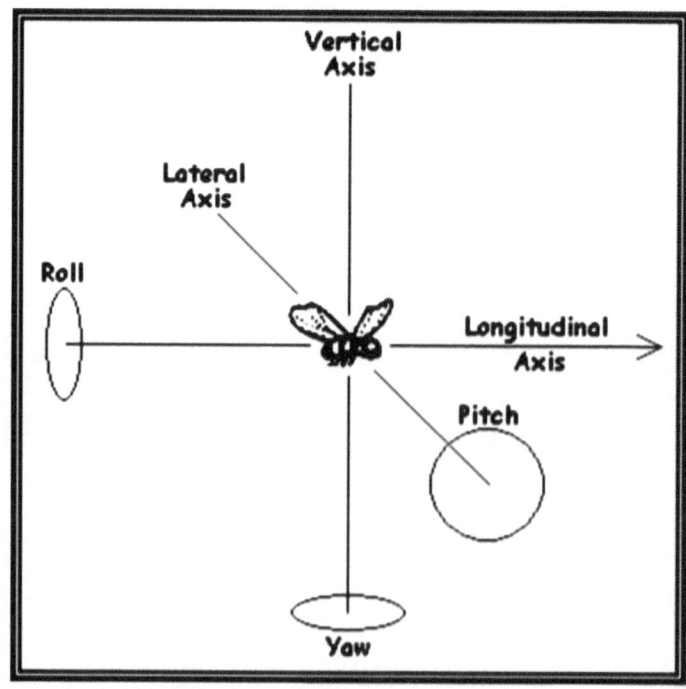

"Is that a bee?" Rini asked.

"We could use some of those," Kibi asserted, cracker in hand. "Honey's getting low."

Ilika smiled. "If I do forward somersaults, like this fragment is doing, that's called . . ." He looked around.

"A biscuit?" Kibi proposed with a goofy grin, her head cocked.

Ilika frowned at her lovingly.

Mati flashed Kibi a dirty look, studied the screen for a moment, then stuck out her arms, as if they were wings, and tucked her head down. "Pitching, around the lateral axis, one of the things I'm gonna do after I get my knee fixed."

Ilika grinned at his pilot.

A few more examples clarified the new words for everyone, with the possible exception of Kibi, who couldn't quit talking about food.

Boro passed her another cracker.

＊

"As I look at the huge thing turning out there," Mati began as she secured her inertia straps, "I know in my gut we'd crash if I tried to land the usual way."

Ilika nodded. "Your intuition is correct. Manessa, what is fragment five-three-three's nickname in the Transport Service?"

"The Meat Grinder," the ship said in its pleasant voice.

Boro made spooky noises. Sata looked at Mati with big, round eyes.

"We'd be the meat," Rini said through a shy smile.

Ilika turned to him. "Remember how to find a center of gravity?"

The slender lad started selecting functions on his console. "Um, um, um . . . reference grid . . . motion analysis. Yeah, got it."

"Send that to Sata," Ilika continued. "Now find the highest point on the fragment, Sata, add a hundred meters, and draw a solid sphere around ol' Meat Grinder. Then create a latitude and longitude grid, and place the north pole at the pitch axis."

"Yeah!" the navigator said as she worked. "Now it'll just look like a ball, and won't make us sick!"

"A ball with a monster inside," Kibi mumbled.

Ilika smiled to himself. "Rini, cancel all visual channels, but keep an occasional eye on reality for us . . . without getting sick."

Rini smiled. "I'll put it way down in the corner of my display."

"Anti-mass one and maneuvering thrusters?" the pilot proposed.

"Yes," the captain confirmed. "Both thruster sets, each one on a separate flight control."

Boro frowned with confusion for a moment, then shrugged. "All green."

"I've simulated that before," Mati said. "It's like patting my head and rubbing my belly!" She touched a symbol to raise a second flight control.

"It's not so hard," Ilika continued, "if you can take care of one at a time, and in this situation, we can. Start by moving Manessa right over the pitch axis at the north pole."

Everyone else watched their displays as the pilot concentrated for half a minute. "Here it is . . . but it's moving."

"That's the yaw — follow it," Ilika said.

The bridge was silent as Mati got comfortable with her task of following the axis of rotation as it slowly moved around the asteroid fragment. "Okay, flight control locked."

Ilika nodded. "Now there's only one motion left, that extreme pitch. Take your other flight control and cancel it."

Mati began by accidentally going the wrong way. After growling at herself, she slowly brought the ship into a matching spin.

"We have tamed the Meat Grinder!" the captain announced.

Clapping filled the bridge for a moment. Mati only grinned, as one hand hovered near each flight control in case they needed adjusting.

"Now we can switch back to visual, but first black out the background, Rini."

"Yeah, I was wondering about that. The more we matched the movement of the fragment, the more the stars and other rocks looked like they were spinning and swirling around. Visual on channel four."

They clapped and cheered again as they all beheld fragment five-three-three, seemingly still in space, against a black starless sky.

*

"Kibi, as steward, you have command for the landing," Ilika said.

She looked at her lover with a gleam in her eyes for a moment, then began studying the visual on her display. Although their destination appeared still in space, the many shadows cast by the metallic spikes were in constant motion, moving from side to side, stretching out to merge with the dark side, or shrinking to join the glare of the sunlit side.

For the next eight minutes, as the steward talked the pilot toward a level area deep down among the fragment's jumbled spikes, more and more details of its metallic structure came into view. Dark crystal shapes sparkled on nearly every surface.

Mati slowly reduced the power of her anti-mass drive, already at a low setting. When she arrived at zero and the ship was still descending very slowly, she chuckled.

Kibi smiled when she realized the landing site was not completely natural, but had been leveled to make room for a small ship.

As they descended past the last jumble of metallic crystals, Rini's eyes sparkled with curiosity when he noticed a dark cave opening.

Mati gave them a nice, soft landing without using any power from her engines.

* * *

Chapter 25: The Meat Grinder

After looking around to see if anyone else was dying to learn the steward's job, Kibi sighed and dragged her feet to the lift, pulled on a space suit with a slight pout on her face, and stepped cautiously onto the metallic surface of fragment five-three-three. After several slow, deep breaths, the shaking in her legs finally relaxed.

The smooth landing site, not much bigger than the little ship, was surrounded by dark metal shapes, some low and easy to walk upon, others thrusting skyward with jagged points towering hundreds of meters above the ship.

Just then, Kibi happened to tilt her head back far enough to see the black sky. The countless points of light wheeling above quickly made her head spin, and a heartbeat later she fell over sideways.

To her surprise, she floated to the ground in slow motion and landed like a feather.

Those watching from the ship frowned with worry for a moment, until they heard through the intercom, "I'm not going to puke . . . I'm not going to puke . . ."

After Kibi slowly picked herself up, the first step she took away from the ship propelled her nearly four meters, ending at a jumble of metallic crystals just outside the landing area. "Uff!"

"You okay, Kibi?" Sata asked.

"Um . . . yeah. Just need a few more minutes to get used to the place. No one comes out until I say so."

Inside the ship, several eyebrows were raised at their steward's newfound strength of will.

*

"It seems to be pretty safe since it's almost impossible to fall hard," Kibi reported. "Just don't look at the swirling sky unless you've got an iron stomach!"

Ilika smiled. "The micro-gravity does create one danger. It's possible to climb one of the spikes, then jump so high you'd achieve escape velocity and float off into space."

Boro frowned. "And because this thing is tumbling, the first asteroid you'd come to would smack you hard!"

"Fatally hard," Ilika added. "I think Rini might have been tempted to try that . . ."

"Not anymore!"

"Good," Mati said with a tender look in her eyes.

Rini grinned at her.

Ilika gave the couple a moment before speaking. "We'll explore our little Meat Grinder in pairs. Mati and Sata, Kibi and Boro, and I'll keep Rini from floating away."

Everyone laughed, then headed for the lower deck.

✳

"I can walk!" Mati nearly screamed.

Ilika had insisted she leave her crutch behind in the ship. Now she knew why. It had taken a few steps to get used to the micro-gravity, but Mati soon discovered that the pressure on her right leg was below the pain threshold, and she could actually walk with both legs.

"This is so wonderful, Sata! I don't care about jumping and floating and stuff, I just wanna walk around the landing site, so if I die before I get to Satamia Star Station, I'll know what it's like."

The navigator smiled through her face plate, crouched down, and sprang upward. "Wee!" She ascended to about twenty meters, then floated down slowly.

Mati laughed, and kept on slowly walking.

Ilika, watching from a hundred meters up one of the metallic spikes, smiled.

"She's gonna have fun once her knee's fixed," Rini said from eight meters higher up. "You coming?"

Ilika bent at the knees, then sprang right over Rini, landing near the cave entrance.

Rini laughed, and bounded to join his captain.

With bracelet lights shining, they crept into the darkness, finding an irregular tunnel about three meters across slowly tapering as it pierced deeper into the asteroid. From all sides, crystals of many colors jutted into the passage, sometimes half a meter in length.

Rini looked all around. "So pretty! Can we take one for our display containers?"

"Crystals grow very slowly, taking thousands, maybe millions of years to get to this size. If every ship took one, they'd be gone already."

Rini frowned and nodded.

"But I see some broken pieces on the floor," Ilika continued, "that would go nicely in our containers."

Rini grinned and began to look around.

*

When Rini and Ilika returned to the landing site, Mati was still walking, almost skipping, while humming little tunes, mostly off-key. Sata was near, sometimes walking with her friend, sometimes jumping up to the top of the ship or one of the nearby jumbles.

Just then Boro and Kibi appeared over a rise.

Sata landed near Mati. "Didn't you guys go off in the other direction?"

Kibi snickered. "Yeah."

"We just walked around the world!" Boro announced proudly. "And I found a little piece of asteroid metal for the display containers."

Rini arrived and pulled out three small broken crystals: deep blue, fiery red, and bright purple.

"Fantastic!" Kibi said with a grin.

*

The three crystals seemed to glow when placed in the display container in front of the dark metal of the asteroid. Memories now peeked out of five containers, most of them natural objects, from stardust to feathers. Only the display for Sonmatia Two held objects made by hand.

At dinner, Kibi talked about her initial discomfort with the asteroid, and Ilika nodded his understanding. Then he invited her to climb to the highest point with him. Her eyes nearly smoked for a moment, then softened as she agreed.

Mati declared her intention to walk all the way around the asteroid, and Rini asked if he could come. Boro and Sata planned to peek in the cave, then climb the second-tallest metallic spike.

*

A few hours later, after the last pair came in the airlock, the entire ship was soon very quiet with six exhausted explorers collapsed on their beds.

Manessa lowered the temperature a bit as Kibi had programmed any time they were asleep, monitored all systems for anything unusual, and watched the stars turn overhead.

* * *

Chapter 26: Gas Giants

The crew demanded another day at fragment five-three-three once stories were told of deeper caves and a metallic spike gentle enough for Mati to ascend. Both Kibi and Boro, at first unnerved by the constantly moving sky, spent extra time looking up, determined to conquer more personal demons. Mati and Rini looked up and shrugged.

On the third day, Kibi took command as they reversed the landing process, first floating up to a safe distance while watching the stationary asteroid below, then turning to see the inside of the solid sphere Sata created on their displays. Mati cancelled the pitch, then the yaw, and once again they beheld the stars, now behaving themselves.

Another quarter hour of bumping and nudging brought them to clear space. Sata plotted an elliptical flight plan with a course change at Sonmatia Six, Mati requested engines, and the Manessa Kwi streaked deeper into space at one-eighth the speed of light.

None of the five new crew members could keep their mouths closed as the huge gas giant filled their displays with mysterious bands of color — oranges, yellows, violets, even brilliant white with tinges of blue and green.

Rini tried to swallow. "We're not even very close yet . . ."

Suddenly a thin, straight band of rocks flashed across their view screens.

Boro nearly jumped out of his skin. "What was that?"

"Sata?" Ilika prompted.

She studied her chart for a moment. "Sonmatia Six has a little asteroid belt around it. We're still several light-seconds out, crossing into the northern hemisphere."

While monitoring their progress along the flight plan, Mati looked deep into wells and canyons among the multi-colored clouds, swirling so slowly the movement was difficult to see.

"Hard to believe we're still at ion seven," Boro commented, "but my board says we are."

"Mine too," Sata confirmed.

Kibi glanced at the empty passenger area behind her. "My passengers are on the edge of their seats!"

Ilika turned and grinned at her.

The bridge fell silent as the giant planet loomed larger and larger, slowly moving into the lower-left corner of their displays.

"The gravity is enormous," Rini reported. "Almost five hundred times our little world."

Boro looked worried, then relaxed. "I'm glad we're using anti-mass and ion drive!"

Silence lingered again as the gas giant grew slowly larger and lower on their screens.

"Nav point in twenty seconds," Sata announced.

Mati looked at the flight plan again, glanced at Ilika, and he nodded. "Course change approved," she said.

A few seconds later, the gigantic sixth planet moved quickly out of their forward view and the Manessa Kwi streaked into the darkness of space toward Sonmatia Seven.

✳

"Rini and Boro are right," Ilika began from the steward's station as a bowl of snacks worked its way around the table. "Without the anti-mass drive, we couldn't go anywhere near a gas giant, unless freeloading. The gravity is just too great. We *might* be able to achieve escape velocity using every bit of our remaining fuel . . . once."

"Is the seventh planet just as beautiful?" Kibi asked.

Rini nodded vigorously as Ilika tapped at the console, and the image of another ringed, multi-colored gas giant appeared on the big screen.

Mati beamed with excitement. "We get to land on that one?"

Ilika squinted for a moment. "Sort of. First we'll descend through thousands of kilometers of turbulent, poisonous atmosphere. Eventually it changes to a liquid at extremely low temperatures. Finally, it solidifies, but the solid surface is very unstable, constantly melting and refreezing. We can take a peek at it, but not really land. Far, far down, below an immense depth of ice, is a small rocky core, about the size of your planet."

Sata's eyes grew large. "Sounds dark . . . and spooky."

✳

During the eight hour transit from Sonmatia Six to Seven, Ilika gave only one command. "Get some sleep, tomorrow's a big day. Sata has first watch."

After everyone else filtered away, Boro took a few steps toward the lift, then stopped himself and looked back at Sata. She seemed nervous as she selected pictures and videos to arrange on her display, alongside the star-studded blackness of space on her forward view. He smiled to himself, then went down to the bridge and started massaging her shoulders. "Want some company?"

She turned her head and grinned. "Yeah. I guess . . . I've got knots in my stomach. I'm not sure I'm gonna like gas giants."

Boro took the pilot's chair. "Because they're so big, or because they're way out here where it's almost dark?"

Sata twisted her face. "Not sure. Maybe I'll understand it better after we visit one."

Boro nodded. "Want to show me how to find charts?"

"Sure!"

✳

Hours later, at the end of Kibi's watch, Ilika awoke in a passenger seat when others started coming up the lift and talking about breakfast.

Kibi looked over her console one more time before giving him a kiss on the cheek. "You're in command," she whispered, then stepped into the galley.

He stood up and stretched. "Manessa, flight plan status?"

"On flight plan, seven light-minutes to destination."

Most of the crew had already glanced at the little screens in their cabins, but seeing the ringed gas giant on the big screen was much more exciting. Soon everyone was sipping tea and staring with wide eyes.

"This one's more special," Rini suggested. "We get to touch it!"

"Have you checked the planet's temperature?" Boro asked, squinting.

Rini smiled. "I know. Only Manessa can touch something that cold."

Everyone quickly ate as the enormous planet, even more colorful than Sonmatia Six, grew larger and larger on their displays.

"We're out of flight plan," Mati reported from her station as soon as everyone gathered on the bridge.

"Bring us to a relative stop at the outer edge of the rings," the captain said. "I have to give you a few warnings before we go down."

Sata provided a chart and Mati kept an eye on the visual display. With the ship still weightless, she brought it to an instant stop within sight of the first rocks.

"We'll start with a fly-over of the planet's ring system," Ilika began. "You'll see gaps with almost no rocks because of the interaction of the planet's gravity and the sun's. Any rocks still in those gaps tend to be unstable and move in unpredictable ways without warning."

Mati blinked a few times, then nodded.

"The atmosphere is mostly hydrogen, so space thrusters might act strangely. There have been cases where a gas giant was large enough that a passing ship, using thrusters, ignited a chain reaction and the planet became a small sun."

Boro swallowed and looked a bit pale.

"This planet isn't big enough for that."

The engineer breathed again.

"The turbulence down there is worse than anything on your planet, but there's nothing to hit but the liquid surface, so we just cancel all inertia and enjoy the ride."

*

The little ship glided over the rings, just far enough for safety, near enough for excitement. No flight plan was used — Mati kept her hand on the flight control and her eyes moving from chart to visual to console.

Even without mass, the descent from the innermost ring felt like falling, as the intricate swirling surface of the planet's atmosphere grew closer every second. Kibi had to close her eyes part of the time.

"Mati, start slowing our descent," Ilika instructed.

She spoke without turning. "Um . . . ion two, Boro."

Boro confirmed the power reduction, and the visible surface of the planet ceased barreling toward them.

No one could feel a thing as the ship punched a small hole in a huge purple cloud. Their displays gradually became foggy, then slowly dimmed as they pierced deeper into the atmosphere.

"Ion one," the pilot requested.

Occasional shafts of brilliant sunlight penetrated deeply into the clouds, but soon the ship was once again surrounded by colorful mists growing darker and darker.

"This is creepy," Kibi muttered with a tinge of fear in her voice, "not knowing what's coming."

Mati smiled without letting Kibi see. "The chart on channel five shows our position and the liquid surface. It's no worse than flying in a thick fog back on our planet."

Kibi swallowed as she looked at the chart. "I'm glad *you're* the pilot!"

Mati smiled again and activated the ship's lights. "Ilika, I think we should float down from here."

"Good call, pilot."

"Finished with ion drive."

✳

As the deep-space response ship, with its crew-in-training from a medieval world, approached the gaseous-liquid boundary of Sonmatia Seven, the pilot slowed their descent by requesting higher and higher power levels for the anti-mass drive. The navigator, with little to do, arranged pictures of butterflies and flowers on her display. The watch monitored his sensors and squirmed with excitement. The steward looked around at the walls and ceiling, took some deep breaths, and checked her internal views for anything loose. The engineer frowned when the pilot requested his highest anti-mass power level, and prepared an alternate fuel, just in case. The captain smiled.

As Mati watched the ship's position indicator approach the boundary, she brought in more and more of the power at her fingertips. Half-way through level seven, the ship's lights finally revealed the eerie churning surface of liquid hydrogen, with plenty of other elements adding color.

"I don't suppose the fishing's any good," Boro said with a smirk.

Ilika burst out laughing. "There are creatures in there, but you couldn't eat them, nor could they eat you, although they might try. Take us in, pilot. As with water, it's calmer below."

Mati lowered the ship into the strange, cold liquid. The ship's inertia canceling kept them from feeling the surface roughness, but the swaying motion on their view screens brought moans, and several fingers quickly poked at channel selectors to study the chart. Kibi now knew what clothes felt like in her laundry machine.

The turbulence soon faded as the gravity of the planet pulled them downward. The ship's lights became useless as the liquid hydrogen reflected most, and distorted the rest.

"All stations, report," Ilika requested.

"Pilot is good, though I don't have anything to steer by. And I don't want hydrogen-fish for dinner."

Boro chuckled.

"Up and down is all that matters," the captain assured. "Sata?"

"Um . . . I guess I'll never love dark places, will I?"

"Maybe not."

"Well ... um ... I'm okay, and the only useful chart is on channel five. The transponder is active, although the Tirilana Kril should be gone by now, so we might be alone in the solar system."

Ilika nodded. "Rini?"

"I'm ... a little nervous. Visual is useless. Sonar shows chunks of ice that are getting larger as we go down. Channel four."

"Boro?"

"Engines are happy, but ... I'm worried because we have to use so much anti-mass."

"Atmospheric thrusters will work here," the captain pointed out.

Boro scrunched his face in a moment of anger at himself, then laughed.

"Kibi?" the captain continued.

"Ship's getting smaller again, but as long as there's room to dance to a little music, I'll survive. Everything's secure."

Ilika turned and smiled at her.

"Bottom's coming up," Sata announced.

"Ice chunks are becoming ice boulders," Rini added.

"Slow our descent, Mati," Ilika commanded.

"Eight meters per second," she reported.

Ilika touched the selector on the arm of his chair. "Everyone switch to channel four."

Boro switched to Rini's sonar image of orange ice and clear yellow liquid. "Much better!"

"Four meters per second."

Suddenly a huge bubble appeared beneath the ship, white on the sonar image. The Manessa Kwi dropped like a rock into the gas pocket before anyone could respond. Hundreds of ice boulders began to plunge downward into the same void, pounding the top of the little ship and forcing it into a deep, dark crack in the planetary ice.

✳   ✳   ✳

Chapter 27: Darkness

"Full anti-mass!" Ilika yelled.

By the time Mati moved her hand, the ship had plunged far down into the dark crack in the icy core of the planet. Boulders of frozen hydrogen rapidly filled the opening above, and the ship only quivered when the pilot pushed the anti-mass drive to its maximum power. "Oh, no, not again!" she wailed.

Ilika frowned. "This is different — and worse. Atmospheric engines, full power!"

Boro worked with shaking fingers. "Ready!"

"Inertia straps!" Ilika commanded. "Quickly, Mati."

Mati got her straps on, saw that everyone else was secure, and grabbed her flight control. The ship at first vibrated, then shook, and finally bucked and lurched, but went nowhere.

"Damn!" Ilika cursed, popping his straps and stepping to the engineer's station. "Anti-mass seven, thrusters seven," he muttered to himself, looking over Boro's settings. "Damn!"

"Continue thrust?" Mati asked, looking over her shoulder at her captain, a tinge of fear growing in her eyes.

"Yeah," he replied, stepping to her station. "Try rocking the ship, spinning, anything you can think of."

Mati tried every trick from Sonmatia Two, and a few she made up on the spot. Seconds ticked by. Sata, Rini, and Kibi barely breathed.

"Thrusters are going red!" Boro yelled.

"Any progress, Sata?" Ilika demanded.

"At first we were going up and down a fraction of a meter, but now . . . almost nothing."

"One thruster just went purple," Boro reported with despair.

"Cut thrusters," the captain commanded. "Ice is starting to choke them. How's the ice above, Rini?"

"It's starting to form between the boulders."

"Boro, space thrusters, all of them, full power."

The engineer looked at his captain, saw desperation in his eyes, and turned to his console. "You've got it all. At that level, we've got fuel for about

. . . four minutes."

"Mati, go," Ilika said, taking his seat and strapping himself in. "Cut-off at two minutes, Boro."

Blue flames quickly ate away the ice around the bottom of the ship, and worked their way up the sides.

"One minute," Boro announced, fingers poised as he watched the clock.

The heat soon reached the top of the ship, and the Manessa Kwi slowly began to move upward.

"Maintain full anti-mass," Ilika ordered.

"I am," Mati muttered.

"Eight seconds to cut-off," Boro announced.

"Progress, Sata?"

"About three meters."

"Thrusters off."

Boro sighed. "Space thrusters off."

"Damn!" Ilika spat out.

In the silence that followed, Kibi knew she had to be more than a steward. She popped her inertia straps, stepped down to the bridge, and stood beside her captain.

Their eyes met and she could see moisture in his eyes. She suddenly knew, deep in her heart, that this was no test or training exercise.

"Rini," she began, "we need to know how thick the ice is above us."

He turned to his console and looked over the sonar options. "Ah!"

"Boro, how long can we keep the anti-mass drive running?" she asked.

"Months, but there's no point once the liquid under us solidifies again."

"It already has," Rini said, "and I just found out the ice above us is about a hundred and twenty meters thick, and now completely frozen to the walls of the crack."

Kibi took Ilika's hand. "With your permission, I think we should let Boro shut down the engines. We all need to rest and eat something before we can think."

Ilika scrunched his face several directions as the first tear rolled down his cheek. "Yeah. We gained three meters. We could gain another three with the other half of our space thruster fuel. No point."

"Engines off, Mati and Boro," Kibi commanded.

The ship fell silent, and no one said a word.

The mood, as the crew gathered at the large table in the passenger area, had only been experienced by this group once before. When the high priest and guards moved to arrest them outside Doko's Inn, about a year before, they knew it was no test. Every situation since had been an exercise of some sort, or a problem with a solution.

Rini wasn't smiling, but he had enough presence of mind to successfully make tea. The others received their cups with shaking hands.

"I'm in command for a while," Kibi said. "Nothing's getting any worse, so Rini and I are going to cook something. Everyone else, relax, especially Ilika and Mati."

Those not in the galley moped around while soup was reheated and crackers broken. They ate in silence, glancing at Ilika often to see if he had thought of anything.

Ilika finally broke the silence. "Kibi remains in command, but I'm going to work with Manessa to make sure I understand our situation fully. We should all get some sleep before we try anything else."

✳

Ilika spent most of the next hour at the watch station, using every possible tool to peer into the strange ice on all sides of the ship. While he worked, most of the others wandered down to their cabins.

Next Ilika moved to the engineer's console, and after checking all the engines and fuel levels, he looked long at the star drive at the top of the display board. Even though he touched several symbols, it remained dark and silent.

After a few minutes at the navigator's console, he returned to the passenger area and took Kibi's hand. Last of all the crew members, they disappeared into their cabin.

She could tell by his eyes and his slumped shoulders that he had not yet found any reason to hope. Once the lights were out, she wrapped her arms around him and let him cry himself to sleep.

✳

During the next fourteen hours, different crew members wandered up to the silent bridge at different times. They sat at their consoles, ran diagnostics, asked Manessa questions, then dragged themselves back to bed.

✳

Sometime the following day, Ilika cooked a hearty breakfast. Rini appeared next, anxious to help with trays, but had to wait for the aromas to circulate throughout the ship before he had anyone to serve.

Everyone kept to light and happy topics during the meal. Once dishes were done, Ilika cleared his throat and sat back down at the table.

"You are not children. I'm not going to lie to you or sugarcoat the situation. We're in big trouble, and this is nothing contrived by me or Manessa. Sata, please activate the Nebador distress beacon."

With big, round eyes, Sata walked to her station, made the selection she had only simulated before, and returned to the table. "Manessa says only a tiny fraction of the signal is getting through the ice."

"Yes," Ilika confirmed. "That means another ship will have to be very close to hear us. We can't count on that happening, so we probably have to find our own way out."

"Can't we melt our way through," Boro asked, "like we did at the north pole of our planet?"

"We'll try, but I've done some calculations, and I'm worried. One piece of information we need, which I think you guys can figure out better than me, is how long we can live on the food and water we have, at absolute minimum usage."

Kibi tapped Boro, he grabbed a knowledge pad, and they went to work pawing through every cabinet in the galley.

Back at the table, Mati put into words what several people were wondering. "Did we . . . do anything wrong?"

"Not that I can see," Ilika answered. "And . . . as much as I wish I could take the blame . . ." He paused to take a deep breath. "Ships visit the liquid-solid boundary on gas giants all the time."

Kibi looked over the galley counter, then ducked back down to continue her counting and estimating.

"I've never heard of this happening," Ilika continued, "and neither has Manessa. It's just one of those rare geological events that can't be predicted."

After hearing those words, everyone breathed a little easier, but no one was ready to smile.

✳

"One month, max," Kibi announced. "That's using every scrap and every drop."

Ilika cringed. "Any way to stretch that?"

"Food . . . a little," Boro replied. "Water, no way. I know what people can get by on. We'll be dying in a month, dead in a month and a half, no matter how careful we are."

Ilika blinked a few times, then nodded. "We'll try melting our way out with Manessa's radiant hull. Sometimes simulations are wrong. Stations."

Happy to be trying something, anything, the crew was soon ready. Ilika worked with Rini for a few minutes, as precise measurements of the ship's movement were necessary. Boro and Mati had the simple task of making the hull glow with infra-red radiation, and applying all the anti-mass they could muster.

The experiment lasted half an hour. Rini reported three centimeters of movement. Ilika did a quick calculation. "It would take two and a half, maybe three months, to get up to the solid-liquid boundary. We don't have the food and water . . . or the fuel."

Sata burst into tears and ran off the bridge. Boro was half out of his seat before he stopped and looked at Ilika. The captain nodded. "Shut down your stations, everyone."

"Why was it so much easier on our planet?" Mati asked, standing up with the help of her crutch.

"That was barely-frozen water ice," Ilika explained. "This is far colder, and part of the massive core of the planet, which acts like a sink for any heat we apply."

Mati nodded and sniffed, then hobbled up to the table where Rini swiveled a chair for her, leaving Ilika alone on the bridge.

✳ ✳ ✳

Chapter 28: Cold

For the next three days, the joyless crew moped around the ship, half-heartedly making simple meals, or just sitting with friends, holding hands and remembering past moments of happiness.

Ilika spent most of his time researching every possibility he could think of, and reading every account he could find of a ship in any similar situation. When his eyes would no longer focus, he spent more hours asking Manessa questions and doing simulations. When he could no longer think, he found Kibi, snuggled close, and listened to her thoughts and feelings.

On the fourth day, Boro was poking at a bowl of barley and vegetables when he finally found his courage. "Ilika, I was a slave. I was hungry most of the time. I don't want to die of starvation . . . if there's any other way. I know some of the others feel the same."

Ilika looked at his engineer. "I understand." He looked around the table and saw nods from Mati, Rini, and Kibi. "Manessa can survive this . . . by hibernating . . . by lowering the internal temperature, conserving fuel, and occasionally sending a distress signal. It might be hundreds of years until that signal is received. Maybe thousands. Either way, she'll be okay. Unfortunately, we cannot use that same method to survive . . . at least, as mortals of flesh and blood."

Ilika could see tears on Mati's face, and remembered how close she was to getting her knee fixed.

"So . . ." Sata began between sniffles, "what would happen to us?"

"Once we all give our permission, of our own free will, Manessa will lower the temperature on the lower deck. Anyone who goes to sleep at that temperature will not wake up in this life. When everyone is asleep, she will do the same with the upper deck, and then patiently wait for rescue. Once that happens, our story will be told and all Transport Service crews will do their best to avoid the same fate."

Rini couldn't hold in his tears any longer. "It makes me feel cold just thinking about it." He left his uneaten meal and shuffled to the lift without looking at anyone.

*

Sometime in the hours that followed, everyone thought one of Manessa's engines had activated itself even with no one on the bridge. With nothing else to do, several of them followed the sound, and arrived together at the door to the engineering ring. Poking their heads in, they found Boro growling his anger and frustration to the engines, waving his arms and sometimes stomping around. They slipped away before he noticed.

*

After dragging herself aimlessly around the ship for most of a day, Kibi curled up in her own bed for the first time. With the exception of a couple of trips to the toilet room, which no one saw, she didn't show her face for the next two days.

*

Sometime the following day, Sata made a pot of soup, but rushed away before it was finished, hiding her face.

At the time, Mati was distracting herself with easy piloting simulations at her station, not even noticing the tears trickling down her cheeks. About an hour after her friend left the soup simmering, she wandered up to the galley, added some salt, and ate a bowl without tasting it.

*

Once Boro yelled himself hoarse and slept two nights in the engineering ring, he dragged his feet to his cabin where he found Rini staring at the knowledge processor on his desk.

Rini's eyes were red, but he was too dehydrated to cry. He gazed longingly at an endless stream of pictures — strange planets and moons, colorful nebulas, and gleaming star stations.

Boro put his arm around his friend and coaxed him up to the big table to drink cold soup.

*

Ilika went back and forth from researching any possible way out of their icy trap, to silently keeping an eye on each of his crew members.

Seeing Kibi in bed, usually not asleep but lying as if dead, tore at his heart almost more than he could stand. He left quickly each time, spoke his pain and anguish in the utility room to anyone who cared to listen, then returned to the upper deck to do more research or sleep in a passenger seat.

*

A day or so later, Mati wandered down to her cabin and found Sata under her desk wrapped in blankets. With some pain, she lowered herself to the floor, scooted in beside her friend, and they talked and cried together for hours before finally falling asleep.

*   *   *

Chapter 29: Emptiness

Two weeks passed with the little ship trapped in the icy core of Sonmatia Seven.

The captain occasionally tried to get his crew together for a meal or a video, but most often they gave him blank stares, challenging him to give them a good reason. He could think of none, so he backed away with slumped shoulders and returned to nursing his shame.

*

At some point in time, days after Ilika had quit trying to boost morale on the ship, he was alone on the upper deck. He leaned back in the steward's chair and stared with sad eyes at the results of another failed simulation, another useless attempt to find a way out of the trap.

Suddenly Rini flew up the lift. "I've been so stupid! I've had a wonderful life, I got to see the aurora, fly in the air all over the world, and visit six other worlds! No one in my kingdom has *ever* been so lucky, not even the king! There's only one other thing I want to do. I want to make a video. Please teach me how."

Ilika blinked for a few moments, trying to get used to the sudden burst of life from one of his crew members. "Um . . . okay. Your station is as good as any . . ."

Rini smiled for the first time in many days as he got comfortable.

"Open the video editor and select New Project," Ilika began. "You have four visual channels, each with a sub-channel for filters and effects. Visuals can come from Manessa's memory, a bracelet, or the high-resolution camera in the excursion cabinet. You also have four audio channels . . ."

*

Ilika wasn't sure what was happening, but he decided to be as supportive as he could. While Rini learned to use the video editor, and often called out questions, Ilika began to clean the galley. He found messes nearly two weeks old, and spoiled food that should have been refrigerated.

As the hours passed and the galley once again looked usable, some of Ilika's guilt and shame melted from his shoulders. Rini continued to work happily on his video project, sometimes hopping up to grab a bracelet and record something, including, at one point, Ilika scrubbing the galley floor.

The lad's excitement was infectious, and Ilika decided to cook a nice meal, even if only he and Rini could enjoy it. The food stocks were getting thin, but he found flour and made a batch of biscuits. Once those were in the oven, he turned his attention to a tasty stew, using the last of their dried fish.

*

Several hours later, Boro appeared in the lift. "I'm done feeling sorry for my ..." He froze and took in the unexpected aromas of fresh biscuits and fish stew, and the sight of Ilika with a bracelet recording Rini dancing in a clumsy free-form style to some lively music.

Boro waited, a smile growing on his face, while the song finished.

"Hi, Boro!" Rini greeted excitedly. "I'm making a video!"

"Wow. I didn't know we could do that."

"It's going to take me a few days, and I'll show it to everyone when it's done."

Boro cleared his throat. "I've got something I want to say." He stood at one end of the table as Ilika and Rini sat down.

"I ... um ... I've been thinking about how lots of my masters said I wasn't a ... you know ... a real man."

Ilika and Rini listened intently, sensing how hard this was for Boro.

"I guess I'm not sure what a real man is. Okay, I'm gentle and quiet, and I'm not very good with an axe. Whatever. I don't care about that stuff any more. I'm the engineer of a deep-space response ship, and I've been thinking real hard about what I should be able to do right now. I finally figured it out, and I want you guys to hear me say it."

Ilika and Rini both nodded slightly to show they were listening.

"I've had a good life, and I'm ready to be a man, my own kind of man. Manessa, you have my permission to begin hibernation as soon as everyone else is ready."

"Acknowledged," the ship said softly.

After a moment of respectful silence, Rini smiled. "I told her that too, but I said I wanted to finish my video first."

*

The three men of the crew sat around talking about what it meant to be a man. Boro shared what he knew from his culture, the ways he fit into the concept, and the ways he didn't. Rini admitted he didn't really relate to the concept much at all.

During a moment when no one was speaking, they started hearing voices from the lower deck.

"Can't you smell the biscuits?" Sata's voice asked. "Others must be getting over it too, and someone cooked!"

"I know," Mati's voice began. "I just don't want to do it looking like this. Tell them I'll be up soon."

The three males waited, and a minute later, Sata appeared in the lift, smiling. "Do I smell fresh biscuits?"

Boro smiled back at her.

Sata stopped part way to the table and stood firmly, with her feet somewhat apart, as if steadying herself on the deck of a sailing ship in rough seas. "Mati and I just spent three days ... maybe it was four ... dragging each other through every kind of grief and self-pity you can think of, and we both realized what we want to do ... what we *need* to do with the rest of our lives. Manessa, this is Sata, your navigator."

"Greetings, Sata," came the ship's pleasant voice.

"I never thought standing on my own two feet, with a smile on my face, would be this hard. Of course, I didn't know I'd have to get ready to die. Manessa, you have my permission to hibernate, in about a week, after we've done the simulations I want to do, had one last feast together, and ... done something else Mati wants to do."

"Acknowledged."

Sata let out a sigh and shivered. After a deep breath, her eyes fixed on Boro, and she began taking slow, measured steps toward him.

Wearing a slightly unsure smile, he stood up to face her.

"Boro, will you be the engineer of the Manessa Kwi for the next week while we travel all over Nebador with simulations? And at the end, after our last meal together, will you be there, with your arms around me, as the cold puts us to sleep?"

Boro took a slow breath. "Yes ... to both questions."

Sata pulled him close, touched her lips to his, and they kissed long and deeply. Ilika and Rini slipped silently into the galley to work on the stew.

Boro suddenly felt he knew a lot more about being a man — his own kind of man.

*

About an hour later, Mati appeared in the lift wearing her nicest tunic, the one from the desert gathering. Her long hair was nicely combed but not quite dry, and her eyes sparkled with a special light that had not been seen in weeks.

The four already on the upper deck fell silent and looked at her. Rini quit stirring the stew, came around the table, and stood facing her. His gleaming eyes met hers.

"I wanted to do this from my knees," Mati began, looking right at Rini. "I wanted to do it on Satamia Star Station, but I have to do it right here, because this is the only place I have, the only place I'll ever have."

The others, sensing the importance of the moment, gathered around. Sata was grinning from ear to ear.

"I'm still a cripple, Rini, but I've walked all the way around fragment five-three-three. That was one of the happiest moments of my life, and this is another."

Rini was turning several shades of red and squirming with embarrassment, but continued smiling.

"A desert girl once asked you to marry her, and even though there was a little confusion . . ."

Everyone chuckled.

". . . you found the courage to walk away . . . so you could be with me."

Rini nodded through his embarrassment.

"Now, here in the last place we can ever go, I finally found *my* courage. Ilika," she said, still looking at Rini, "you're a captain, and on our world, any captain can perform a wedding. I know we're not on our world any more, but we're still in Sonmatia, and there's no one else here except a few dying people on Sonmatia Two, so I think the rules of our world should apply."

Ilika grinned. "In the eyes of Nebador, you are married if you choose to be, and you can have anyone you want perform a ceremony."

Mati took a slow breath. "I don't have a special pastry to share with you, Rini. Maybe . . . we could use one of these fresh biscuits?"

Rini, still red with embarrassment and still smiling, grabbed a biscuit from the table and stepped close to his sweet friend Mati. No one else made a sound as the biscuit was broken, each of the slender youth offered their half to the other, then slowly chewed and swallowed what they had been given.

Just then Kibi rose in the lift. "Did I . . . miss anything?"

Boro and Sata burst into laughter. Rini and Mati didn't seem to notice the new arrival, and slipped their arms around each other. Ilika quickly strode to the lift, took Kibi by the hand, and pulled her into the room.

Unlike Mati, Kibi's eyes were red and her face crusty with dried tears. Her hair was completely tangled and matted, and her cheeks looked hollow. Ilika coaxed her along and gestured at different people as he narrated.

"Rini has decided to use the rest of his life to make a video, and he's been learning the video editor and collecting pictures. Of course, that might go slowly now, because Mati just asked him to marry her, and it appears he has accepted, so there will probably be a wedding ceremony sometime soon."

Rini nodded vigorously.

Kibi's mouth opened in amazement.

"Boro has made some decisions about what it means to be a man, and he and Sata have promised to go into hibernation together. But before that happens, Sata plans to navigate the ship all over Nebador using simulations."

Kibi tried to close her dry mouth and swallow, but couldn't manage it, so she just nodded. When she was sure Ilika had finished, she struggled to find her voice. "I . . . um . . . feel completely empty . . ."

Rini and Mati found seats side by side, and Sata stepped into the galley to get Kibi a cup of water.

After drinking deeply, she tried to collect her thoughts again. "For the first time in my life, it seems like I've felt every feeling and cried every tear, and there's nothing left inside me. This might sound funny, but . . . it almost feels good. For the first time, I'm not worrying about the next emotion that might . . . you know . . . slap me around. I've been to the bottom. There's nothing left. I'm completely empty and . . . um . . . when we've done everything everyone wants to do, I'll be ready to go to sleep in the cold."

"Acknowledged," Manessa said softly.

*

Ilika and Sata took a minute to get bowls of stew onto the table, and Boro promised to do the dishes.

Mati and Rini immediately began chatting and giggling about their upcoming wedding. Sata volunteered to cook the feast, and Boro thought of things he could use to decorate the ship. The engaged couple tossed out several possible dates, then settled on four days in the future.

Kibi remained quiet, her color and sparkle only returning very slowly as she ate. Eventually, when everyone else had fallen silent as they scraped their bowls, she let out a deep sigh and looked at Ilika. "I'm sorry I've been so . . . distant. It's part of the curse of being a feeling person, I guess. I thought I knew about every kind of emotion, and could handle them all, at least . . . after getting used to a moving ship."

Ilika smiled at her.

"The one I wasn't ready for . . ." she continued, ". . . and now I am . . . is dying."

"That's a hard one to practice!" Boro pointed out.

Kibi grinned shyly.

Ilika reached over and took her hand. "I don't think anyone's ever completely ready for that. But one of the things we can give each other, as fellow crew members, is the knowledge that if it must happen, we'll be together."

Rini and Mati both grinned.

Boro hopped up and collected the dirty dishes.

Kibi leaned her head on Ilika's shoulder, closed her eyes, and just listened to the sound of her own breath going in and out.

* * *

Chapter 30: Simulation

"What sort of simulation shall we start with?" the captain asked his crew, all of whom had just decided to die with their eyes open and their friends at their sides. "Manessa has memories from all over Nebador, and many places in deep space that are completely uninhabited and have not yet been assigned to a local universe."

"Somewhere pretty!" Rini suggested.

Mati frowned slightly. "Except . . . not Satamia Star Station. That would make me too sad."

"Me too," several others echoed.

"Hmm . . ." Ilika pondered as he stroked Kibi's matted hair. "Manessa, full simulation mode, Zekoria Comet Observation Platform. Stations, everyone."

This time, they didn't bolt to their consoles like excited children, but a subtle light of curiosity shone in their eyes, and perhaps a tiny bit of fear of the unknown.

While everyone else brought their stations to life and did their basic pre-flight checks, Sata searched for a chart of a place she had never seen or imagined. Her eyes opened wide as soon as she saw the large swaths of space colored red and marked *Extreme Navigation Hazard*.

Rini soon gave them simulated visual displays. "We're on a landing platform beside a supply dome on a tiny airless planet."

"Oh . . . wow . . . look at the sky!" Boro breathed.

They all tapped at their display selectors until they beheld a black sky streaked with twenty or more large, glowing comets, some plunging inward toward the system's primary star, others moving away. No matter which direction they moved, their shimmering tails pointed into deep space. Even as the crew watched, two of the comets silently collided, sending a spray of glowing ice in all directions.

"Let's get a closer look," Ilika began. "Departure pattern two."

Sata found the pre-defined flight plan in Manessa's memory. "Channel five."

Mati studied the plan. "It follows a band of space that's protected from the comets by the fifth planet, a small gas giant. Anti-mass one and ion five, please."

Just as Boro was announcing that the requested engines were ready, Kibi felt the hairs on the back of her neck tingle. She slowly turned her head to see what could have caused that sensation.

"Ilika . . . we have a passenger."

✳ ✳ ✳

Chapter 31: The Passenger

Ilika quickly stood and looked. "Greetings, Melorania. You are a very welcome sight. Manessa, cancel simulation."

Kibi continued to stare with wide eyes. The lady in her passenger area smiled and sparkled like a happy girl-child, and at the same time radiated a subtle light of ancient and timeless wisdom. Her gown of many colors shimmered and flowed around her, obviously not made of any cloth. Kibi's eyes opened even wider, seeing that her guest was not sitting or standing, but instead just hovering effortlessly. Even as Kibi watched, the mysterious visitor floated closer and spoke.

"Hello, Kibi."

"Um . . . er . . . um . . . I know that voice."

"The last time I spoke to you, dawn light was barely in the sky, smoke swirled everywhere, and I had to take a simple form that was easy to see and follow."

Kibi suddenly grinned. "You saved Neti, Miko, and me from the fire!"

"Actually, I just saved you. You saved Neti and Miko."

By this time, the rest of the crew had gathered around Kibi's console. Except for Ilika, fear showed in every pair of eyes.

"I am well-pleased, Ilika," the passenger said, looking at the captain for the first time. "For monkey-mammals, they are certainly the best you could have found."

Sata remembered her navigator-friend using the same term, and shriveled her nose for a moment.

Ilika smiled. "Everyone, this is Melorania, head of the Nebador Transport Service. She was there when the fire drove us out of Lumber Town, she was near when we buried Miko . . ."

"And she responded to our question," Sata cut in, "when we found Risan Gor and her father."

The strange visitor nodded as her gown swirled around her. "Yes, Sata, and a hundred other times when everything in the Transport Service was going smoothly and no one needed me."

Rini chuckled.

"You may all sit," Melorania said. "We have much to discuss."

❋

The simulation and its comets were completely forgotten as the passenger area was quickly rearranged into a circle of chairs. Kibi offered tea and left-over stew to her guest, and apologized for the lack of variety.

Melorania floated all the way around Kibi, her face twisted into a smirk that reminded them of Buna. "Kibi, do I look like I need tea or stew?"

Kibi lowered her eyes. "I'm sorry."

Melorania stopped to reach out and touch Kibi's face. "You need never cower before me, Kibi. Just keep learning, moment by moment, and you will be precious to me. You are prepared to die, are you not?"

Kibi couldn't keep herself from shaking. "I . . . I think so."

"Decide."

"Y . . . yes. I am."

Melorania brought her face close to Kibi's and looked deeply into her eyes. Kibi knew, in that moment, that her entire mind, heart, and soul were laid bare for the visitor to see. Time stood still.

When Melorania finally smiled, Kibi felt completely raw, as if every part of her being had been scraped and was in need of ointment and time to heal.

"You have a strong heart, Kibi, and even though you feel very empty right now, you will recover soon and find that many demons from your past have much less power over you."

Kibi's face twisted several directions and her eyes glistened with moisture as the mysterious visitor watched. Finally, a somewhat-forced smile appeared on Kibi's face, and she began to breathe easier.

❋

Melorania became a blur as she spun around in the middle of the circle, then came to a stop looking right at Rini.

Lost for a moment in her child-like beauty, the lad grinned, then turned red as he realized she knew his every thought and feeling.

Melorania moved back a little. "Even though you claim to not understand what it means to be a man, I know lots of young ladies who would love to explore the subject with you."

Rini's eyes sparkled for a moment, then he chuckled. "I'm . . . taken."

"Yes you are. But are you ready to die with your fellow crew members and your ship?" she asked aloud.

"Yes," Rini began with confidence, "just as soon as I finish my . . ."

"I don't take conditions, Rini. Death can come at any moment, just as you might be needed at your watch station at any time of the day or night. Being in the Transport Service is not like a boy reluctantly doing his chores, or a slave dragging his feet to a work site."

Rini completely lost his smile, and tears were close. "I understand. Miko would have loved to say good-bye to Neti, but all he could do was whisper her name one last time."

"And what about you?"

"I . . . want to be there for Mati . . . and my ship . . . as long as I have breath. Then I'll willingly die if I must."

Melorania smiled and kissed Rini on the cheek.

　　　　　　　　　　　　　　*

The mysterious visitor swished around the inside of the circle and stopped right in front of the navigator. Sata nearly jumped out of her skin.

"Sata, when you asked to be tested by Ilika, I saw in you great potential, but I was worried about your age."

"I know. My mother had a little trouble letting go of me, and I got homesick a few times."

"You misunderstand me, Sata. I was worried that you might be too old."

Sata frowned with confusion.

"You are somewhat set in your ways. For example, you don't like being called a monkey-mammal."

Sata looked at her hands in her lap as they twitched against her will. "Um . . . we call ourselves people."

"The only problem is that 'people' now includes all the sapient races — insectoids, reptilians, avians, mammals, and others you know nothing about. And even among mammals, your species is just a small part of the incredible variety of sapient life in Nebador."

Sata took a deep breath. "I know that now. I talked to an avian navigator, and we were going to meet on Satamia Star Station, maybe . . . you know . . . be friends."

"Drrrim-na is sweet, and an excellent navigator. Are you prepared to let go of all the friends you have, and all the friends you might have made, and then die?"

Everyone else was so quiet that Sata's breathing and swallowing could be clearly heard during the next half minute. Eventually, she spoke in a tiny voice. "Y . . . yes."

"I know you are ready if Boro's arms are holding you tightly, and if it's a painless death, like a ship going into hibernation. What I really want to know is if — you know the saying by heart — if you are ready to stand on your own two feet . . ."

"With a smile on my face?"

Melorania nodded.

Sata glanced at Boro, then took another deep breath. "Without Boro, I'd probably cry like a baby. But I'll do my job for as long as I can, and then I'll die, alone if necessary. I . . . don't know if I can give you a smile."

The head of the Transport Service looked deeply into Sata's eyes, mind, and soul for a long minute, then nodded.

　　　　　　　　　　　　　　*

"Boro," Melorania called softly, turning to him slowly.

"Yes . . . what should I call you?"

She laughed. "The titles of respect in your language don't translate very well into the language of Nebador, do they?"

Boro shook his head.

"You may call me by my name."

"Melorania," he whispered.

"I really like the kind of man you have become, Boro."

He blushed.

"Too gentle for man's work, too clumsy for woman's work, but just right as a deep-space response ship engineer."

Boro grinned with embarrassment.

She came close and looked deeply into his soul. No one else made a sound. Boro soon started to tremble. His entire life seemed to parade before him in just a few seconds.

Melorania backed away. "You are often strong when others are weak. But will you be able to let go of your responsibilities when it is time to die, so you can be fully present in yourself, and fully experience the great mystery that lies beyond?"

Boro swallowed several times. "I . . . don't know. Not long ago, I wouldn't have even understood what you mean. After meditating at the monastery, and talking about death after Miko died, I think I understand a little."

"Perhaps . . ." she mused, "the last two weeks have helped with that understanding . . ."

"Oh, yes!" Boro declared.

"And maybe the next week will help also . . ."

Boro swallowed hard and nodded.

✳

Melorania swirled around the room while looking into each of their eyes, and eventually stopped at Mati. "You have carried your burdens so bravely, precious one."

"I've never felt very brave."

"I know, but if you had seen the countless big strong men I've seen who were reduced to whimpering babies when they lost a leg or an arm, you'd understand what I mean."

Mati blinked several times, then nodded.

"Ilika guessed correctly that Kibi would not be ready for the Transport Service without her years in slavery. You would not be able to pilot this ship without your time as a crippled slave, and your long journey on donkeyback."

Mati glanced at Kibi, their eyes met for a moment, and tiny smiles were exchanged. Then Mati took a deep breath for courage and turned back to the mysterious visitor. A tiny bit of anger colored her words. "But I might have lived a little longer."

"No," Melorania corrected, shaking her head gently, "you would not have. You would be dead already."

"Oh . . ." Mati said with a thoughtful look as her eyes shifted back and forth nervously.

"So . . . are you ready?"

"You mean . . . to die?"

The visitor nodded.

Mati looked at Ilika, then at Sata, and finally at Rini. "So much of me just wants to cry, and let someone hold me and tell me everything's okay."

"That's natural. But right now it's your job, as pilot of the Manessa Kwi, to give me an honest answer to my question."

As Mati blinked, tears began streaming silently down her cheeks. "No conditions, right?"

"No conditions."

A long minute passed as Mati searched her heart for the courage to die. Tears continued to drench her best tunic. Suddenly she wiped her face on her sleeves, sat up straighter, and looked directly into the visitor's eyes. "Yes, I am ready to die."

The strange lady with a face of both beauty and wisdom smiled and nodded.

Mati cleared her throat. "Melorania, may I ask you a question?"

"Of course."

"I know we're going to die, but . . . you don't *mind* if Rini and I get married first . . . do you? I mean . . . if we have time . . ."

"Not at all, Mati! I love weddings! Being able to form a loving, working bond with another person is one of the things that separates the many barely-sapient creatures in the universe, from the few who might be called to universe service. I'll even come to your wedding, if you want me to, and if no one in the Transport Service is having a crisis that I have to go fix."

Mati grinned, and everyone else laughed.

✳

Finally, the head of the Transport Service looked at Ilika. "You, I have already tested many times."

"And no doubt will again before I draw my last breath," Ilika said with wide, smiling eyes.

Melorania grinned. "Is that a dare?"

"No," Ilika said through his own grin. "Just a fact."

The rest of the crew tried to hold in their snickers and chuckles, but some slipped out.

✳ ✳ ✳

Chapter 32: Melorania's Gift

Melorania of Nebador floated back to the center of the circle of chairs and turned slowly, looking at each of them as she spoke. "I must go. Others need me, and you all have preparations to make for a very important moment in your lives."

She then swirled around each member of the crew, leaving them feeling tingly and alive. Last of all she embraced Ilika and began fading from sight, her mouth still smiling like a sweet child, her eyes still sparkling with timeless wisdom. Then she was gone.

*

The six crew members of the Manessa Kwi sat in the silence that lingered and looked at each other. Before anyone could think of anything to say, the ship began vibrating, then shaking, and loud cracking sounds came through the hull.

"Manessa!" Ilika shouted as he sprang to his feet and dashed for the bridge. "Emergency departure, all engines!"

After a half second to recover from his surprise, Boro grabbed Mati under her arms, pulled her out of her seat, and a few strides later, lowered her into the pilot's chair.

"Kibi, do what you can with the galley!" Ilika ordered. "Sata, flight recorder! Boro, be ready to cut the space thrusters as soon as the atmospheric engines are working!"

Everyone was in motion, finally realizing what was happening. The cracking and groaning sounds grew louder every second.

"Rini, color-coded sonar!" the captain continued. "I need to know what's solid and what's liquid, and I need it on the big screen!"

They all worked frantically with shaking fingers. Kibi stuffed dirty bowls and spoons into a cupboard and latched it. The ship began bucking and lurching, and she could barely keep her feet under her.

"Boro, inertia canceling, but fuel priority to the engines. Inertia straps, everyone!"

The Manessa Kwi was now jerking up and down violently. Kibi was knocked into a passenger seat before she finally reached her console and strapped herself in.

"We're moving up!" Sata shrieked with joy. "Four meters. Seven. Twelve.

"Boro, call engine status!" Ilika yelled over the scraping and bumping sounds from the hull.

"Space thrusters down to one minute of fuel. Atmo engines still purple. Wait! One of them is warming up ... blue-green ... green ... yellow. Another one!"

"Cut space thrusters!" the captain ordered. "Rini, where's my sonar?"

Kibi looked and saw Rini desperately trying option after option on his console, none of which gave him the needed sonar image. She could see sweat pouring down his face, and his efforts to wipe his eyes on his sleeves only made his work harder. She popped her straps, grabbed the galley counter as the ship lurched again, and reached for a towel. A moment later she was on her knees beside Rini, holding his chair with one hand and wiping his face with the other. "You focus on your console, I'll keep your face dry."

A quick nod was all he could spare to express his gratitude as he struggled to clear his mind and find the right controls. "There it is! How did I miss it the first time?"

Kibi continued to care for her friend, knowing all their lives might depend on it.

"Sonar!" Rini cried as the image appeared on the big screen in front of Ilika.

The captain beheld freshly-cracked orange boulders of hydrogen ice swimming in yellow soup as the ship continued to push its way upward. The solid wall of the planet's core was still visible not many meters away. Crystals of ice tried to form between the floating boulders and the wall, and the ship was barely outrunning them.

"Ion drive status?" Ilika demanded.

"Green," Boro replied.

"Mati, get your flight control ready. You'll need a planetary chart."

"Coming," Sata promised.

Suddenly the icy walls of the crack in the core of the seventh planet came to an end, and everyone could see liquid hydrogen before them, with only a few small boulders floating about.

"Whoopee!" Boro cheered as he waved his arms while keeping an eye on his engine status board.

✳

Rini soon quit sweating, but Kibi stayed with him, as he was now in danger of being unable to see because of tears of joy. Suddenly she realized that in the past it would have been *her* dealing with overwhelming emotions. Now, for some reason, her mind was clear and she was able to help someone else. It felt very good.

Ilika gazed at the sonar image in front of him. A few small hydrogen ice boulders floated about leisurely. "The rest should be easy. Anti-mass seven, Boro."

After several seconds, Ilika began wondering why his engineer hadn't verified his engine request. "Boro?"

"Um . . . sorry. I was just trying to figure out why all my anti-mass drives are purple. Diagnostics are fine. Everything looks like it should work."

Ilika was beside Boro a second later. "Manessa? Do you know anything about this?"

"Melorania asked me not to use the anti-mass engines, except for inertia canceling, until we arrive at Satamia Star Station."

Ilika frowned. "Manessa, over . . ."

"Wait, Ilika," Kibi said unexpectedly from where she knelt beside Rini.

He looked at her, his mouth still open to speak.

"I don't . . . really know what Melorania is," Kibi said as she struggled to put her thoughts into words, "but she's someone very important and . . . very powerful. She just looked into our hearts and she . . . you know . . . accepted us. No one's ever done that before . . . except you. We always try hard when you ask us to do things. Couldn't we . . . try it . . . before overriding?"

Ilika thought for a moment, then looked around the bridge. He saw a smile from Rini and little nods from the two girls at the front of the ship.

"I'm willing to try it," Boro said, "as long as we don't risk getting trapped in the ice again."

The captain thought for another few seconds, then smiled. "Okay, we have to figure out how to break free of the gravity of this gas giant with very little space thruster fuel. How much is left, Boro?"

"About a cup, maybe a cup and a half if I scrape the bottom," Boro said with a grin.

The captain looked at his engineer with stern eyes.

"Sorry," Boro mumbled.

"I understand, but I need a number."

Boro's fingers were already moving on his console. "At full power . . . forty seconds."

Ilika turned back to the big screen and sighed. "Melorania didn't make this easy. Guard that forty seconds with your life, Boro. Mati, begin pitching down. Bring us to thirty degrees relative to the planet's surface."

"We've got plenty of atmo thruster fuel . . ." Boro pointed out.

"Yes, and a very strong gravity well between the top of the atmosphere, where those thrusters will cease to work, and free space where the ion drive alone can get us out of here."

"Coming to thirty degree pitch," Mati announced.

"Time to liquid-gaseous boundary?" the captain asked.

For a moment, everyone was silent.

"Oh, that's me," Sata said with a guilty voice as her hands started moving on her console.

Kibi gave Rini one last squeeze on the shoulder, left the towel for him, and returned to the galley. A minute later she had a cup of water in the drink holder at each console. "Sorry we're out of pinkfruit juice," she mumbled.

"Twenty-three minutes," Sata read from her console.

"Thanks," the captain said in a kindly tone, sipping his water. "Give me a planetary cross-section with ship's position. Continue monitoring sonar for obstacles. Pitch down to twenty degrees. Ion drive power level one. Recalculate time to boundary."

The four crew members who had just received commands all looked at each other like blinking owls as they figured out which of the tasks was theirs. Sata swallowed when she realized she had just received two orders at once.

From beside Ilika, Kibi started massaging his neck. He looked up with grateful eyes.

"Does this mean we're not going to die?" Mati asked without turning around after stabilizing the ship's pitch at twenty degrees.

Ilika was silent for a moment. "Ask me again in an hour."

✳

"Two minutes to boundary," Sata announced.

"Mati," Ilika began from right beside her chair, "when we reach the boundary, Manessa will naturally gain speed and pitch up. We want the speed, but not the pitch. The moment we're clear of the liquid, bring us parallel to the surface. The tricky part is, there might be a wave or two in your face, and you need to make sure they don't scare you. Go right through them, get your pitch down, and stay as close to the surface as you can. Practice visualizing that before it happens."

Mati thought for a moment. "This is critical, isn't it?"

"Very."

"Maybe you should do it . . ."

Ilika took a breath for courage. "The problem is, Mati, that could be said about almost every piloting maneuver you've ever done and ever will do."

She gave her captain a long look, and saw respect and trust in his eyes.

Ilika returned to the command chair. "Full inertia canceling. Real-time topographic of the liquid-gaseous boundary. Pre-select hydrogen atmosphere filters for the forward view, maximum contrast. Ship's lights."

Boro, Rini, and Mati all confirmed, and Mati merged the topographic and the visual channels on her three-D display.

"One minute to boundary," Sata reported.

"I never thought I'd be so calm in a situation like this," Kibi said from her station as she secured her inertia straps. "I guess it was getting ready to die that did the trick."

Ilika flashed her a grin, then turned back to the bridge. "Magnify our current position on the big screen, Sata."

The small gold dot grew to a circle and rapidly approached the line where the yellow liquid ended and the white atmosphere began.

"Critical communications only," Ilika ordered. "Prepare to go to ion two, and select an alternate fuel."

Boro programmed the new fuel from memory, than began a diagnostic. When the indicator turned green, he smiled.

"Eight seconds," Sata announced.

Mati took the flight control in her hand and narrowed her eyes as she gazed at her display and waited to breach the surface.

✳

Even with full inertia canceling, they all felt the sudden transition from ocean to atmosphere. Kibi thought she heard dirty spoons rattling in the cupboard.

Mati was prepared for a wave or two in her face. Instead, her lights revealed a twisting tornado of liquid hydrogen, looming over the tiny ship and threatening to suck it into the dark, swirling clouds. Mati banked the ship so quickly that the entire visual scene turned sideways. "Ion two!" she yelled and pushed forward on her flight control.

A heartbeat later, the little deep-space response ship picked up speed and dashed away from the spinning funnel, streaking along less than a hundred meters above the eerie liquid hydrogen surface, just as fast as her engines could make her go.

✳

As soon as Mati had time to think, she rolled the ship so the surface of the ocean was once again beneath their feet.

"I don't think I could have done any better," Ilika admitted with a smile.

Kibi started clapping, and everyone else joined.

The pilot grinned without letting anyone see.

"Our next trick is all about speed," Ilika explained. "We need to gain as much as possible while deep in the atmosphere, but you'll need more clearance from the ocean the faster we go, Mati. I'd love to make one-hundredth light-speed before we lose the atmospheric engines, but we probably won't be that lucky. That's where Boro's forty seconds of space thruster fuel comes in."

"It's ready," the engineer assured.

"We need a vertical cross-section of the planet, Sata, so Mati can avoid the rings."

Sata wiped her brow and went to work.

"Other than that, it doesn't matter which way we go, as long as we get a few light-seconds away from Sonmatia Seven's gravity well. Then we party."

Laughter filled the ship, and hands started waving for toilet breaks. Ilika took the pilot's seat, and Kibi brought Mati her crutch from the passenger area. Then Kibi stepped into the galley, determined to do something about the dirty bowls and spoons.

✳   ✳   ✳

Chapter 33: Manessa's Secret

When everyone was back at their stations, Ilika looked around. "We'll be okay. Melorania has left us a challenge, but it would feel good to do this on our own."

Everyone nodded.

"When you're ready to die," Boro began, "having two feet under you again feels *very* good."

Sata flashed him a grin of understanding.

Ilika cleared his throat. "Pilot, do you have your chart and forward display?"

"Yes, Sir!" she replied, using a word from her native language.

Ilika smiled. "I'll give you thruster levels and altitudes, but take us higher if it feels too close. Remember, you always have flight command."

Mati nodded as she rearranged the images on her display.

"Ship's status?"

"We're still about a hundred meters above the hydrogen ocean," Mati reported, "skimming along at ion two. I've seen a couple of twisters in the distance, nothing on our flight path."

"Full inertia canceling," Boro said, "with higher levels of atmo engines at my fingertips. Forty seconds of space thrusters, warmed and ready."

"The galley is secure," Kibi informed. "I'm worried that everyone's gonna need food and rest soon."

Ilika nodded. "Thanks, Kibi. I agree, and seeing the stars again will help, whether we're free of the planet's gravity or not." He turned to the watch station.

"Oh, my turn," Rini chuckled. "Real-time topographics on channel four, and . . . I just figured out how to give Mati a long-range chart of those twister funnel thingies."

"Thanks!" Mati said, making room on her display.

"Flight recorder still active," Sata reported, "but I don't have any other useful charts unless we get into the rings or moons."

"I hope that doesn't happen," the captain said. "Pilot, one thousand meters, ion level three."

Mati was amazed at the sudden increase in speed, but felt high enough above the ocean for safety. The liquid hydrogen surface became a blur, so Mati concentrated on her topographic display. She noticed from her console that Manessa had changed into the double-ended needle shape she used for space travel.

"Four thousand meters, ion level four."

The pilot was suddenly grateful for the tornado map, and changed the ship's course slightly to avoid one.

"Pitch up to twelve degrees, obstacle check."

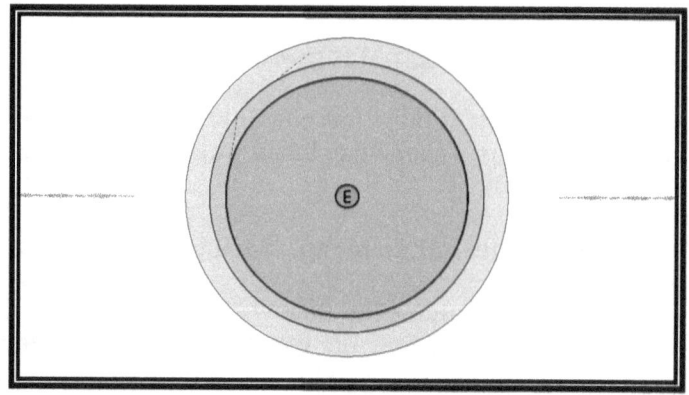

Mati focused on her planetary cross-section, and judged they would leave the atmosphere not far from the north pole. "No obstacles."

"Ion five. Ready space thrusters."

Mati gained all the speed she could, but her instruments and her gut both told her that the last increase made little difference.

"One atmo engine just went red!" Boro reported. "Another one!"

"That's okay," Ilika assured. "Just keep them from going purple by bringing them down, a level at a time, for as long as you can. Go to ion six, Mati."

"Stars!" Sata breathed as the last of the thick hydrogen clouds began to fade from her visual display.

Boro growled. "Atmospheric engines are dropping like flies, Ilika. I can't keep them going any longer. That's it. All purple."

"Ion seven! Space thrusters, full power!" the captain ordered.

Boro grinned as he touched the symbol for his most powerful, and most thirsty, engines.

"Now we're going somewhere!" Sata announced. "Escape velocity in thirty seconds!"

Everyone waited, hardly breathing. The captain glanced at each crew member while searching his memory for anything else they could do, any reserve of power his little ship possessed ... other than the forbidden anti-mass drive.

"Five seconds to escape velocity," Sata reported.

Before she had finished speaking, the space thrusters sputtered and died.

"Damn!" came from the engineer's station.

Ilika quickly stood and stepped to the pilot's station. "Adjust your pitch, Mati, and bring us into a close orbit. Sorry, Kibi, we tried."

"I thought Melorania would give us a way," Kibi began, "but I guess I was wrong."

Manessa's gentle voice broke the silence that followed. "Boro, I believe you will find eight liters of space thruster fuel on supply line fifteen."

Boro frowned and looked at his control board. "Manessa, that's a spare line with nothing attached to it!"

"I know the fuel is there. You can trust me, or you can look for yourself."

Boro turned and exchanged puzzled expressions with his captain.

Ilika stepped close. "This is news to me. Your call, engineer."

After a deep breath, Boro's hand moved. "No harm in trying it, I guess. You ready, Mati?"

"Sure! You give me thrust, I'll get us out of here."

As soon as Boro touched the symbol for supply line fifteen, it lit up and the fuel began to flow.

"Hooray!" Mati cheered as she pulled back on her flight control. "I won't have to dodge rings and moons!"

✳ ✳ ✳

Chapter 34: Space At Last

It didn't take long for everyone to notice that the space thrusters were not running smoothly, but instead surging and sputtering almost constantly.

"Manessa," Ilika asked, still standing beside Boro, "how old is this fuel?"

"Two hundred and seventy-four years."

"Wow. And how did it come to be on supply line fifteen?"

"My engineer at the time, a very capable insectoid named Trrist'ku, put it there not long before she died. She said I might need it someday. I have not needed it . . . until today."

"Do you have any other secrets?" the captain prodded.

"By definition, if I told you, they wouldn't be secrets, so of course not."

The entire crew burst into laughter.

Kibi wagged a finger at her lover. "Us girls have to keep a *few* things to ourselves!"

After more laughter rolled around the bridge and finally died down, Manessa spoke again. "But Kibi, I'm not a girl."

Kibi grinned. "I know, Manessa, but you're one of us anyway."

"Thank you, Kibi."

"If anyone cares," a voice came from the pilot's station, "we are free of Sonmatia Seven's gravity, but I have no idea where we're going next."

✳

Ilika didn't request a flight plan. He just made sure they were pointed into deep space, and asked Kibi to take first watch.

She arranged the necessary visuals and graphs on her display and lowered the table while everyone else came up from the bridge. Boro and Sata stepped into the galley.

Mati lowered herself into a seat with a deep sigh. "It looks like . . . we're gonna live . . . .right?"

"We'll die someday, somewhere, Mati," Ilika replied with a grin, "but not on Sonmatia Seven today."

Boro laughed deeply from the galley. "The last time we had a meal together, we thought we were *done!*"

Rini laughed nervously and looked at Mati beside him. She couldn't help but grin. When all the laughter faded, they continued to look into each other's eyes.

"Now . . ." she began, "I can get my knee fixed . . . and ask you again from my knees."

Everyone else remained silent.

"You don't have to ask again," Rini said softly with smiling eyes. "But you can if you want, just for fun."

Mati smiled, and continued looking into Rini's eyes. "Ilika, is a star station a good place for a wedding?"

"It's a great place. Satamia is small, with only a few thousand people, and most of them will come to your wedding if you want."

Mati's eyes grew large. "Even though they don't know us?"

"If you're in the Nebador Services, they know you've been through . . . experiences like we just went through. That's all they need to know."

*

Sata and Boro quickly made sweet tea to warm nervous stomachs, then Boro got flour for biscuits while Sata started a pot of soup.

The three at the table, and Kibi at her station, chatted about everything that had happened in the last few hours. Boro and Sata jumped in whenever they remembered an important moment. With warm tea in hand and friendly eyes all around, they soon began to feel alive and safe again.

"Are we heading for Satamia Star Station now?" Kibi asked after looking over her console display.

Her question was answered by a long moment of silence.

"Um . . . we don't have to rush . . ." Mati began, peeking over her cup with courage in her eyes, ". . . if there are other things we should do first."

Ilika looked at her with surprise.

"I've made my peace with . . . the universe," she explained. "I'm ready to die whenever my time comes. I found the courage to ask Rini, and I have his answer. I can't think of any reason to rush. I want to savor every moment of my life, however long or short it is."

Ilika nodded. "There are two more gas giants . . ."

"Ilika!" Boro cut in after sliding biscuits into the oven. "We don't dare go anywhere *near* a gas giant with only a couple of liters of old space thruster fuel . . . unless we're gonna use anti-mass . . ."

"True," the captain said. "And they aren't much different from the ones we've seen up close — different colors because of different trace elements, but the same basic structure."

"And Manessa has oodles of pictures of them," Rini added from where he sat holding hands with Mati.

"There's also a small, rocky world far out in the solar system," Ilika went on. "The twelfth planet has no air, no sentient life, just crystals that grow slowly over millions of years."

Mati smiled with curiosity. "Much gravity?"

Ilika pulled a knowledge pad from the middle of the table and tapped at the keys. "More than fragment five-three-three, but I think you could walk there, maybe with a friend at your side."

The pilot grinned as the aroma of biscuits in the oven started to make their mouths water.

✳

After eating, the captain worked with Sata and Boro to see if they could get onto and off of Sonmatia Twelve without using the anti-mass drive.

Kibi listened from her station as she kept an eye on the ship, currently streaking farther and farther away from the Sonmatia sun. She noticed some surprised looks from both Boro and Sata as they huddled with Ilika to discuss the landing and take-off.

Eventually Sata turned around and announced that it could be done.

Kibi smiled, remembered the glow of happiness and wisdom on Melorania's face, and realized how much she wanted to be like that . . . maybe . . . a little bit . . . someday.

✳

Many hours later, Sata was alone on the bridge, sitting in the command chair with her knees up. Views of the stars, several graphs, and all the important status displays were arranged on the large screen in front of her.

"Manessa, please put my butterfly pictures around the edge of the main bridge display."

A dozen different creatures with delicate wings appeared.

Sata smiled. "Thanks. Now put out all the other lights."

The bridge and passenger area lights faded.

Sata's eyes became large as she gazed at the shimmering colors of the little creatures' wings. After a minute, her eyes were drawn to the visual displays of the stars. The forward view contained only stars, but the sun, much smaller than before, still glowed in the aft view.

For just a second, she thought she saw something in the stars she'd never noticed. She squinted and blinked, but all the bright graphs and butterflies made it hard to find whatever had caught her attention.

"Manessa, remove the butterflies, please."

They disappeared, but too many other distractions remained.

"Manessa, remove the radiation graphs and status displays, but tell me if anything happens that I should know about."

The other bright displays vanished.

Sata's mouth opened as she began to see colors and textures.

"Manessa, remove the aft view."

Suddenly the one remaining display, the forward visual of the stars, seemed to come alive and jump out at her. Reds, blues, and every color in between looked back at her from countless far-away stars, nebulas, and galaxies. The space in between was no longer empty, but revealed many different textures. In places it seemed thick with glowing mists. Elsewhere, it rippled and folded like a mysterious fabric. Sometimes it became thin, hinting at openings and passageways to . . . whatever might lie beyond.

"I never thought I'd see you sitting in the dark," Kibi's voice came from behind.

"Come see, Kibi! It's so . . . I don't know what to call it! I've missed so much by . . . always having lights on."

"Wow," Kibi breathed as she came down the steps and stood beside the command chair. "I never imagined . . ."

"Me neither!"

"Too bad Boro's not here to see this."

"He tried to stay up, but was yawning so much, I poked him until he went to bed."

Kibi chuckled. "And the darkness isn't bothering you?"

"I'm almost afraid to say it, but . . . not yet! I mean, I still like butterflies . . ."

Kibi smiled as she continued gazing at the textures and colors in the star field before her.

"What about you?" Sata asked. "Are the walls and ceilings closing in again?"

Kibi nodded. "Yeah, but it's okay now. They no longer have any power over me. After spending two weeks in the core of Sonmatia Seven . . ."

Sata began snickering, Kibi joined her, and they both turned to gaze once more at the mysterious universe into which they were flying as fast as their little ship could go.

✳   ✳   ✳

Chapter 35: A Strange Landing

Ilika emptied the last of the porridge grains into the cooking pot, and Kibi managed to find a little dried fruit in the back of a cupboard.

Others appeared one by one after getting baths and scrounging for clean clothes. For the first time in two weeks, Kibi announced she would start a load of laundry after breakfast.

While they ate, Rini displayed pictures of little Sonmatia Twelve on the screen over the steward's station, and shared what he knew between bites of porridge. They peered at frozen landscapes with a pitch-black sky even at mid-day. In places, vast level plains were covered by ice and snow. Elsewhere, jagged mountains stood like sharp teeth on the horizon. The ice, Rini explained, wasn't water ice, but frozen gasses that would be an atmosphere somewhere slightly warmer.

However, Rini didn't know the answer to the most burning question.

"Boro, would you brief everyone on the landing procedure?" Ilika asked as he began to collect dirty dishes.

Boro stood a little hesitantly, then drew himself up to his full height and took a deep breath. "This is going to be a little different than anything we've ever done. I've asked Manessa three times, and she swears it's okay."

Kibi, Mati, and Rini still looked clueless.

Boro continued. "Our problem is getting to the planet before we run out of food . . ."

Several people chuckled nervously.

". . . and then slowing down enough to land. We're saving the last of the old thruster fuel for take-off. There's no air, so we can't use atmospheric braking. We've got some tricks we'll use on approach to minimize the relative motion, like coming in from behind the planet in it's orbit. Luckily, parts of the surface are smooth, or this wouldn't be possible."

"What wouldn't be possible?" Kibi butted in, unable to contain herself any longer.

Boro grinned. "The final deceleration will be done with friction between the ship's hull and . . . um . . . the ground."

✳

With twenty-two hours and several course adjustments before arrival at Sonmatia Twelve, those who had not already done so had plenty of time to ask Manessa for themselves.

Kibi asked from the utility room when she got the clean laundry.

Mati asked from a bathtub later that day.

Rini asked from the crawlway under the lower deck where he was pretending to inspect his sensors.

"The landing procedure will not harm me in any way," the ship assured each of them. "It is rarely done, as more elegant methods of landing are usually available, but it works. It is, of course, necessary to have complete inertia canceling."

"What would happen if something went wrong with inertia canceling?" each of them asked in slightly different words.

"All of the crew members would die . . ." Manessa began.

After a moment of reflection, Rini, Mati, and Kibi, at different times and places, each shrugged.

". . . and any cooking pot on the stove would spill," the ship added.

After rolling with laughter, which brought tears to all three crew members, they each went back to preparing for the strange approach and landing on the icy little planet.

*

Everyone managed to get a nap that day, but excitement was high, and Rini, Sata, and Mati all had duties at each course adjustment.

Repeatedly, during the hours of waiting, Ilika was asked if there was anywhere else in their home solar system they should explore. He soon realized what they were feeling. Satamia Star Station was far, far away, accessible only with the mysterious star drive, and they all knew it.

Boro settled the issue when the entire crew was at the table getting a snack before the last course adjustment. "If we explore anything else, it's gonna be on empty stomachs."

Several heads nodded slowly.

"Stations," Ilika ordered.

After checking all his sensors and sending displays and graphs to the other crew members, Rini quickly located the little planet. "It's hardly moved since the last time we checked."

"Because it's so far from the sun, right Ilika?" Boro asked.

"Right. Remember your orbit velocity equation? When orbital radius is large, velocity is low, and the other way around."

Boro made a selection on his console and looked at the equation and diagram for a moment, then nodded. "I can picture that."

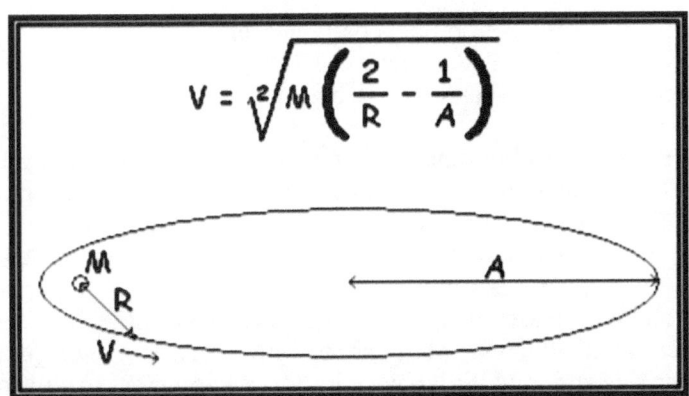

"Sata?" Ilika inquired. "How do we look?"

"Just a tiny adjustment, and we should nail the ... what do you call it? Landing? Belly-flop?"

Everyone laughed, releasing some of the tension in the air.

Ilika smiled. "Mati?"

"We just need a little puff from the maneuvering thrusters, Boro."

"All warmed up."

Mati approved the course adjustment, and Manessa did the work. Rini and Sata rechecked, and declared the course perfect. "Twenty minutes to ... um ... landing," Sata said with a somewhat-twisted smile.

As they approached the small, airless world, Kibi appeared at Ilika's side. "It's about time I got some command practice, isn't it?"

He looked at her with surprise. "This is the first time you've asked to command a maneuver!"

"Yeah. And it'll be our first landing since you-know-where."

"The slave market?" Ilika asked with raised eyebrows.

"That was the you-know-*what*," Boro corrected without turning around.

Ilika laughed as he stood up.

As Kibi got comfortable and looked over the displays on the main bridge screen, Sata started squirming. A moment later she stood, and stepped beside Mati. "This landing doesn't need any great piloting skill, right?"

Mati looked up at her friend. "Just a little maneuvering as we make contact."

"Want to ... let me try?"

After a moment of thought and a glance at Ilika, who nodded, Mati reached for her crutch. "I'll give flight commands and talk you through it."

Sata refreshed her memory of the basic piloting controls as Mati strapped herself into the navigator's chair. "Eleven minutes," Mati announced, "and the navigator's station is closed."

"We already have the only useful chart," Ilika said, putting on his inertia straps at the steward's station. "Make sure Manessa has the right shape, Kibi."

"Oh, yeah. Manessa, round like a ball, please."

Sata chuckled. "That's called spherical."

"Yeah, that word," Kibi replied with a grin.

Boro ran every possible diagnostic on his inertia canceling system, each one several times, during the remaining few minutes. The little planet, gray on the sunlit side, black on the night side, began to fill their screens.

"Sata will need both maneuvering thrusters," Mati informed the engineer.

He announced them ready and in tip-top shape.

"See that light area just north of the equator?" Mati asked her friend in the pilot's chair. "That's the level plain we're aiming for. The flight plan will put us down near this end, and we'll have a hundred kilometers to slow down."

Sata magnified her flight plan display. "I have a three-degree glide slope right down to the ground."

Mati studied the same view on the navigator's display. "We just need to be ready for things too small to see on the chart."

Kibi took one last stroll around the bridge.

"Rini," she said from over his shoulder, "be ready to cancel the visual display as soon as Mati says."

He nodded.

"You see anything else we should worry about?"

"Looks like some rough ground on the edge of the level plain."

"I see it," Mati said.

Kibi moved on. "Sata, Mati has flight command, so if she speaks, you listen."

Sata nodded. "I may be ready to die, but that doesn't mean I *want* to!"

"No one talks during this landing, except Mati, unless it's *really* important," Kibi said to the entire bridge.

Ilika smiled and nodded.

Kibi stepped beside Boro. "Do we have a back-up plan?"

"Two of them. Old space thruster fuel, and the forbidden anti-mass drive."

Kibi thought for a moment. "Warm them both up. I'll decide which, if it comes to that."

"Two minutes," Mati announced.

The bridge was very quiet as they watched the dimly-lit planet grow larger and larger — no clouds, no weather, no air, just gray rocks and white ice. Soon jagged mountain peaks became visible as they swooped lower.

Sata followed the glide slope on her flight plan with white knuckles and tense muscles, determined to do a good job.

"Okay, here comes the fun part," Mati began. "We're going to come very close to that last row of pointy mountains. Forget the flight plan ..." She reached up and canceled that part of the display. "...just follow my lead."

"Okay," Sata promised with a shaky voice.

"Nudge us a little higher, and aim for the largest gap between those peaks."

Sata worked with the flight control as sweat started forming on her brow.

"Good," Mati said. "Keep us up, don't let gravity get us yet."

The last of the jagged rocks swished by just a few hundred meters below the ship.

"Follow the curve of the land down, but not too closely until we pass those rough hills."

Kibi was concentrating on the visual display with her eyes, and Mati's words with her ears, when she suddenly saw a green light off to one side. It started flashing, as if trying to get her attention. "To the left! About twenty degrees! Now!"

Mati didn't see the green light, but she knew that tone in Kibi's voice, and gave Sata about half a second before yelling, "Do it!"

With sweat dripping into her eyes, Sata jerked the flight control and quickly banked the ship.

"Good," Mati continued more softly, "now steady your flight . . . come back right about four degrees . . . keep your altitude up just a little longer . . ."

Sata tried to blink away the stinging water in her eyes as the broken hills quickly passed beneath the ship.

"Okay, there's the ice," Mati pointed out. "Take us down, pilot!"

Sata wanted to smile, but was too close to tears to accomplish it. She tried to nudge the flight control downward, but her hand seemed unwilling to move.

"Don't be afraid of it. Either get us down, or I'll have Boro cut your maneuvering thrusters."

The engineer brought his hand close to his control board.

With a supreme effort of will, Sata jerked the flight control downward. A second later, the little ship hit the ground at a sharper angle than Mati would have liked, but in a pinch, it would do. "Visual off!" she ordered.

The entire crew saw the scene on their displays begin to tumble for no more than a second, but it was enough to bring moans and voices begging for bowls.

"Sorry," Ilika said as he gripped the arms of his chair tightly against the vibrations that were getting through. "No one moves until we come to a complete stop."

✳   ✳   ✳

Chapter 36: The Littlest Planet

Soon after contact with the ground, Mati and Sata reached out and clasped hands. The bone-jarring vibrations seemed to go on forever.

All the crew members of the Manessa Kwi had learned to trust their faithful ship in many different situations, but as they slowly decelerated on the icy plains of the twelfth planet, they knew that not even Manessa had any control over what was happening. The situation felt strangely familiar to at least four of them.

Boro kept his stomach under control by sheer force of will. When he thought the vibrations might be lessening, he knew from his console they had only been rolling through the ice and snow for about two minutes. He was sure, however, that he would need at least two hours to recover.

Rini at his station, Kibi in the command chair, and Ilika at the steward's station, all managed to keep their teeth from rattling too much as the ship finally rolled to a stop, somewhere in the half-light of a frozen little planet far out in the solar system.

*

After a deep sigh, Kibi remembered she was in command. "Um . . . status reports, everyone. Pilot?"

Sata hung her head. "I'm sorry, Kibi," she muttered. "I don't know why I . . . froze back there when you said turn. I think . . . I really like *navigating*."

Kibi smiled. "Will it be easier next time?"

Sata nodded as she made eye contact with the acting commander.

Mati, until that moment still and silent, grinned and touched the navigation console to get the ship's position, one of the few things she knew how to do at that station. "That was about like riding a donkey at a trot," she informed everyone as a small orange circle appeared on the planetary chart. "We rolled almost sixty kilometers."

"*You* sound okay," Kibi responded. "Boro?"

"Um . . . need to leave . . ." he said in a muffled voice.

Kibi saw that he had his hand over his mouth. "Go, go, go! Rini?"

While Boro dashed to the back of the passenger area, Rini made a selection on his console, then snickered. "Ready for visual?"

"I *suppose* . . ." the commander responded with suspicion.

The external view that flashed onto their displays revealed the surface of the planet on top, and a star-studded sky below.

Ilika, Kibi, and Mati burst out laughing. Sata managed to smile.

"You still have maneuvering thrusters, Sata?" Kibi inquired.

"Um . . . yes."

"Could you . . . you know . . . turn us over?"

"I . . . think so . . ."

Sata's first try caused the ship to spin completely around several times. Luckily, they felt nothing and only the external view tumbled.

Mati laughed. "We're on ice!   Manessa, minimum power on the maneuvering thrusters."

Sata tried again, with much better control. After a few tries, she got the little ship almost upright. Mati pointed out the landing strut controls, and a moment later the Manessa Kwi rose out of the ice and snow and became perfectly level.

"You okay up there, Ilika?" Kibi asked, turning her head.

"I'm just sitting here feeling very proud of my ship and crew!"

✳

With frayed nerves, everyone carefully checked the status of all systems, then shut down their consoles. Rini stepped into the galley to make tea.

"Welcome to Sonmatia Twelve," the captain said, taking a seat at the table. "The commander will brief us about that mysterious course change."

"Oh, that," Kibi said from the head of the table, brushing the concern away with her hand. "It was Melorania. Who else?"

Rini nodded knowingly from the galley.

"Any idea . . . why?" Mati inquired.

"No idea," Kibi admitted with a shrug. "Maybe she'll tell us someday."

Ilika laughed. "Don't hold your breath! She did things during my training that I *still* don't understand."

"Mysterious lady!" Boro concluded, returning from the toilet room.

After a moment of silence, Kibi took a deep breath. "The navigator will tell us about interesting things we can walk to."

Mati and Sata looked at each other, and Mati pointed at her friend.

"Um . . ." Sata began as she craned her neck to glance at the chart. "Just about nothing, but ice and snow, for a long way in every direction. Oh . . . except now there's a gouge in the ice about sixty kilometers long going back the way we came. That might be kind of interesting."

"Yeah!" Boro proclaimed with a big grin while others chuckled. "I wanna see that!"

When the laughter died down and cups of tea arrived, Ilika took on one of his serious looks. "Something you all have to understand."

They looked at him over their steaming mugs.

"It may look like ice and snow, but it's actually solid hydrogen and helium, and it's just as hard and sharp as any metal."

Rini pretended to pout for a second. "No snowball fights?"

"No," Ilika answered. "Extreme caution, every step."

"Can we . . . get a sample?" Kibi asked.

"It would probably explode as it warmed up, and soon be nothing more than a little bit of invisible gas."

She frowned.

"But the mountains look like they're made of rock . . ." Rini pointed out.

Ilika nodded. "And they're a long way from here. We might have to wait 'til we have all engines running."

Kibi looked forlorn. "I guess souvenir hunting would be a pretty poor excuse for overriding the head of the Transport Service."

Everyone else nodded and laughed, and Kibi cracked a tiny smile.

✳

Ilika, as acting steward, led the first excursion through the airlock.

The tiny crystals they called "snow" crunched as Sata carefully placed her feet. Boro examined the larger crystals, sometime half a meter high, and found them tough and sharp, and determined to snag his space suit. All three soon retreated to the nearly-smooth avenue the ship had created as it rolled to a stop.

Sata looked around at the dimly-lit landscape and the starry sky. "About like our planet at night with a quarter-moon out."

Boro chuckled. "Except that it's early afternoon!"

Sata looked up at the sun, now just the brightest star in a black sky. "Our world is up there somewhere, right Ilika?"

"Very close to the sun, from this point of view."

"And yet . . ." A long pause followed as Sata continued to gaze in the direction of her home planet. "And yet, I'm safer here than I would be most places in my kingdom."

"And you could get to your parents' inn quicker from here," Boro added, "than you could from the monastery in the mountains."

"We could do it in seconds with the star drive," Ilika informed as they all began walking along the avenue, away from the Manessa Kwi.

"The star drive . . ." Boro pondered aloud. "That's next, isn't it?"

"Yes," Ilika replied. "This is the end of Sonmatia, not counting a few little asteroids and comets. Thousands of years from now, if your people take good care of their planet, they'll come this far. But try as they will, they can go no farther."

Boro nodded. "That seems like . . . enough. Why would anyone want more than one beautiful planet, and a few hotter and colder ones to explore?"

"I don't know, but they usually do want more."

"I can see that," Sata said as they walked along. "On our world, ship captains get all boastful when they find a new island with no one around to claim it. They talk like they're masters of the sea, but more often than not, they drag their ships home with broken masts and leaking hulls."

"And sometimes they never return," Boro added.

Sata nodded slowly.

They walked for another minute, then drifted to a halt.

"All looks the same," Boro observed, "and no sign of any rocks for a souvenir."

The others silently agreed, then began slowly crunching back toward the ship, a golden sphere gleaming in the dim light about half a kilometer away.

✳

After hearing Boro's report on the complete absence of souvenirs, Kibi, Rini, and Mati agreed it would be best to stay fairly near the ship.

They examined the snow and ice, wandered a hundred meters down the avenue, and gazed at the black daytime sky. Mati reported a little pain, but could walk if someone held her right hand. Rini was happy to be that person.

When they were just about to turn back, the eastern horizon began to glow.

"Looks like the moon is coming up," Mati said.

Rini frowned. "That's impossible!"

"Ilika?" Kibi called. "What's causing the horizon to glow? Anything we should worry about?"

"I'm looking into it. Rini's right, it's not a moon."

"I think we should . . ." Rini began.

At that moment, a bright, white ball appeared on the eastern horizon and quickly grew larger and higher in the sky.

"Comet!" Ilika yelled into the intercom. "Get under the ship, quickly!"

Rini started to stride toward the ship, but remembered too late he was holding Mati's hand. She spun and lost her balance, then instinctively leaned where her crutch should be. Rini's outstretched arm was not ready to catch her. He tried to hold on as she fell, but was pulled off balance. Mati slowly tumbled onto the ice and cried out in pain. A half second later, Rini landed on top of her, causing her to scream again.

"I'm so sorry, Mati, it's all my fault . . ." Rini began pouring out his guilt as they struggled to untangle themselves.

The bright ball of light was now almost directly over them, and had grown huge. A sparkling hazy glow seemed to spread from horizon to horizon in every direction.

Before Rini could make any sense of the situation, Kibi lifted him to his feet. "Under the ship! Run!"

"But it's my fault . . ."

"I can carry Mati, you can't!"

Rini couldn't make his legs move until he witnessed Kibi scoop up his precious friend and begin striding toward the ship. He ran along beside, his mind spinning with guilt and the desire to help. Before they had covered forty meters, tiny chunks of white ice and black rock started pelting the ground.

"Don't stop for anything!" Ilika commanded. "I'm rotating the ship so the airlock will be right in front of you!"

Suddenly something knocked Rini's legs out from under him, and he slid onto the ice, face first. He looked up to see Kibi's back getting smaller, and Manessa's airlock coming into view. A feeling of happiness filled him, knowing Mati would be okay.

A second later he was overwhelmed with anguish, realizing the grief she would go through if he died there on the ice.

He focused on the falling rocks, hitting the ground hard and often burying themselves deep in the ice. One of them had knocked him down. The next, he knew, would probably end his life. With all his might, he scrambled to his feet, ignored several flying shards of ice, and ran as fast as his legs would go.

✳

The airlock was too exposed, Kibi decided.

Mati screamed again as she was dropped onto the ice, then quickly dragged under the ship. A few seconds later, Rini dove under and skidded to a stop beside her.

Kibi breathed once to clear her mind. "Suit checks!"

Both Mati and Rini felt for their bracelets and tapped in the code.

"I'm . . . good . . ." Mati began with a shaking voice, still dealing with pain, ". . . as long as . . . I don't have to . . . bend my knee again."

Rini's heart throbbed in his throat. He had to blink away tears before he could remember Kibi's command. "My suit knows something hit it, but there's no breach. I'm so sorry, Mati . . ."

"It was an accident, forget about it! What hit you?"

"Rock, I guess. That's why I was a little behind."

The couple fell silent as they listened to Kibi and Ilika talking on the intercom. A moment later, the ship above them began to change shape, extending a wide brim over the airlock. Beyond, ice and rocks continued to fall from the sky, but seemed to come less often as the comet neared the western horizon.

"Rini," Kibi began as they all started wiggling out from under the ship, "would you like to take Mati in? I'll come after."

Kibi could see the gratitude in Rini's eyes, even through his face plate.

✳

Inside, Ilika quickly spotted the place where a rock or ice fragment had caught Rini in the leg. The suit was tagged purple for repair.

Rini continued to apologize to Mati several times each minute as they stowed the space suits. Kibi and Ilika kept their mouths shut.

The problem was solved when Mati stepped into the lift. Instead of making room for Rini as she usually did, she turned and blocked the entrance. "*You* stay down here until you quit feeling sorry for yourself." Then she rose out of sight, leaving Rini nursing his guilt, and Kibi trying very hard not to laugh.

*

"That was close!" Ilika began as Boro and Sata reheated left-over soup. "Comets don't often come that near a planet without . . . worse things happening."

Boro, in the galley, demonstrated an explosion with his hands. "Boom!"

Rini, now happily holding hands with Mati, chuckled.

"Everyone did well," the captain continued. "You were about one layer away from a suit breach, Rini. I noticed you hesitate when Kibi ordered you to run."

The freckled lad turned to his second-in-command with a slight cringe. "I'm sorry, Kibi. It was my guilty feelings . . ."

Kibi smiled. "I used to be the one who acted on feelings too often. I learned. You?"

Rini nodded. "I realized that if I died out there, Mati would go through even more pain . . ."

Mati looked him in the eyes. "And don't you forget it!"

Ilika smiled. "It's very natural to want to help after causing a problem. It's the honorable thing to do. But honor is a human value. Comets and other dangers don't know about our values. Next time your commander says run . . ."

Rini turned red as everyone looked at him. "I'll run, I promise!" he squeaked.

Everyone else clapped.

"Want to watch my back on a short excursion?" Boro asked the lad as he passed out bowls and spoons.

"Sure . . ." Rini agreed, "but why?"

"An hour ago there wasn't a souvenir in sight. Now they're all over the place!"

Rini smiled and nodded, and felt Mati squeeze his hand.

"First we all get some sleep," Ilika declared. "Tomorrow we say good-bye to this little planet . . . and the entire Sonmatia system."

All around the table, the eyes that looked up from their soup bowls sparkled with much excitement, and squinted with more than a little fear.

* * *

Chapter 37: Final Departure

Ilika and Kibi were up early. Kibi, still in command, studied the planetary chart while Ilika scraped together all the grains he could find and made a thin mush. Alas, no sweetener or fruit was to be found in the nearly-bare cupboards of the little ship.

After getting a warm breakfast into their bellies, Boro and Rini easily found rocks from the comet. They brought back a fist-size lump for Kibi's display, and smaller ones for each crew member.

After souvenirs were stowed, Sata instinctively sat down at the navigator's station.

"Sorry, Sata," Kibi corrected. "I'm still in command, and you're still the pilot."

The innkeeper's daughter frowned. "But I stink at it!"

Kibi smiled. "Exactly."

Sata sighed and moved over. Mati, waiting nearby with her crutch, didn't say a word.

While everyone did their pre-flight checks, Kibi spoke. "Ilika promises me this will be easier than getting away from Sonmatia Seven."

The acting steward nodded. "And Boro's going to run that old thruster fuel through a couple of filters to clean it up."

"I am? Oh, yeah, I am." The engineer began working at his control board.

"It's easier, he tells me," Kibi went on, "because the gravity's a lot less, and we can use high levels of ion drive as soon as we're off the ground. We're going to look like ..." She switched to her native language for a moment. "... like a bat out of the Underworld."

Everyone chuckled as they completed their preparations for flight.

"Straps, and inertia canceling," Kibi said, getting serious. "Flight recorder, universe transponder."

Mati had to get instructions from the real navigator.

"Equatorial and polar charts, real-time topographics," Kibi continued.

Mati and Rini provided the data while Sata arranged her display.

"Space thrusters, ready at full power. Ion drive, prepare for level five, ready for levels six and seven."

Boro touched several symbols, then smiled.

The commander of the Manessa Kwi, an ex-slave who used to have lice in her hair, listened as each of her crew members gave status reports.

"Have I forgotten anything, Ilika?" Kibi finally asked.

"Yeah. Preview the flight path with the pilot so she can begin to visualize it."

Kibi described what they were about to do, prompting Sata to add another graph to her display.

Finally Kibi took a deep breath. "I've got knots in my stomach."

"Welcome to the Transport Service," Ilika said from behind her.

She flashed him a grin that expressed several emotions, some professional and some personal, then turned back to the pilot. "You have flight command, Sata. Destination, deep space."

Sata breathed while looking over everything on her console and display. Finally, she couldn't think of anything else to do but activate the thrusters. She thought of Boro, at the next station over, and touched the symbol.

*

Slowly at first, then faster and faster, the icy plains of the twelfth planet moved lower in their visual displays.

"One hundred meters," Mati called.

"Come to a sixty degree pitch," Kibi ordered.

Sata moved her flight control and watched her vertical cross-section chart.

"Two hundred meters."

"Forty degrees."

Sata confirmed.

"Three hundred meters."

"Twenty degrees and ion five."

Sata made the course change and touched the ion drive symbol.

"Aha!" Rini exclaimed.

"What?" Kibi demanded.

"I found out why Melorania changed our course."

"Passing the south pole," Mati announced.

"Ion six," Kibi ordered.

"Escape velocity," Mati said.

"Ion seven."

"Nothing but deep space ahead."

*

Ilika took back command, and everyone gathered around the watch station.

"Manessa couldn't see it during landing because we were at a shallow angle, then rolling along the ground. But look what she spotted on take-off!"

The topographic on Rini's display showed the entire level plain where they had landed. About forty kilometers from the last range of jagged mountains, and right along the path they would have taken but for Kibi's course change, a deep meteor crater interrupted the smooth surface.

"It's not on the chart!" Sata declared with a tinge of guilt.

"Must be too recent," Ilika explained. "But now that Manessa's seen it, it's on the chart."

Sata, out of curiosity, stepped to her station and selected the equatorial chart. "Wow. It is. But how do we tell other ships?"

"Manessa already has. She's in contact with Nebador whenever we're in space."

"Will Melorania always watch our backs like that?" Kibi asked.

"No, very rarely," Ilika replied firmly. "I think she felt a little responsible for us this time because she's the reason we're flying without anti-mass."

"That's fair," Boro said, nodding.

✳ ✳ ✳

Chapter 38: The Star Drive

After a few hours of free time for everyone to get baths and otherwise relax, Ilika called them all back to the table. Rini stepped out of the galley were he had been putting the last few scraps into a small cooking pot.

Ilika looked around at his crew, all of them wondering what was next. "In some ways, you guys were handicapped because you'd never experienced air travel, never seen a space ship, and you knew nothing of ion propulsion and anti-mass drives."

They accepted their humble origins with nods and sheepish grins.

"In others ways, the fact that you're from a simple world with little energy and power, but what the wind and muscles can provide, means you can easily avoid a trap that people from advanced planets usually fall into."

"Power always goes to people's heads," Boro declared with a shrug.

Ilika nodded. "On most planets like yours, there are solid or liquid deposits of concentrated energy deep in the ground. As soon as people find them, they go crazy building cities, having babies, and making all kinds of machines to make life easy. It lasts for a century or two, then the energy starts running out."

"What do they do then?" Sata asked.

"It's often quite ugly. They've usually multiplied their population by eight or more. When the energy runs out, most of those people . . ." He paused to swallow the lump in his throat.

The other crew members nodded understanding.

"Those who are left are accustomed to very easy lives, and suddenly have to be farmers and laborers again, tilling the fields by hand, or at best, with animals."

Boro blinked several times. "I can't feel too sorry for them. Every gift has to run out someday. Anyone but a child knows that."

Ilika sighed. "Yes, but before that happens, they get some very strange ideas about the universe, and some very unhealthy attitudes. They start thinking they can have anything they want, go anywhere, just because they desire it."

Mati laughed out loud. "They should trying having a bad knee and a crutch! I get to go where Tera, Manessa, or Rini wants to take me, and that's about it."

Ilika nodded with understanding. "During their time of plentiful energy, they start dreaming of going to the stars. They invent countless ships, few of which can ever be built, and imagine engines that can take them wherever they want to go at the touch of a button."

Boro frowned and shook his head slowly. "I'm new at this space travel stuff, but even I know it doesn't work like that."

"After centuries of trying," Ilika continued, "if and only if they've saved some of the energy pockets on their planet, they learn how to carefully poke around their solar systems. But they still dream of the stars, and still imagine engines that can take them anywhere."

"You told us before that the end of the solar system is the limit," Kibi said, "but you never said why."

"The stars are far apart for a reason. Between the stars lie vast stretches of dark interstellar space. No ship made by mortal hands can cross those distances. No mortal mind or body can survive the journey. Manessa could do it, just as she could wait in the ice on Sonmatia Seven for thousands of years if necessary. But when she arrived at Satamia Star Station, the nearest outpost of Nebador, we would all be long dead."

The others nodded thoughtfully, remembering their recent preparations for exactly that.

"The universe is structured that way so that immature people will stay in their . . . what do you call it when a mother fences off part of the house for a child?"

"Play pen," Sata informed. "Mine was in the kitchen by the wood box."

Ilika smiled at his twelve-year-old navigator.

"So . . ." Boro pondered aloud. "This is where the star drive comes in, right?"

"Yes . . . the star drive. It is completely different from all the other engines. It uses no fuel, and has no moving parts. It does not *make* us go anywhere."

Puzzled looks greeted Ilika all around the table.

"People who are intoxicated with energy and power dream of flying to the stars as an act of will. Their make-believe ships and imaginary engines *make* them cross the vast distances between the stars, just because they want to.

"The real star drive, on the other hand, does the only thing that allows a flesh-and-blood person to make that journey. It *asks* the powers of the universe to move us from one place to another."

*

Silence lingered as all his crew members tried to absorb what Ilika was saying.

"Does it ask ... Melorania?" Kibi inquired with a very confused expression.

"No. The universe powers that the star drive contacts are far greater. But I assure you, if Melorania doesn't want us going somewhere, we'd have to get out and walk."

Nervous laughter circled the table. Several of them glanced at the large display over Kibi's station, currently showing stars in the vacuum of space.

Mati's face revealed a question forming. "Um ... how does Manessa fit into all this?"

"The star drive is part of Manessa. She sends a complete description of where we are, where we need to go, and why. Since I'm a new captain, and you're a new crew, every star drive request will be checked carefully by Melorania. But as Sata found out back on your southern ice continent, she usually decides things very quickly. Later on, when we're all highly tested and deeply trusted, our requests will happen instantly, unless Melorania or someone else in charge thinks of a good reason to delay."

Boro took a slow, deep breath. "Wow. That really is ... a different kind of engine."

"And that means," Rini began with a straight face, "we can't do stupid things with the star drive."

Ilika's eyes grew large. "I hope we never do stupid things with *any* of our engines!"

Mati snickered. "He means ... you know ... have fun."

Ilika smiled. "Having fun is okay, sometimes, even with the star drive."

Rini nodded and looked content.

*

"So, jumping between solar systems with the star drive is gonna be easy!" Boro proclaimed. When the captain didn't immediately agree, the excitement drained from Boro's face. "Right ... Ilika?"

They all looked at their captain and teacher. He appeared worried.

Kibi poked at him. "Spill."

Ilika took a deep breath. "To jump between the stars, Manessa ... and all of us ... must pass through a reality state where space ... and time ... don't exist." He looked around at his crew and saw mostly blank faces. Rini appeared curious, but clueless.

"That spaceless, timeless reality state has some rather ... um ... unpleasant effects on anyone who isn't ... prepared."

Kibi swallowed. "What kind of ... effects?"

"It ... um ... tends to make them go ... insane."

"Oh," Sata said, her eyes shifting back and forth as if looking for a way out.

"But you guys are about as prepared as any new crew can be," Ilika continued. "You've practiced clearing your minds in meditation. That's the key to visiting non-spatial, non-temporal reality states. If you don't have expectations of finding space and time dimensions to relate to, you won't be bothered by the lack of them."

His crew started to breathe again.

"And you've had the extra preparation of preparing to die on Sonmatia Seven. That helps because the experience of star transit, if it can be compared to anything, is most similar to . . . you know . . . dying."

"So the sisters at the monastery," Rini began with sudden realization, "would be right at home with it!"

Ilika smiled. "They'd be better prepared than anyone else on Sonmatia Three."

"What would happen to the high priest?" Boro asked, squinting.

Ilika laughed and shook his head. "It wouldn't be pretty!"

"But what about passengers?" Kibi asked with concern. "Can I only have passengers who know how to meditate?"

"No. There are those in Nebador who have the power to shield others from the effects of the star drive. One of them will come along any time you have passengers who aren't Nebador Services people."

Kibi nodded, for the moment satisfied.

✳

"Actually, neither Manessa, nor any other ship, would ever cause anyone to go insane in star transit. The drive will simply not engage until everyone is prepared, or shielded."

"That's good!" Mati burst out. "I couldn't imagine Manessa hurting anyone on purpose."

"Thank you, Mati," the ship said.

"You're welcome, Manessa. So . . . when do we go? I think there's a healer I want to talk to at Satamia Star Station."

Everyone else chuckled.

Ilika looked around. "I need to spend about half an hour with each of you, going over your responsibilities before and after star transit. Most crews like to get their ship clean and tidy first, whenever they have time, because star transit is sort of like . . . well, dying and coming back to life. Also, we need to be well-nourished, but not have too much in our stomachs, especially the first time . . ."

"Yeah," Boro agreed, "if it's anything like *flying* the first time."

Kibi and Mati both nodded.

Ilika smiled. "So let's get Rini's soup finished, have our last meal in your home solar system . . ."

"And that's the last meal we're gonna get out of *these* cupboards!" Kibi declared.

"I'll help with the soup!" Sata volunteered.

"Everyone, tidy your cabins when you're free," Kibi requested, "and I'll do the common areas."

"Mati," Ilika began, standing up, "let's go down to your station and talk about piloting during star transit . . ."

✳ ✳ ✳

Chapter 39: Star Transit

A special, tingly mood filled the Manessa Kwi for the next few hours as the crew learned what they needed to know, ate the very last of their food, and shared excited glances or touches as they passed each other, going from task to task. The cabins had not been so clean and tidy since the five new crew members moved into them, many months before and nearly six light-hours away in space.

Kibi and Rini gave the toilet rooms and the galley a good cleaning. Sata, at her station, glanced up with a guilty look, but had more study and preparation for star transit than anyone else.

Eventually everything was ready. Ilika went to the steward's console, raised the big table, and asked Manessa to arrange six seats in a close, inward-facing circle. "Soon this will be as easy as ion flight, and you'll be able to do it from your consoles without a second thought. But for your first time or two, holding hands really helps."

Everyone waited until Mati was comfortable, then Rini took one side and Sata the other. Boro seated himself beside Sata. Kibi looked over her console one last time, then she and Ilika took the last two seats. Hands found each other all around the circle, most a little sweatier than usual.

"Kibi," Ilika prompted.

She took a couple of slow breaths to focus on her task. "Manessa, secure all fluid systems. Switch all internal energy to standby. Lock hatches and the lift. Shut down my station and the big screen."

"Acknowledged," the deep-space response ship said.

The subtle background sounds of the ship suddenly ceased, leaving a profound silence. All of the passenger area and bridge lighting faded out, leaving only displays and instruments casting a soft glow.

"Rini," Ilika called.

He glanced at Mati with sparkling eyes for a second. "Manessa, shut down all sensors. Auto-restart on return to normal space and time."

"Acknowledged."

The watch station went completely dark.

"Sata."

"Manessa, feed ship's position and flight plan Satamia Five B to the star drive. Shut down navigation and communications."

"Acknowledged."

"Boro," the captain prompted.

"Manessa, lock all fuel lines and initialize the star drive."

"Acknowledged."

Boro's station became dark except for six tiny blue lights, high up on his control board, in an area he had never before used. Even as he glanced that way, they changed to blue-green, showing him the star drive was warming up and testing itself.

"Mati," Ilika began, "as always, the pilot has the honor, and responsibility, of making the final determination that we are ready for flight."

The handicapped pilot, who had hopes of not being handicapped much longer, looked around at her captain and fellow crew members. She didn't see anything in their eyes that worried her. "Manessa, shut down all remaining systems. Activate the star drive as soon as we're ready."

"Acknowledged."

The last displays and control symbols went dark. The only light now came from the six little indicators on the star drive at the engineer's station, all still blue-green.

*

Rini felt Mati squeeze his hand as he closed his eyes.

Old memories, of a family who didn't understand him, fleeted across his mind for a few moments. Scenes from his years as a slave came and went. The painful moment, when Mati decided to stay with the goatherd, lingered, then the pleading face of a desert girl pulling him toward her tent.

Finally Rini cleared his mind and drifted into the timelessness of meditation.

One of the lights on the star drive changed to green.

*

Kibi closed her eyes and reviewed many painful scenes from her childhood, always out-thinking her parents with ease, and always being punished for it. Her time in slavery passed in a blur, except for a sweet memory of Miko that lingered for a moment. She smiled slightly, accepting the part of her life that had made her strong.

The memory of seeing Ilika for the first time burned brightly in her mind, and the warm, almost hot feeling of wanting something with all her heart.

Realizing he was beside her now, holding her hand and sharing her bed, allowed her to relax into the comfort of the darkness around her.

The second light on the star drive changed color.

*

Boro felt his heart throb from holding Sata's warm, sweaty hand, but let the feeling pass, knowing he could treat her to a nice meal or a gift at Satamia Star Station, and more of the deep kisses they had begun to share.

Memories of cattle, sometimes taller than he was, came and went. Painful scenes from slavery made him cringe, scenes of masters telling him he was good for nothing.

Eventually he relaxed, remembering his beautiful engine and fuel control board, and knowing that even now it was preparing to take them on a long journey. Thoughts fell away until only his breath remained, without measure in time or space.

Another light change to green.

*

Mati was so filled with the hope of getting her knee fixed that she couldn't relax. The faces of slave owners, soldiers, and a lonely goatherd peered at her, but had no power compared to the overwhelming dream she clung to with every fiber of her being.

Finally, she realized that as long as she held tightly to her hope of someday walking, running, and dancing, she would not be able to relax and clear her mind. Many long minutes passed as she wrestled against her deepest desire, its claws sunk deep into her heart. Sweat poured down her face and dripped onto her clothes.

Suddenly a memory came to her, a scene from the recent past in which she asked the most beautiful boy in the world to marry her, and he accepted. And he hadn't, she remembered, set any conditions, such as first getting her knee fixed. Her breathing slowed, a slight smile appeared on her wet face, and her mind cleared.

The fourth light on the star drive changed to green.

*

Sata's mind visited countless fond memories of mother, father, and brother. She could see every timber and board of the inn, and had personally scrubbed or swept most of them, except a few on the ceiling.

Then the anger returned from the day she overheard her parents talking about giving the inn to her brother, because girls just got married, they said. Slowly the anger faded and a smile grew on Sata's face as she remembered the navigation and communications console of the Manessa Kwi, just a few steps away, where she did a job her parents and brother could never understand.

Coming fully back to the present for a moment, she felt Boro's hand in hers, and her friend Mati's hand on the other side. She let her mind clear, and drifted into timelessness.

Another light changed color.

*

Ilika took his time relaxing.

Memories of his parents and sister were not overly painful, and far in the past. The faces of a few girls visited, girls who had liked him during his years of training. Zini appeared for a moment, then danced away into the crowd at some social event for the nobility of her medieval kingdom. Only one face lingered, a face of longing and desire, framed by lice-infested tangled black hair, first seen in the common room of Doko's Inn. She was the first girl to ever really love him, and she was beside him now, his second-in-command, his partner and companion for travel and service in the stars.

The captain of the Manessa Kwi took a slow breath and let his mind relax and go dark and quiet.

The last blue-green light changed to green.

✳

A moment later, all six green lights changed to yellow at once.

Manessa Kwi Habishu Glinta, deep-space response ship of Nebador, currently floating in the blackness of space on the outer edge of a little solar system called Sonmatia, began to shrink. Soon she was just a tiny speck of gold, barely visible in the dim light on the edge of deep space.

Then she was gone.

✳   ✳   ✳   ✳   ✳

Buna's New World

By Karen Buchanan

This story takes place when Buna and Toli are buying sweets in the marketplace in *NEBADOR Book One: The Test*.

Buna danced into the marketplace.

"What are you doing?" Toli asked. "Everyone's gonna stare at us!"

"So what! There's nothing wrong with dancing."

"But Ilika said to watch out for each other, and so I'm watching out for you."

Buna stopped prancing and thought about it. "I guess you're right. I'm just ... really happy! I haven't been able to just walk around since ... I don't know ... since I was a little kid. It feels *wonderful!*"

"We're supposed to buy something for dessert."

"Hmm ..." Buna started to say, looking around. "There's tarts at the bakery ..."

Toli scanned the marketplace, looking over most people's heads. "I think we should look at everything, then decide. Everything sweet, I mean."

Buna pouted for a moment, then grinned and nodded.

✳

After whispering to the tall boy and the tangle-haired girl, the sweet biscuits thought about standing up on the table and dancing, but the woman who made them was watching, so they didn't.

Candies winked and wiggled, especially when the candy maker had his back turned. The girl holding hands with the tall boy caught a glimpse of them, but when she got close, the man was looking, so they stayed still.

A big bowl of plums, from a farm in the southern valley where hot water gushed out of the ground, could feel the girl's feet moving to the music. They wanted so much to jump up and dance, and then send plums home with her and the tall boy. They started to wiggle, but the farmer turned around after selling carrots to the innkeeper's son, so they stopped moving and tried to look like a plain, innocent bowl of plums.

✳

As they walked among the carts, Buna leaned on Toli and looked up at him. "What do you think of this weird master we have?"

"He's not a master, he's a captain."

"Oh, yeah. What's it like working on a ship?"

"About like being a slave, I think. I've unloaded ships, but not sailed on them. I think you have to be good with ropes and stuff to be a sailor."

Buna frowned. "But you can leave, right?"

Toli laughed. "Only at a port!"

Buna thought about it, then snickered.

✳

A donkey eating hay saw the girl prance by, her feet still tapping to the music as she walked. The donkey listened, and heard the drum rhythm that was the same as what the girl's feet were doing.

The shaggy brown animal felt something special, like it had just seen a spirit. It knew about wolf spirits and mountain lion spirits, and how dangerous they were. But this girl seemed like a different kind of spirit, a nice spirit.

In a burst of courage, like it had never felt before, the donkey decided to try it. Front hooves started lifting up from the ground, one at a time. Once in a while, they tapped against each other.

Feeling its heart beat faster with the thrill of doing something a spirit could do, back hooves started lifting, then tapping.

Suddenly a booted foot jabbed the brown donkey in the ribs, it stumbled sideways over some wooden crates, and landed on its side, calling loudly in pain and confusion.

"Stupid donkey!" the man said, almost spitting out the words.

The donkey stayed on its side until the man left, then slowly got back to its feet.

It always remembered the girl-spirit, now long gone, but never again tried to dance.

✳

Buna and Toli sat down on a log to think about what they had seen.

"I think we should get plums!" she said excitedly.

"They looked good, but I don't think they were ripe."

Buna frowned. "Okay, sweet biscuits!"

"There were only six left. We need ten of something."

Buna sighed.

"*I've* never had a sweet biscuit . . ." a timid voice said.

Buna and Toli both looked. On the other end of the log, a little girl sat holding a bundle of cloth in her arms, and looking at them with big brown eyes.

Buna hopped up. "Maybe *we* can't decide, but *you* are getting a sweet biscuit, little friend!"

"But we're not supposed to . . ." Toli started to say, but Buna was gone.

A minute later she returned, sat down beside the little girl, and handed her the sweet biscuit. "Now there are only *five*," Buna said, looked at Toli, and stuck out her tongue.

Soon a poor woman came by and the little girl hopped up.

"Mommy, she gave me a sweet biscuit!"

The woman looked at Buna with eyes that said *thank you*. She looked in her bag for something to give in return, but found only a crust of bread.

Buna shook her head, fished in her pouch, and handed a silver piece to the woman. It brought a smile that was missing several teeth.

When the girl and her mother were gone, Toli stood beside Buna. "I'm sorry I snapped at you."

Buna looked up at the tall, handsome boy, and kissed him on the cheek. "I think the baker probably still has plenty of pastries."

"Let's go see!"

✳

Three crows perched on the inn roof.

"I could have snatched that sweet biscuit, right out of the little brat's hand, if her *mommy* hadn't shown up!" said Ke.

Te cackled. "Afraid of an old hag? That's not like you, Ke! Did you see the crust of bread she had?"

"What I see, I eat!" said Re.

"In your dreams!" Ke taunted. "Let's see what the tangle-haired girl and the tall boy get. They're heading for the bakery."

"You do recon, Ke. As soon as we know what's on the menu, I'll create a diversion, then Te swoops in for the first grab. Ke and me will be right behind for clean-up."

The three cawed at once.

✳

A slave boy, about nine years old, was cleaning up the marketplace that evening after all the wagons and carts had left. He liked working in the evening because he could look up and see the stars come out.

He didn't dare look up for very long, of course, or a whip would make him get back to work. But he knew how to take a quick look, memorize what he saw, then cherish it in his mind until he could glance up again.

As he was picking up some scraps of rope and broken pottery near a log, he happened to spot a small piece of a sweet biscuit down in the dirt, partly hidden by the log. He quickly picked it up but just held it in his hand with two fingers and continued to work.

A guard glanced at him but didn't see anything wrong.

The boy waited until he tossed the junk into the trash wagon, then as he turned to go back to work, popped the little piece of sweet biscuit into his mouth.

Even with a little dirt, it tasted heavenly.

As soon as he could, he glanced up at the darkening sky to see what stars were out. Only the brightest ones were shining.

He smiled to himself and wondered if maybe he could somehow visit them someday. Maybe he could find a way if he got free and climbed the highest mountain.

As he started picking up horse droppings, he wondered if they had sweet biscuits in the stars.

✳

It was nearly midnight before Te came out from under the little cart where he had been struggling with his painful broken wing for hours. He hadn't seen the baker's broom handle coming, but clearly remembered the guard's sword slice through Re's body, then seconds later Ke fell from the sky, pierced by a feathered shaft.

Te looked around, and wondered how he was going to find somewhere safe before a dog or cat found him.

✳ ✳ ✳

First Taste of Freedom

By Katelynn Persons

This story takes place when Miko and Neti are buying pouches in the marketplace and the nearby streets of Rumble Town in *NEBADOR Book One: The Test*.

Miko and Neti stepped into Rumble Town for the first time on their own, with nothing but each other and the money pouch Ilika had given them with two small silver and eight copper pieces inside.

"Where do we go?" handsome Miko asked uncertainly as he stared uneasily into the busy streets of Rumble Town.

Neti looked around, more determined than frightened. "Well," she said, thinking, "Ilika said we need to do some of the shopping for the group. We need money pouches, enough for all eight of us, so we need to find somewhere that sells them, preferably somewhere close."

Miko looked at Neti with shifting eyes. "What if we get lost?"

"We won't," the pretty girl said as she took her love's hand. "Trust me."

He nodded as he looked timidly down the street, and followed Neti's lead into the crowd, in hopes of completing their first task.

*

"Look!" Neti exclaimed as she pointed to a group of large, rich-looking men on horses coming toward them.

Miko watched the men approach as his stomach tightened. "Our old slave masters," he whispered under his breath.

They stood frozen for a few moments of panic before Neti took Miko's hand and led him into the crowd, going away from the terrible men. Miko stopped in his tracks.

"No, Neti!" he said firmly.

She turned around, almost running into him. "What are you doing?" she asked with a hiss.

Miko took her hands in his as he looked into her startled eyes. "Neti, we aren't slaves anymore, there's nothing to be afraid of! Ilika said to treat everyone we come across with respect, so we can't run from them. We have to continue what we're doing, or they'll think we're acting suspiciously."

Neti looked at him anxiously, but gave him a small nod of understanding.

He smiled and touched her cheek gently. "Come on, there's a leather wagon over there, maybe they'll have what we need."

Without a word of disagreement, Neti followed Miko to a small wagon filled with different leather goods. Miko reached down to make sure the coin pouch was still on his belt as he and Neti looked around the wagon with eager eyes.

"There!" Neti said with excitement as she rushed to the other end of the cart, picking up a brown coin pouch off the wagon. "How much for this?" she asked the leather man as Miko scurried to her side.

The leather man turned to face the pretty girl, and saw the nervous boy standing beside her. With a pause for thought, he responded, "One copper piece and it's yours."

Neti smiled at Miko as he untied his pouch and dug out a copper piece, handing it to the man.

"Thank you very much!" he called back at the man as he followed Neti into the crowd.

✳

"Those sweet biscuits smell so good!" Miko said as they ambled past the baked goods cart.

"I know," Neti said slowly, "but Ilika might be mad if we spend his money on treats. We have to find money pouches for the rest of us."

"You're right," Miko said slowly with disappointment.

"One copper for three biscuits!" the man said to Neti and Miko as they passed.

"Really?" Miko said, then received a disapproving glance from Neti. "I mean, no thank you."

Neti smiled and took his hand again, leading him past the lingering aroma of sweets.

They passed one of the bread carts, stocked with good-smelling breads and rolls, but with their stomachs still full from breakfast, it wasn't as hard to pass them up as the sweets had been.

"Hey, Neti," Miko began as they continued walking, "what do you think of Ilika so far?"

"Ilika?" she responded, her eyes examining the ground in front of her. "He's alright, I guess. I don't really understand the point of all this, though."

"Me neither," Miko said, shaking his head, "I was just curious. He seems so different from the rest of us. I don't get why he's treating us this way. For all he knows, we could be escaping right now."

"I know, it's weird, but I'm not going to complain. He bought us our freedom. He said that we could leave whenever we wanted and he wouldn't try to stop us."

"But he trusts us with his money, why would he do that if we're free to walk away?" Miko asked, noticing Neti's thoughtful expression as she pondered the question.

"I don't know. He's just a very trusting person, I guess. I just hope he's not so blind that he trusts Kodi with his money."

"Or anything, for that matter," Miko said with a smile.

Neti smiled back and kissed her man.

"Alright," she said, looking around, "where would we find more money pouches? I don't remember."

Miko looked around. "What about that little shop over there?" Miko said as he looked at Neti for approval before heading that way.

Inside, they found exactly what they needed, money pouches of all different colors and designs.

"These are perfect!" Neti said with excitement, picking one up. "The different colors will make it easy to tell them apart if they get mixed up!"

"Right!" Miko said as he chose two colors. "How many more do we need?"

Neti thought for a moment. "Well, if we need eight, and we have one . . . that's eight minus one."

Miko put down the pouches and subtracted slowly on his fingers. "Seven pouches!" he stated as he picked up a few more. When they had all they needed, they joyfully approached the shopkeeper.

"We'd like to buy these, please," Neti said in her most polite voice, setting the seven pouches in front of the shopkeeper.

"Alright," said the large man slowly, "that'll be seven coppers."

Neti looked eagerly at Miko as he slowly counted out his coppers from the money pouch.

"Seven coppers," Miko said, handing them to the shopkeeper.

"Thank ya kindly," said the man. "Have a good day now!"

Neti and Miko smiled as they carried their new merchandise away from the counter. Suddenly they heard the large old man holler at them. "Hey you kids! Get back here with them money pouches!"

They stopped in their tracks. Their skin became cold and pale as they turned to face the man, who approached them and took the pouches from their hands.

"Trying to steal one of my pouches?" the man quickly accused. "Do you know what the penalty is for stealing?"

"We . . . we didn't steal anything," Neti said, trying to keep her voice from shaking.

"You've already been caught, stop lying!" the man said as he went back to the counter and set the pouches in a row. "You see these right here? You bought seven pouches from me, yes?"

"That's right . . ." Miko replied cautiously.

"Then would you mind counting how many of them are lying on this counter?"

Neti, lacking good counting skills, turned to Miko in fright, who slowly approached the counter. He counted out loud, one by one.

"There are eight pouches here," Miko said softly, "but we had already bought one from another place."

"You expect me to believe that crud? Get out of here, and don't you two dare come back!"

"No, honestly!" Neti said, fighting back tears. "We would never steal from you! Please believe us . . ."

"Prove your innocence!" the man said firmly.

Neti, with determination written on her face, approached the counter and picked up the money pouch from the cart. "See this one? It's different from all of these you sell. The ones we bought from you have different colors and patterns, so there's no way we could have stolen this one if you don't sell them!"

The man examined the pouches with careful eyes before looking back at Neti, trying to hide her trembling. He sighed and handed the pouches back to them. "My apologies," he said in a deep, rough voice. "Be careful, and don't bring things like that into other stores or you'll get yourself in some *real* trouble, do you hear me?"

"Yes, sir," Neti and Miko said at once as they picked up the pouches and hurried out of the shop.

They stopped and sat on a street corner, setting the pouches next to them. Neti broke into tears.

"Oh, Neti," Miko said, wrapping his arms around the pretty girl, "there's no reason to cry, we didn't do anything wrong!"

"I know," Neti said between sobs, "but we could have let Ilika down! What if the shopkeeper didn't believe us?"

"Shh," Miko coaxed, "no reason to talk like that. Your quick thinking got us out of there, and that's what counts." He wiped the tears quietly from her face as she calmed down. Then he kissed her forehead before saying, "Let's get back to Ilika before he thinks something's wrong."

Neti nodded and thanked him softly, but Miko only smiled and took her hand as they stood up, each of them carrying a few of the pouches.

*

Neti and Miko walked side by side the entire way back to the inn, making small talk about their friends, and about Ilika.

"This life is a lot better than the one we had, that's for sure," Miko said with a soft smile.

"Yeah . . . it's sure different."

Miko smirked as he thoughtfully said, "Remember that time where you, me, and Kibi honestly thought we could escape?"

"Yeah," Neti said dryly. "I do."

"Doesn't seem so crazy now!" Miko declared.

Neti looked down and shuffled her feet, something she hadn't done before.

"I hit a nerve . . ." Miko began softly. "What is it?"

Neti shook her head quickly. "It's nothing, just remembering."

"Remembering what?" Miko questioned with raised eyebrows.

Neti stopped and put her hand on Miko's shoulder.

He turned around to face his girl. Seeing her seriousness, he whispered, "What is it?"

"Miko," Neti said softly, "do . . . do you still have feelings for her?"

The handsome boy's face flushed, as he immediately knew she was speaking of Kibi.

Neti looked at him anxiously. "Well?"

"No . . . no, Neti . . . not at all." He wrapped his arms around her. "It's just me and you, I promise. I care about her, but she's a close friend, nothing more. She will never be anything more, no matter what."

"Tell me this much," Neti said, fighting back tears, "tell me that you've never actually loved her."

"I swear to you, Neti," Miko said softly.

Neti gently wiped the tears from her face.

Miko leaned in to kiss her. "You're my girl, Neti, and you always will be. No need to worry about silly things like that, alright?" he said tenderly.

"Alright."

Miko kissed her again. "Let's head back, and let other people have a chance to go out, okay?"

"Okay," Neti said as she took her man's arm, and wandered back through the streets of Rumble Town, not knowing when she'd get another moment alone with Miko.

✳   ✳   ✳

About the Authors

Born in the Mojave Desert, J. Z. Colby now lives and writes deep in a forest of the Pacific Northwest.

He has studied many subjects, formally and informally, including psychology, philosophy, education, and performing arts, but remains a generalist. His primary profession as a mental health counselor, specializing with families and young adults, gives him many stories of personal growth, and the motivation to develop his team of young critiquers and readers.

All his life, he has been drawn toward a broad understanding of human nature, especially those physical, emotional, mental, and spiritual situations in which our capacity to function seems to reach its limits. He finds fascinating those few individuals who can transcend the limits of our common human nature and the dictates of our cultures.

In his spare time, he flies helicopters and airplanes.

He may be contacted at the email address listed on the internet site www.nebador.com.

Karen Buchanan, 14 at the time she wrote *Buna's New World*, is a native of Quebec, Canada. She speaks both English and French fluently, is learning Spanish, and wants to learn German and Chinese someday.

Born and raised in Portland, Oregon until the age of fifteen, Katelynn Persons now lives and goes to school in Sandy, Oregon, where she continues her journey through her teenage years.

Although she is only seventeen, Katelynn finds much enjoyment in her passions for writing and theater. She'll be graduating high school in January 2012, and plans to attend Mt. Hood Community College immediately afterwards.

This is Katelynn's second published piece of literature, and she hopes it won't be the last. If she isn't locked in her room typing away, you'd most likely find her with her few close friends, or out meeting new people, and trying to change the world one step at a time.

www.ingramcontent.com/pod-product-compliance
Lightning Source LLC
Chambersburg PA
CBHW031349170626
46807CB00002B/891